3/12

Married *but* *Looking*

Daniel S. Libman

Livingston Press
The University of West Alabama

Copyright © 2011 Daniel S. Libman
isbn 13: 978-1-60489-078-5 library binding
isbn 13: 978-1-60489-079-2 trade paper
Library of Congress Control Number 2011931134
Printed on acid-free paper.
Printed in the United States of America by
United Graphics

Hardcover binding by: Heckman Bindery
Typesetting and page layout: Joe Taylor
Proofreading: Joe Taylor, Stephanie Murray,
Tricia Taylor, Jim Carroll, Danielle Harvey, Eadie Caver
Cover design: Chris Mann
Cover Photo: Mari Stewart

Previously Published Acknowledgements:

The author thanks the editors and staff of the literary journals where these stories originally appeared: *The Paris Review, Confrontation, The Laurel Review, Other Voices, Columbia, Southern Humanities Review, Pushcart Prize XXV, The Beloit Fiction Review, Northwest Review, Carolina Quarterly, Tartts IV: Incisive Fiction from Emerging Writers,* and *Fifth Wednesday Journal.*

Livingston Press is part of The University of West Alabama,
and thereby has non-profit status.
Donations are tax-deductible:
brothers and sisters, we need 'em.

first edition
6 5 4 3 3 2 1

Married

but

Looking

for Molly

Table of Contents

In the Belly of the Cat

THE same day that he canceled all his newspaper and magazine subscriptions, Mr. Christopher deveined a pound of jumbo shrimp by hand. He had never done this before, and used nearly a whole roll of paper towels wiping the snotty black entrails off his fingers one by one. He also grated a package of cheddar cheese with a previously unused grater he uncovered in his silverware drawer, kneaded a loaf of oatmeal raisin bread, then called the escort service and arranged for a girl. "I want Carlotta. She's a Latina, right?"

He had called The Tribune earlier that morning. "Stop my subscription. The relationship is over; deliver it no longer. The advice columns just rehash the same situations—alcoholism, smoking, infidelity—although sometimes those columns are titillating, which I appreciate. The comic strips are contrived, and the punch lines aren't ever that good. That cranky columnist on page three ought to have his head examined; I think he's finally lost it, and your media critic is always biased towards the TV stations you own. But what I object to mostly, the reason I'm canceling, is because it comes too often: once a day, and anyway what good is it? I don't have that much time left and do you know how much I've wasted over the years slogging through, reading and cringing, hands and fingers covered in the ink, hauling paper-bloated garbage bags stuffed with Sports and Food sections, which I never even touch, down three flights of stairs every week?"

Mr. Christopher was hurt by the cavalier way the man at the Trib took care of the cancellation. After so much loyal readership he felt they should have put up some sort of struggle, a little token of respect: "But Mr. Christopher, please think about it; you want to throw away sixty years just like that?" Not that it would have gotten them anywhere. His mind was made up.

He had been a widower now for a year and a half, retired, down to only two-thirds of what he weighed at forty, dentures, a toupee he no longer wore but kept hanging off his hall tree, an artificial hip, and a brother a couple of states to the east whom he didn't like with a mouthy know-it-all wife. This had come to him one evening earlier in the week, a cold-cut sandwich and a pickle on a plate in front of him, eyeing the pile of papers; he had enough of them.

Mr. Christopher canceled all the magazines too: *The East Coast Arbiter, Harbingers', World News Ruminator,* even *The Convenience Store Merchandiser,* a holdover from work that they sent him for free.

He was bundling up the last week of *Tribs* he would ever receive, when his hands landed on a Food section. "Special Dishes to Commemorate Any Event," the headline said. I'll give you an event, he thought. How's finally ending 60 years of crap sound to you, Mr. Tribune?

Mr. Christopher decided to open up the Food section for the first time and cook those commemorative dishes. He mapped out what he needed to do in his head: buy fresh fruit, two pounds of shrimp; he'd need to take a bus to that specialty food store for some of it.... He even scanned the tips on what makes a good party: fancy utensils, music and special friends.

He was cubing the honeydew for the fruit slaw when she buzzed. He gave a start and walked to the intercom and thought how odd it sounded. No one had buzzed him for...weeks? months? decades? He leaned down to the grill, painted the same off-white as the rest of the apartment, and pressed.

Talk: Yes?

Listen: You call for me?

Talk: Who is it?

Listen: This is Monique. You call for me?

Talk: No. I called for Carlotta.

Listen: I'm Carlotta. Buzz me in.

Talk: Who are you?

Listen: Carlotta. You want me, baby?

He touched *door* and heard the far away buzzing. She was in the building now; his heart raced. It would take a minute or two to climb the three flights, and then she would have to decide which direction to walk; that would take a few seconds. He was in 3A, towards the front of the building, so she would have to look at 3B first, because it was right across from the stairs, and then make a choice, and she might choose right, which would take her to 3C—and in all this time he could back out, decide not to go ahead with this. He slid the security chain across the door.

But he had already gone to so much trouble. He had found the escort service in another part of *The Tribune* never before looked at, the match ads. At the very end were listings for adult services; these included descriptions of women, measurements and height and weight, and he wasn't born yesterday.

Mr. Christopher heard her footsteps and a knock. She had gotten to his door very quickly. Nervously, he touched his front pocket where he had put the money. It was a lot of cash to have at one time, the most he had carried in years. He looked down, considering himself, his paunch and his house slippers; he saw that the end of his belt was loose. He tucked it behind the proper loop in his corduroys, and she was knocking again, harder and faster.

"Yes, yes," he said quickly. "Hello."

"It's me," she answered, as if it might really be someone he knew. He was suddenly grateful that she hadn't said, "The call-girl," or something provocative that his neighbors might hear, and he quickly undid the chain and opened the door.

She was about a foot taller than he was, starchy white, with large fleshy legs and a tiny skirt. Her midriff was showing, and her shoulders were bare, too. It was a lot of flesh for Mr. Christopher to mentally process, and he sputtered once before speaking.

"No," he said. "You are not a Carlotta. Not petite and not a coed."

"Carlotta sent me. I'm her friend, Monique."

She pushed passed him. Mr. Christopher squinted against her redolent perfume as she breezed confidently to his living room. She had a small purse and tossed it onto his reading chair as if she had been in the apartment many times before.

His apartment building had once been a three-flat, but it had been sectioned off into nine uneasy units. His living room was long, but narrow; a wall had been added to make a bedroom where the other half of the living room had been. Knowing that the other three units on the floor had once been part of his apartment made him curious to know what the other units looked like. On those rare occasions when a neighbor left the door open—like if they were getting ready to go out or trying to get a better breeze in the summer—and Mr. Christopher happened to be walking by, he would linger, just a little bit, craning his neck slightly to get a peek. He always wanted to know how the units fit together, and it vaguely irritated him that two-thirds of his apartment were being lived in by other people.

"Smells good," she said.

"You're smelling the onions and green peppers which I will be using to stuff the pork chops, our main course."

"Having a fancy party?" she asked, turning slowly and eyeing the elaborately set table for the first time. Although Mr. Christopher usually ate on his couch with his plate and a magazine on the ottoman, tonight he had set out the best plates he had, the good silverware, and had even put two candles right in the center.

"No no, it's just us," he said, taking a step to his cassette player.

"I already ate."

"No no. I told the man on the phone this was for dinner and... that it would be for dinner as well as the other stuff."

A tinny version of Benny Goodman's clarinet came out of the box.

"No one told me," she said. "I don't have that much time."

"I need you here for at least three hours. I told the man that; I told him. I can't get all the food prepared in an hour, let alone eat it. We're going to have salad and soup and appetizers and bread—the bread's not even completely baked yet."

"You have an hour from when I got out of the car, and that was a couple of minutes ago. If I don't get back to Mickey by then—"

"Who's Mickey?"

"Look out your window. Across the street."

The blinds were shut, but he shuffled between the table and the window and lowered a couple of slats with his hand.

In the no-parking zone, an enormous man sat on the hood of a town car, feet spread-eagle on the pavement, reading a newspaper. Even though it was a large and bulky car, it dipped under the weight of the man's bottom.

"What's he doing?" Mr. Christopher asked.

"Wasting time, now. But I'm telling you, if I don't get down in... fifty-three minutes, he'll come tearing up here. You've never seen anything like it. You won't be able to reason with him, you won't be able to stop him. He'll come up those steps, bust down your door, and he'll clean your clock."

Mr. Christopher pulled his hands off the blinds and looked towards his kitchen. "Okay," he said. "We'll do it first, what you came here for, and that will give time for the bread to rise and also for the sugar—this is part of the dessert—to caramelize so that I can pour it, drizzle it, onto the flan. I need forty-five minutes for dinner. That gives me fifteen minutes for the rest of it. Can we do that in fifteen minutes, not even fifteen, but now it's already just twelve or eleven as you pointed out. Can it be done that fast?"

"Normally I have a routine I do, dancing and a rub down, and tickling on the genitalia to arouse you. If you want to skip all that, go right to it...well, it's your money."

"I wasn't picturing dancing or a rub down, but now that I hear about it, it does sound like fun. This is my first time, Monique, and so you'll have to guide me."

"Your first time, a guy of your age?"

"First time with a call-girl. Okay, we're wasting time. I need to finish sautéing the onions. We better do this in the kitchen."

The kitchen had once been the hallway that connected Mr. Christopher's third of the apartment to the rest of the building. It was narrow and ended abruptly in a sheetrock wall. The floor changed from hard wood to linoleum about a foot away from the wall, giving the impression that it might have led to a bathroom or a utility closet at one time. One side of the corridor was a narrow countertop, now covered in fruit peelings, shrimp shells and other food debris. Across the corridor was the sink, mini-refrigerator and a two burner stove that was already covered with large pots. Another small counter top separated the two appliances.

He found the Food section and brushed some cheese shavings off the page and put his finger on the right passage. He took a sniff of her perfume and knew she was behind him. "Clear and soft...I'm going to add the green peppers and the cumin and then cook that.... Then I have to slice the fat off the chops and carve little pockets—" He put a wooden spoon into his sautéing onions and turned his neck slightly so he could see her bare shoulder.

She reached around him unceremoniously and unbuckled his belt and lowered his pants. His legs were hairy with thick blue veins, but his underwear was shockingly white. When she pulled it down to his knees she reached under and grabbed his limp penis. Her hand was so cold and dry that he jumped, but didn't scream. He reached over to the small counter without moving his feet and began to scoop the melon pieces into a large blue bowl.

"I can't get around you here," she told him from the floor. "Can I open one of these cabinets by your knees, so that I can move my head closer, and I'll be able to reach you while you're working?"

He said, "Hang on a second, I'll be able to turn around in a second. Do you think...," he took a pair of black food scissors and slowly began snipping away at the tips of a large artichoke. "Do you think you could take off some clothing too, maybe just your top? Otherwise I'd feel too self conscious to enjoy it."

She pulled her tank top over head, and when he turned around she was kneeling in front of him with her hands folded in her lap. Her shirt was lying next to her, and he allowed himself to stare at her breasts. They were the largest he had ever seen, which made him feel a flash of pride, as if he had gotten a surprisingly good return on a shaky investment. Her nipples were oval, straining to keep their shapes on top of such large breasts.

Monique looked right at him and took his balls in her hand. Uncomfortable at the strangely clinical turn this had taken, he cleared his throat once. "My, eh, testicles...they're much larger than they should be for the size of my..."

She waved the comment away, which did make him feel better. She surely had seen all sorts of genitalia; and she leaned down and put him in her mouth.

The tail on his kitty-cat clock swung back and forth with each second, matching the absurd ping-pong eyes in the cat's head. The clock, painted into the torso of the cat, showed that he had only six minutes left for this part of the night if he was going to have the minimum amount of time he needed to serve the meal. A burning spit of grease from the onions hit him on the back of the neck.

Concentration was difficult for Mr. Christopher, and without moving from his spot, he picked up the big wooden spoon and pushed his onions around in the oil. When he felt his legs getting wobbly, he put the spoon down and held the countertop.

He was losing time now, it was going by quicker than usual; the kitty-cat's eyes and tail had been sped up by some strange force. But he had to admit that it felt good, what she was doing. His legs shook and he was afraid he might fall. He dug in with the heels of his house slippers and gripped tightly to the countertop, his hips involuntarily moving closer to the heat of her face. He wheezed from the back of his throat and felt her breasts against his legs, and he let himself go.

"Okay," he said. "You can spit that out in the sink."

She waved that comment away too, and put her shirt back on.

"Don't spoil your appetite," he said, as he did the top button on his pants and pulled his belt snug against his waist.

"I told you I ate already."

"Look," he told her. "I've got you for another thirty-three minutes. Go take a seat at the table."

She left, and he turned around and scooped the last melon pieces from the counter and used his hands to mix it all up in the bowl. He felt tired for a second, useless. He steadied himself against the counter and realized he just wanted to sleep—to pull the blanket up to his chest and open a magazine and relax. But the pot on the far burner began to bubble, and he remembered the magazines weren't coming anymore, although he couldn't remember why exactly. Mr. Christopher put the artichoke into the water and watched it simmer for a second before covering it.

She was already sitting when he walked back into the living room. He used a book of matches and lit the candles.

"You're going all out for this dinner, huh?" she asked.

Mr. Christopher wanted to smile, but he felt the pressure from the kitty-cat. The soup was done, and he went back into the kitchen, aware of the pathetic way his hip made him look when he was in a hurry. He ladled out two bowls, making sure each serving had the same number of shrimp and pineapple chunks.

"Lemongrass soup," he said, walking slowly out with the bowls. He placed them on the table and sat across from her.

"What is that smell?" she asked, cocking an eye at him.

"That's the lemongrass," he told her. "It's spicy, and I hope you like it."

"Should we say grace?"

Mr. Christopher had dipped his spoon in and was stirring his portion. "No time," he said, and slurped a loud mouthful. "Mmmm," he said, dabbing his lips with his napkin. "Okay, you keep eating, and I have to finish the fruit."

When he returned three minutes later, carrying four small bowls, he was breathing hard. Beads of sweat glistened on his forehead.

She looked up from her bowl and said excitedly, "You know, this is really good. Much better than it smells."

"I'm glad."

"You know what? The pineapple was even better than the shrimp. Pineapple in soup!" she said, and shook her head.

"This is fruit slaw, and this is a cheese and pea salad." He put both bowls in front of her and took her soup bowl. Her hand clenched momentarily, as if she might yank the soup bowl back, and this pleased Mr. Christopher, but he didn't have time to think about it.

"Oh God, the wine," he said. He went towards the kitchen but turned around after a few steps and took the soup bowls with him. On the way, he limped to the cassette player and flipped the tape, which had stopped at some point.

The music was back on, and Mr. Christopher poured two

glasses of wine. The song was one that he really liked—one of his favorites—Benny Goodman's "Belly of the Cat," and he suddenly felt self-conscious listening to it while pouring a woman wine. He quickly asked, "So, how do you like the salad?"

"It's okay," she said. "The soup was exotic, and this is sort of everyday type of food, so it's a strange menu."

"The food section said the salad is best served in a glass bowl. That way you can see the layers, the mayonnaise on the bottom, then the peas, then more mayonnaise, then the cheddar cheese, which I shredded myself. It's too bad I don't have a glass bowl."

"Why don't you sit down for a second?" she asked.

He twisted the blinds so he could see out the window. Mickey had put the newspaper away and was leaning against the door now, facing Mr. Christopher's doorway. He was dressed in a bow tie and a sporty tuxedo coat, like a bouncer at a banquet hall or a limo driver on prom night.

"I guess I'll sit down for a second," Mr. Christopher said, lowering himself uneasily into the chair. "And rest. I had planned on a nice conversation with you." He dabbed his forehead with the napkin, but he still felt sweaty. "So," he said, "how many people will you visit tonight?"

"I usually try to get five or six customers a night," she told him. "At least four, but six is a good night. Eight is the most I would do."

"When I worked retail, it was the same. Just like you, get to as many people as possible. So that's something we have in common, me and you," Mr. Christopher nodded once to himself. "But about you, eight times in one night? That's a lot. Good for business, I guess. Right?"

"That would be real good," she said. "Yes. It's not that tough. How many times do you do it a night?"

"Usually, none," he told her.

"But what's the most?"

He made a face.

"Come on, for a conversation. What's the most you've ever done it in a night."

"If I've ever done it twice in a night, then two. But I can't remember.

I usually get tired, and there isn't enough time in a single night to rest up entirely. So we're different, that's why it's so nice to spend time with someone you don't know, to share different experiences...." These sentences that he had prepared and even rehearsed a few times now sounded stilted and ridiculous in his mouth, although she was nodding in apparent agreement with him. Who was he trying to kid anyway? He looked at his watch to cover his embarrassment. "Okay," he said. "Time for the main course. Let's go, let's go."

He took her bowls away and returned a few minutes later with a platter. "We're going to eat dessert now, but save enough room for the pork chops. They're still a little pink and if we wait for them we might not have time for dessert. So we'll go out of turn."

She put her hand on her bare stomach. "That's fine with me anyway, because I'm not especially hungry. I told you that, that I had eaten already. I don't even know if I could eat another bite."

He brought four helpings of flan, each perfectly shaped like a large quivering eyeball. He had hoped she would want more than one helping, but he knew that wasn't going to happen, so he said, "I think it's time to make a toast."

She picked up her glass of wine, which was still full.

"To a lovely night," he said. "A lovely woman, a lovely meal and a lovely time."

He tipped his glass towards her slightly and she did the same in imitation, and they both drank.

"Okay," he said. "Now dessert."

He looked at his watch for a second and saw that he had nine minutes left. When he checked the window, he was surprised to see Mickey was walking back and forth. His legs and arms and were thick, like sausages. Mickey checked his watch and looked up to the third floor of the building.

"It's time for the pork chops," he mumbled.

"Are you sure there's time? You don't want him—Mickey, coming up here. It's better that I should leave a few minutes early than he get mad—come up those stairs and start banging on your door."

"I have eight more minutes of your time," Mr. Christopher answered icily, and he walked into the kitchen.

When he returned a few minutes later, he was carrying a plate with two sickly pink and grey slabs of meat. Corn and onions had been stuffed into slits along the sides of the chops, but they oozed like puddles of sewage. Mr. Christopher skewered the largest one and tried to get it off the tray, but every time he lifted the fork, the chop slid off. Finally he pushed it with the prongs onto her plate and slid the other one onto his plate. He put the serving platter on the floor.

"Bon appetite, my sweet."

"Are you sure these are done?" she said, poking her chop with a knife. "You've really got to cook meat, pork especially; and I thought I saw these out on your counter, raw, when I was in the kitchen."

"That's right," he told her. He cut off a slice. It was dull pink on the inside and she looked away before he put it in his mouth. "But I turned the oven up as high as it would go and had them in since we began eating. Mmmm. Anyway, I don't have any more time." His lips were glistening and he sliced off another piece and waited for her to begin.

"It smells good," she stood up. "But I ate before I got here, and the custard and the soup, and that's it. I couldn't eat another bite. Thank you for the night. That'll be a hundred and forty bones, and that's not including a tip."

"Take a bite of the dinner. The bread isn't done yet and we'll forget about the liqueur; I haven't even begun to make the garlic butter sauce for the artichoke appetizer. So we'll forget all the rest, but I want you to at least try the pork chop. It's stuffed with corn and sautéed onions. You know, festively."

He wolfed down another bite, swallowing it as quickly as possible to show how good it was.

"My money," she said putting her palm out.

"My time," he said into his plate. "This is all I wanted, for you to come here and have a nice meal and a nice time. It's my special day and this was all I wanted."

"Listen, old man. You didn't cook it long enough; I'm going to retch just from the smell and I'm already nauseous from the spicy soup and the bowl of mayonnaise."

He forced himself to take another piece of the pork chop. When it reached his tongue his stomach lurched, and the meat fell apart unnaturally. He put his napkin up to his mouth and spit it up. When he was done gagging and had wiped his lips hard onto the napkin, he said, "The money is in my front pants pocket. Seven twenty-dollar bills." He covered his head with his hands and rested his elbows on the table.

"Give it to me," she said.

"It's too late," he told her. "Check the window."

The door lurched in its frame and then popped open. Monique put her arm around Mr. Christopher's shoulders. "It's okay, Mickey," she yelled. "It's okay, I'm all right."

Mr. Christopher closed his eyes as a hand grabbed his shoulder and pulled him up off the chair. He opened them and saw Mickey's teeth, a row of little rat triangles.

"You see that door, buddy," Mickey snarled. "I suggest you hand over the money right this instant, or that's what's going to happen to your head."

"The money's in my pocket, sir," Mr. Christopher said, dropping back in the chair. "The money's in my pocket," he repeated. He stood up and took a step back. "Here." He put the wad of folded bills onto the table.

"And hold on you two. Hold on a minute." He put up a finger towards Mickey and Monique and ambled into his kitchen. The pot with the artichoke was boiling over, and Mr. Christopher turned off the burners and shut off the stove. A stack of old newspapers were piled under the counter, waiting to be taken to the trash.

"I know your time is valuable," Mr. Christopher called out. "And I know I've wasted some of it. I'm sorry about that...." Brightening up, he slipped on an oven-mitt and took the platter of pork chops from the oven. "And six customers is a lot, and I know you've got to be going.... Believe me, I respect the need for speed. So maybe this will help, with dinner...." As he spoke, he wrapped in newspaper three of the juiciest chops he had. He pulled the artichoke out of the water with tongs and put it into a large Zip-loc baggie. When that was done, he dumped the rest of the fruit slaw into another baggie, and the cheese and pea salad into a third. "I appreciate you coming over, Monique, and you too Mickey! I appreciate the time you spent with me...." Mr. Christopher pulled a brown shopping bag out of the garbage and put the moist newspaper packages and all the baggies into it.

The soup was hot, but he found a square tupperware in a cabinet and poured it in, burped the lid, and put it in the brown bag with the rest of it. The flan was more delicate, but Mr. Christopher emptied an egg carton and filled the cups with the lumpy brown custard.

"I remember on Thanksgiving," Mr. Christopher called while skittering around his kitchen, "or any food holiday like that, Christmas and the Fourth of July—barbecues on the Fourth—and at the end the host always would ask what you wanted to...take home with you, leftovers...."

He had no plastic forks or spoons, but now wasn't the time to worry about his stuff. It would be a long time before he ever had guests over again, if ever, so he put his nice silverware into the bag. Two of everything: two salad forks, two regular forks, two sets of each spoon—fruit, dessert, soup—two sets of steak knives and two butter knives. He pulled the bread loaf out of the oven, slapped the bottom of the pan with his mitted fist, and the oatmeal raisin mass fell solidly into the bag.

"That's when you know you've had a good time—didn't waste your time—when you walked out with an armload of food for the next couple of days..." He folded the top over twice, put his hand on his hip, and walked into the living room.

The room was empty. Mr. Christopher held the warm shopping bag to his chest and looked at his door. It was only attached at the top hinge and looked like it might fall, and he could see past it, into the empty hallway, all the way to his neighbor's closed door.

Lost Languages of Africa

Couzine pulled her long coat closed when the express rocked past; no faces in the window, just warm flashes of white. Holding her breath never helped, she could still taste metallic sweat in her mouth long after the train was gone.

"Missy?" A fiddle-wielding busker, a dark man in overalls and a delightful fedora, stepped near Couzine. "Your hair is glorious!" he told her, pointing with his bow.

She had spent the day getting tiny lights woven into her braids that winked red, yellow and green. Two small watch-batteries glued behind her lobes powered the panoply by way of a thin filament. Before she could thank the busker he bent into his open case and pushed aside the few crinkled bills. He was wearing gloves with fingers cut off and he grabbed a plastic rose with a light in the center pulsing red. He smelled of powerful mints as if he had eaten an entire roll, or maybe it was some kind of syrupy alcohol that smelled that way. Couzine made a grand gesture of sniffing the rose (using stagecraft because she would never take such a deep breath on a subway platform) and gave the man her best curtain-call bow. The busker raised his fiddle and broke into a frenzied outburst of hillbilly bowing and picking which rendered Couzine momentarily giddy, before the sound was lost in the rush of her arriving train.

Her fingers clutched the rose on her lap and she rocked with the unruly subway. Why was she going so far uptown to see David Bernstein again anyway? The first reason, first and foremost, was that Couzine volunteered at an art school for gifted children, and David's little sister was her favorite. Rosie Bernstein was only eleven, but Couzine considered their friendship inevitable, and she delighted in long, rudderless chats with the child; they were like characters in an Eric Rohmer film, not that Rosie would have understood the reference. As for the brother, David, she wouldn't have looked twice in any other set of circumstances. The struggle for even awkward conversation with David Bernstein brought Couzine to all sorts of extremes, listing possible topics in her notebook ahead of time and loading her pockets with gewgaws from home, thrift store costume jewelry mostly, which she could produce during awkward lulls. Couzine sighed at her reflection in the subway window, taken by surprise yet again by the winking lights in her hair, and savoring the ennui of social obligation. *My weariness is a beautiful thing*, she thought.

Couzine knocked on the door, and when David Bernstein opened it she was already fanning open her glimmery notebook.

"What do you think of this for a title?" She cleared her throat: "*A Good Cooking Monkey*."

David Bernstein, who was holding a large wooden spoon still splattered with tomato sauce, appeared momentarily concerned.

"Not for an opera or a drama. But maybe for an off Broadway show, something brief and radical. Wouldn't you come see a show called *A Good Cooking Monkey?*"

"Who's in it?" David Bernstein asked. He had curly blonde hair like a girl's and was at least a foot too tall for her and had kind of a plain face to boot. Rosie Bernstein had the same face, all cheeks and freckles, and on an eleven-year-old it was charming. When Couzine agreed to the date, Rosie had whispered, "I love you, Couzine."

She put her notebook away; it was a prop that had served its purpose: to put David Bernstein on notice that she was alert and paying attention, a trick her father had taught her for getting better service in restaurants. Of course this was just David Bernstein's stuffy apartment, two rooms and a half bath, one window overlooking someone else's window, dreary old couch that had probably passed from tenant to tenant for years but on which Couzine was now sitting, her legs in dark tights and steel-toed work boots, stretched out across the uneven surface of David Bernstein's coffee table.

He handed her a bottle of beer with the top off.

"I have news," he announced. His lips rarely moved, permanently fixed into an oval that quivered when he inhaled. The only reason Couzine knew she was being spoken to was that he tended to look away from her at the start of sentences.

She grandly took her notebook out again. "Pray tell."

David Bernstein turned his back. "It's about my fiancée."

She closed it again. Two nights ago they had slept together for the first time. Not that it mattered, but now she felt suddenly compressed and tired.

"I want to eat out tonight." Couzine answered flatly.

"I'm making pasta in a vodka sauce and peppers."

"Out to eat."

He was looking out his window. "Reductions. I've been cooking since two-thirty."

"If you're eating with me," she slung her scarf back around her neck, "you're bringing reliable plastic."

It was dark already and people were walking briskly, pressing forward into the wind toward the Hudson.

"Your hair," he said suddenly. They stopped for the first time and he stared unabashedly. "I couldn't tell upstairs, but out here," he reached up and stroked the side of her head. "It's like a Christmas tree."

"I wanted an actual crèche woven into the flip," she told him, not joking. "But the girl balked. Down on Astor Place. And the guy who put the wire in runs sound for a disco in the meat packing district and just happened to be in for a weave. How's that for serendipity?"

David fingered a single braid down to the blinking light. His index finger tapped it lightly as if to test the heat.

"Where's the battery?"

"Wouldn't you like to know."

"It's truly amazing," he said to her finally. It was the first confident proclamation he had ever made in her presence and it made her inexplicably sad.

They walked aimlessly, although David Bernstein pressed forward as if with purpose. They fell behind a thick man talking on a wireless headset. He was waving his hands wildly and every other word sounded like a snarled expletive. Couzine remembered the old joke that all the muttering homeless in New York should be paired so it would look like they were talking to someone. Now they could just be outfitted with headsets like everyone else and you'd never know who were the crazies.

Through fogged windows, Pepé Roncini's, a wide storefront near Columbia, looked warm and convivial with a long bar and lots of red checkered tablecloths. David Bernstein ordered an apple martini for himself at the bar and she took a rocks glass of Yellowman Bourbon straight. They hunched over their drinks and she hoped it would take a long time for a table.

"I'm drinking vodka tonight because I don't want to mix," he said to explain himself. "I nipped the bottle a few times while making the sauce."

"Guess that's why you're so loosey-goosey tonight."

He nodded, not hearing the joke or not getting it. A Knicks game was on television and the bartender stood nearby but kept his attention almost exclusively on the screen. They had been in this place two days before, but Couzine hadn't recognized it until just now—that obtrusive television hanging down from the ceiling like aging beef. That night while walking home they'd been approached by a large African in a dashiki and with a thick accent who exclaimed, "Day-veed Bernstein!" before hugging him. He was an informant, David Bernstein had told her later, one of the last speakers of some language in Africa for which he was writing a grammar. The two began an animated conversation in whatever native language the man spoke, a dialogue like two cars struggling to get up a mountain. But it was beautiful, too. The shock of it had utterly gob-smacked Couzine—that David was capable of something so strange and wonderful on a random street corner in New York City. She had taken his hand and stayed the rest of the night.

After sipping half her bourbon in silence she clamped a hand on his knee, startling him. She took a dramatic breath. "I'm ready."

"Her name is Brenda," he said quickly.

"Sounds like a nice name." She was sincere but couldn't help sneering. "Brenda. How long have you been engaged?"

"Forever."

"When you got engaged, did you hire Western Union to sing it, or have a mime come to the house and pull it from a shrinking box while walking against the wind?"

"It was Brenda's idea. She had a magazine with pictures of dresses and she showed one to me and asked me what I thought and—"

"What did you think?"

An aproned busboy arranging olives and maraschino cherries was looking at Couzine. Every time she turned he would look away, but Couzine could see it in her peripheral vision. She smiled coyly, assuming they were flirting and that he was bad at it. But then Couzine realized the busboy was only sizing up her hair, and what she thought was interest was probably something closer to bafflement and probably disapproval. Maybe he wasn't the type who appreciated novelty. Or effort.

"Brenda consulted me in a certain way," David Bernstein was saying. "For example, she asked hypothetically if June after my defense would be a good time for one to get married and then later if I thought Verdurin Banquet Hall was a nice place for a reception."

Couzine sucked an ice cube. "And you just went along with it."

"Over the phone yesterday I told her I was having second thoughts."

"And she said?"

"She said, 'This is because of Couzine Richardson.' And then she coughed, which is her marker of frustration and irritation."

Couzine wasn't looking at David Bernstein any more. "And pray tell, lover boy, how does Brenda know my name?"

"She and Rosie e-mail. I assume Rosie told her."

Tomorrow, before Rosie's class began, Couzine decided she would go behind the kiln and smash the kitty cat figurine the girl had just finished glazing. The hostess waved broadly in their direction; the table was ready.

"I was in a cafe, yesterday," Couzine told him, rapidly scanning the menu. The words weren't penetrating: small type, familiar letters, pasta this, chicken that, veal angel hair, Vesuvius, Fontana, Calabrian, put it any order. Couzine wanted no pause in the conversation. "I guess about the same time you and Brenda were on the phone talking about me, I was in a cafe chatting on my iBook, and I was watching this man and woman, kids really, my age, so younger than you, not a grown-up getting married like you, anyway, they were playing a game of backgammon on the cafe's set. They have a shelf of games and cards and the like, magazines too, and the first thing I noticed was how eager this guy was."

"Should we get the fixed dinner for two?"

"You choose," she told him even as she flipped a page in the menu. "I'm busy with my anecdote." But she stopped speaking.

Couzine had been sure watching the aggressive way this man would nudge the woman's arm when he got a good roll that they were sleeping together and were at the point where he was being deliberately confident to cover for the fact that he was still insecure about their relationship. When they finished the game Couzine had come to so identify with them that she was nearly crushed when they didn't clean after themselves but left the game instead for the employees to pick up. Out on the street the pair split in opposite directions without a kiss or even really a nod to one another, no backward glances or friendly waves. Looking more closely, she thought she saw a similarity in their features. Couzine had no siblings herself and consequently often overlooked this possibility when guessing about the relationships of strangers. Having a brother was a romantic idea for her: the one she imagined for herself was older and jealous and someone with whom she shared vaguely incestuous feelings. Couzine got up and cleaned the game herself and felt, not for the first time that day, that if she should force herself to cry right then and there it wouldn't be at all difficult.

"I'm going to order a 7-Up," David Bernstein said finally, peering out from the menu. "I'm getting a tummy ache from all that vodka."

DURING the antipasto, Couzine improvised a provolone and pepperoni sandwich using a leftover bun from the basket. "Tell me about her. Brenda," Couzine said. "Because I can't picture her." She dragged her sandwich around the oily plate.

"She's seven years older than me," David Bernstein said. He always took small, mincing chews, wringing every scintilla of taste.

"And exactly how old a man are you?"

"I'm 26."

"Which puts her at..." Couzine nodded to herself. "Pepper me," she gestured across the table. This was an actual adult life that had been ruined. Not ruined, that was too dramatic. Affected.

"She's pretty?" Couzine asked.

"Can I have a bite of that?" David Bernstein was looking at her directly, his hand out.

"Finish it." She felt pleasure at his comfort. David was cute, she thought, like Rosie cute, and he was smart, but his intelligence was masturbatory, his knowledge only narrowly useful: good if you should happen to bump into a fully uniformed African in Manhattan, otherwise, not so useful.

It might have been an elevation of blood sugar, but as the food started arriving, so did David Bernstein's story. He met Brenda when she was in grad school learning to teach ESL and he was just starting out in Theoretical Linguistics, and even as Couzine's heart gladdened for this openness, she felt her attention drifting. Eight women at a table just down from their booth, four on each side, were going over the bill as if it were a legal contract. The woman closest to Couzine had removed a smallish calculator from her purse. Probably figuring 18% on her portion to the penny or maybe even just her part of the bill so she didn't accidentally overpay. Why were people so rigorous and stingy? And narrow. If she were one of those women she would say, "Let me treat you all. Get me next time." If she had money she'd go over there now and pay the bill just to give them a story for next time they got together.

Cannoli had been ordered or maybe it just came with the meal, she wasn't sure. With chocolate chips on the outside and bright green pistachios ringing the ricotta, it was more elaborate than it needed to be, and they took turns hacking at it with forks until it was gone. "I read your father's book," David Bernstein said at last. "It was strange for me. I've only read one other book of fiction since high school, really."

"Which one did you read?"

"*Gravity's Rainbow.* It was about World War II but really weird."

"I'm asking which book of my father's did you read?"

David Bernstein's eyes widened. "He's written more than one? It was called *Out of Gas and Other Stories.* I haven't read the other stories yet but I liked 'Out of Gas.' It was pretty funny. I didn't get all the metaphorical elements in it and frankly wouldn't even had looked for them if the book jacket hadn't explained the whole thing. The jacket people really make him out to be a genius."

"He wrote the jacket. The authors always do it in the third person. I'm not saying he's *not* a genius. Just buyer beware, you know, in the future."

I'm giving you back to Brenda, Couzine thought. She imagined herself at home on her mattress on the risers over her desk. She would probably cry tonight in bed except that it was Saturday and she liked some of the short films that showed on the Sundance Channel, so maybe she would wait and cry tomorrow. *Still,* she thought, *my sadness is a beautiful thing.* Maybe someday she would get to sing the Marschallin and use this night as part of her performance. *Go back to Brenda, David Bernstein. I'm giving you back to her. Probably.* She gave a deep, benevolent sigh now at David Bernstein, who allowed an adorable look of confusion to come over his girlish features.

SHE dreaded the moment at his door mostly because that was when he was going to make a move or not, and she would have to react. She hoped the man from Africa would be on the corner again but of course he wasn't, although she felt closer to David just walking through the intersection.

He was thinking of it too. "I'm actually going to Africa, you know. Did I tell you?"

"No. Funny, you've been so open with me since we've met."

"I've been waiting on funding. But I got my letter today and so I'm going to Mali. I've been once before to this region, it's very remote. A fertile plane where the Niger, Bani, and Diaka rivers run within a few hundred miles of each other. You have to raft in and then hike for three days to get to the site."

"Me? You. You're not asking me to come with you, right?"

"Certainly not. But you should come visit. I'll be very lonely. The funding covers a three year commitment. It's an exciting project. We're investigating a dialect of Bombara." He was looking into her eyes and his lips were moving and his cheeks were even getting flush, although it may just have been the cold. "I'll be traveling with Bwa and Tukulor speakers—it's very diverse region, linguistically. We think there must be a sort of 'native lingua franca' so Mande tribes could trade with the Berbers and nomads. Some of the grammar itself might be gestures and facial expressions and we have old *tifinagh* documents that suggest we're correct about this. There had to be a way for all the disparate groups to recognize what was going on with one another."

"Are you going to invite her too?"

"Brenda? I don't know if she'll come. It might be easier if the two of you traveled together but I don't know if your schedules will match. I know you do a lot of performance in the summer, which is when she'd be available because of teaching."

It was so ludicrous that Couzine could actually see it happening, she and Brenda traveling together and becoming dear, lifelong friends. She was going to need someone to replace Rosie anyway.

Over David Bernstein's shoulder, like the rear flank of a defeated army, three street vendors trudged slowly, heads bowed like horses, each hauling a cart from behind. The last one had a closed umbrella pointing up and Couzine thought it was lovely, but a second later the troops turned a corner and were gone. When she looked back at David he was moving in for a kiss and she only had seconds to brace herself and take him, grip his arms, and then gently nudge him back toward his building, where he turned and went without another word.

If the African man had been standing on the corner she might have gone up with David again. But as it was, nothing wonderful had happened, and in its absence it felt like everything was awful; just another corner with too much light and too much noise in too big of a city. Through the frosted glass she watched David pause by his mailbox and then make his way past the security door. Then she went straight home like anyone else, just another girl riding the subway, a girl with a plastic rose in her pocket and the twinkling cosmos in her hair.

Tandem

THE moon was orange the evening he got back and he whistled while wrestling his bicycle down from the car roof. He heaved it over his head and left it to dangle upside-down like a bat in the garage. Then he took a beer into the shower with him and drank it down while a week's worth of street dust and chain-grease washed into the drain. At the sink he shaved and then brushed his teeth twice, savoring running water, and after putting the empty bottle in the blue recycle bin, he crawled into bed and woke his wife.

"I had an epiphany," he said into the darkness, feeling his way into his groove next to her body. "I'm sorry I've been so mad for so long, keeping my anger inside, but I've let it all go and now everything is going to be different."

She thought, *he thinks he keeps his anger inside*, but slid over to make room for him. She re-shifted her battery of pillows, fluffy dark under her head, pinky-feathers clutched tightly against her stomach, a third propped between her knees, and then she took his hand from her breast. "Sounds like you had a peak experience," she said curling his fingers into her fist. "No pun intended on peak. It'll pass and within a day or two you'll go back to being exactly the same person you were before you left. I'm happy you're back."

There would be tests of his new resolve, challenges to the way in which he had decided to live his life post-epiphany, and this was shaping up to be an unexpectedly early one of those. "I'm going to proceed with the conversation as though it were happening the way I wish," he told her, then worried it had come out edgy so he giggled to show no harm meant. He tried to wind himself around her like a helix, arm against her stomach, legs draped across hers while not disturbing her knee pillow. He inhaled the back of her head.

"The epiphany happened when I was coming down Monarch Pass. Summit's 11,000 feet and the climb was nine miles straight up, three hours of relentless pedaling. The air is so thin up there and then you have to go down the other side, 7,000 feet straight down dangerous, twisty road. I was terrified. I was really, really scared. You start to see signs for "Runaway Truck Turnoffs" and then you think about all the things that can go wrong with a bike. I feathered my brakes—do you know what that means? To feather your brakes?"

"Hand me my Blackberry and I'll check Wikipedia."

"Like this," and he took first her breast and then her shoulder, alternately squeezing and releasing. "With the brakes, back and forth, first the back then gently on the front, easing off on both."

"Got it. Thanks for the demonstration. Maybe you're enjoying this part too much?"

He kissed the back of her neck, pressed in tighter, hoping she could tell the bike had firmed the muscles on his lower half. He didn't have those ropey calf muscles like some of the grizzled old timers who'd been biking for decades, but he thought he could sense new hardness to his calves, his ass too—it would be great if he could wheel around and present that to her like a chimp.

"If I spilled, the momentum alone would probably have pulled me over the side of the road and down the mountain."

She pressed back into him. "Sounds scary."

"It is until it isn't. Suddenly, just out of nowhere, the fear lifts, like a blowing veil, leaving the most amazing, free feeling. No fear now, just the wind and the speed and the bike...I started to describe the feelings to myself in my head so I could remember them, the feeling of being connected to something wa-ayyy out of proportion to my size.

"I thought: this is like riding a broomstick. Of course I've never ridden a broomstick, no one has, but that's the feeling, just hanging on to this thing, keeping it steady between your knees while soaring. I kept narrating the descent to myself so I could remember later. Being able to describe coming down Monarch became the most important thing in the world to me. The only thing. I wanted to be able to share it with you. And then suddenly..."

He felt the familiar moistening in the corner of his eyes that this part of the story always brought. It didn't seem to matter if he was telling it in the campground or at the beer garden or even just in his head, practicing. If the lights had been on she could've seen the emotion in his face.

"Suddenly...epiphany. I realized that I *couldn't* keep it. The ride would be over when the ride was over, the elation would be gone. I couldn't go back up and do it again, I couldn't slow it down. And I knew I wasn't even going to remember it again. Not really."

His voice had slowed and halted a few times and he wasn't even forcing it. Her throat tightened a little. They were sharing the moment now, his retelling of the epiphany, and she kissed his fingers laced in hers.

"I was descending Monarch right then on my bicycle, it was happening, but I understood the experience wasn't mine to keep. I started to cry, tell the truth. But I held back because at that speed I couldn't take my hands off the handlebars long enough to wipe my eyes."

"So you—"

"I understood that you get a moment, and then it's gone. Later, reflecting on it in my tent in Salida I recognized it really wasn't anything new that had occurred to me. Fact is my epiphany was maybe the oldest one in the world: that life is temporary, just a series of moments and that the key is to be plugged in to each one as it comes because it's really all you get. Take pleasure in what's happening when it happens. Don't look ahead for something that might be. Don't look back at what was. Somehow coming down Monarch those clichés became real."

"I see what you mean," she said. "Arriving at those ideas in that way is different from just reading it in a self-help book. I can see how you might feel changed."

"I just feel really good. About everything. About you and about us. I feel really close to you." And to show what he meant he put his hands under her nightshirt.

She said, "It's late for me, because I was already asleep. Do you want me to get up and insert my diaphragm?"

The question was deflating. "I guess not, if you don't want to."

"I don't mind. But you have to say it. Tell me to get up out bed and get it."

"I guess...if you're all settled in already..."

"Another time then," she assured him.

"And I have an idea," he murmured. "About a way for us to be different and burn new memories to replace the old, bad ones. But I'll...tell you the rest of it later...."

They clung to each other for a little while until his drifting body released her tangle of limbs back into the ether. His own legs felt rubbery in a dream state, as though still clipped into the pedals, as though pounding over switchbacks, left, then right, then left.... "I'm not mad at you any more," he mumbled into the dark, not certain if she was awake, not sure if he was really saying it, the feeling of the drift, unaware of how long it had been since either one of them had spoken. He reached across the bed for her, worried suddenly she had gotten up to use the bathroom and not returned or gotten a drink and just disappeared, his arm stretched through an obstacle course of pillows and comforters, stretching like taffy, fingers reaching for her....

HE waited for breakfast the next morning to tell her the rest of it.

"It solves all our problems," he told her over the magazine she was hunkered behind. "I saw lots of couples on the BRACE riding them. Nothing can come between a couple on a tandem bike."

She smiled kindly. "Nothing is going to come between us." Her narrow cheater glasses perched forward on her nose.

"And on a tandem, nothing can. Hey, what are you eating?"

His tone startled her and she paused before holding open her palm. "It's an energy bar," she said.

"Oh no no," he said. "Cycle Blasts are only for riders."

"I have a bike. I ride."

He snorted. "Look, when we get the tandem, and we're out on

the road, then you can eat a Cycle Blast."

"I don't want to ride a tandem bike."

"Well you don't eat a Cycle Blast just to go teach kindergarten. What, are you going to bonk out getting the kids to line up single file?"

She folded away her magazine and took another bite.

He pressed closer. "When was the last time you rode your bike anyway?"

Her bike was a Schwinn three-speed she bought at a yard sale for 30 dollars and had owned since high school. It had wide, white-walled tires and a seat commodious enough for a rider twice her girth. Before they met she had loved riding it around the lakefront, from Oak Street Beach near where she worked to her condo in Lakeview, stopping at cafes in Lincoln Park for espressos and bran scones, where she would invariably meet friends from work or maybe even one of the hundreds of her pals from college, all of whom seemed to be living within a pleasant bike ride's distance. She hadn't even needed a car the first couple of years after graduating because she was never far from the red line. Back then, before marriage, she could walk into any tiny Thai place or narrow Indian buffet—sushi at the Tokyo Marina, margaritas at El Jardin—and be pretty much guaranteed to know a handful of other people, men and women near her age also taking leisurely breaks from jobs at nonprofits and environmentals, young adults who shared basic political assumptions and the same taste in movie stars. This was being young and single in this city, the dusky lights of Clark and Belmont on her fat-tired bike, waving to friends drinking against whale-sized windows under Old Style signs. She never locked her bike in those days, partly from a feeling that having her bike stolen was just something that couldn't happen to her. *I'd rather be mugged than live in fear* she told more than a few friends more than a few times. She was also fairly certain she would lose the key or forget the combination anyway. She'd been married now fourteen years, hadn't taken a bike ride in ten, but still had the thing in the garage hanging next to his expensive carbon bike, a dusty youth waiting to be reclaimed, but just for an hour or two.

"The tandem will also mark a fresh start for both of us," he continued. "I've never ridden one, and as far as I know you never have either."

"I never have."

"As far as I know." Despite himself, he was hungry and he fished out the last Cycle Blast from the box.

"I suppose I would be the back rider," she sighed.

"The stoker, natch. But we'll switch sometimes and you can captain. Not at first, but after you get some, you know...experience."

"Do I ever get to steer?"

"From the back?" He used his tongue to pry some of the thick slush from a molar.

She creased her magazine at the picture of the yoga pose she was thinking about trying. "Okay. I'm game. Might even be fun. But I just don't like the feeling that you're making me ride the tandem as some sort of penance for perceived crimes that you think I've committed."

"You know what you did," he growled, but waved his hands to keep the conversation from slipping into this particular rut. "The tandem is for both," he said quickly. "So we can start all over. Clean slate, the whole mishigas. Burn new memories, like Dr. Shiraz says."

"There aren't any bad old memories. You need to stop talking like that."

He took a deep breath. "Anyway, it's not just you that needs penance. I have something I should tell you about. I met a woman on the BRACE."

She stared at him. He took another nibble of his bar and drummed his fingers on the table once before continuing.

"This gal was older than me and she had a bike map holder from REI velcroed to her handlebars. The kind you sometimes see with the Shimano gear shifters?"

She shrugged, cautiously.

"You know. Anyway, it sort of attached to her Trek mileage computer and she and I managed to get lost briefly while coming in to town. Gunnison, which was sort of a college town, not like Hotchkiss or *Boo-wayna* Vista which were both pretty small and not hard to navigate in. But we got to base camp late and it was too dark for both of us to set up our tents so we both just pitched hers, me helping her, being gallant and gentlemanly, and we drank a lot of beer at the beer garden celebration. Remember I texted you about the New Belgium Brewery being a kind of a sponsor? The lady bought my beer, and then she said I could crash in her teepee since we didn't set mine up and then it was getting cold so I moved closer together to generate some heat. This was on the high school football field, and then she took off her clothes and said I should do the same to generate even more heat. She had a pretty good body too, you know, for an older lady."

"Did this really happen?"

"Absolutely! What sort of question is that?"

"I don't know. I know you have that older lady thing so it seems sort of a convenient detail."

"I'm sorry if this is hurting you."

"Also you said it was too dark to see, so I don't know how you all of a sudden can tell she had the nice body—"

"I could tell from earlier, from the way her Pearl Izumi bike pants fit. Anyway all long-time bike riders have nice—"

"And the thing about generating heat reminds me of that MASH episode when what's-his-name was hitting on Hot Lips, and we both know how nuts you are for MASH."

"Why would I make this up? I'm confessing something terrible."

"You want to hurt me. You were hurt, and whether you should or should not have been hurt is no longer the issue, I understand. You were hurt, and you're still trying to hurt me."

"No! That's me before. I'm different now since coming down Monarch. And anyway, even if I am making this up, what difference does it make? Isn't just thinking it bad enough?"

"Thinking what?"

"We had sex, me and the lady! I was cheating on you during this sexual encounter. It was wild too. Well, not that wild maybe, actually pretty standard stuff, but we had our bike helmets on which is at least sort of novel. Oh, and we did it two times in the same night." He leaned back in his chair to let that settle for a moment.

"Weren't you tired from all the bike riding?"

He snorted. "Not *that* tired."

"Did this happen before or after the Monarch Pass ride?"

"Excuse me?"

"Did you have sex in your bike helmet with the shapely older lady like on MASH before or after your epiphany?"

"I...what difference does it make?" He began fiddling with the salt shaker, tapping it a few times, trying to turn the base like a top. "Before, I think. You know when you're on a trip like that, all the days tend to blur. But I already told you it happened in Gunnison and that was before Monarch, the night before in fact. I'm sorry if you feel devastated by this."

"I would be devastated, if I believed it. Which I don't. I think your epiphanic moment didn't have as much lasting effect as you thought it would. But before you say anything else, I take the point that this is something important to you. That's all you needed to say, that it's important. I'll try a tandem. Let's rent one and go around the subdivision. Could be fun."

"Sure! You'll want your own bike in no time. You'll probably even want to be on next year's Bike Ride Across Colorado's Environs with me."

"Don't register me for the BRACE just yet, I'm just trying it out. Don't get me any gear until I see how I like it. No jerseys or pants, and for god's sake don't buy me a 'Livestock' bracelet."

"Livestrong! Wait, don't tell me you're against curing cancer too."

THE bike arrived at the shop several days later and they went to be fitted, the technicians lowering her seat, raising the stoker pedals, adding bottle cages to the frame, pushing the captain's handlebars forward a few centimeters. By the time he was disassembling the frame so it would fit on his Yakima hitch she understood they were buying and not renting, but the process had gone on too long for her to say anything. Which is why the morning of the first ride, when he laid out her new bike pants, fresh jersey, shoes with clips on the bottom and a new helmet, she was determined to be a good sport in the spirit of shared endeavor. They dressed in silence, naked by the dim light of the closet. She tugged at the bike pants—hadn't worn anything so tight since high school. She had to admit that the biking had changed him, and not all for the worse. Physically he was better off, a good twenty pounds lighter. Plus he no longer wheezed during sex, although it hadn't done anything for the sweating, which tended to make him as moist as seaweed, turning their connubial bed into a damp eco-system before it was over.

By the time he got the water bottles filled and caged, checked pressure in the tubes, retopped the Presta valves with Schrader converters, the sun was just beginning to rise, bleeding purple slashes into the morning sky.

"Are you sure these pants are even the right size?" She slapped herself idly to keep warm. "It feels like I'm wearing a diaper." He had already told her she would feel differently in the saddle and didn't see any need to repeat himself. He made sure their bike helmets were secure but not constricting and then, after giving a few swings from his hips to loosen everything up, he rolled the bike to the lip of the driveway, just at the edge of the lawn.

"I dub thee," he officiously patted the seat with his gloved hand. "Fresh Start."

This was the name she had negotiated, having objected to his first suggestion "Penance" as being a clear attack on her and his second idea, "Peacemaker" as being too loaded and backward looking. He thought her first ideas, "Dream Horizon," and "Tomorrow's Treat," corny and more suited for a racehorse, but agreed "Fresh Start" caught something in the spirit of what he was after.

Throwing his leg over the seat he situated his rump and gave his fingers a flashy wiggle before leaning low toward the handlebar. Just as he was about to plant the balls of his shoes and stabilize the bike, the frame began jerking back and forth.

"Whoa! What're you..."

His arm stiffened to keep from upending, but against his effort the bike suddenly lurched right and he was face down on the dewy grass, bicycle pressing heavily upon him.

"Oopsy," she said. "Sorry."

"You need to tell me what you're going to do before you do it." He picked the bike up and ran his fingertips over the cables to make sure nothing had been damaged. "It's okay. We had to have our first spill at some point." He gave his best confidence building, captain's smile. "And now look at your right leg! Chain grease. Those smeared ovals are a real badge of honor among enthusiasts. Shroud of Bontrager. Now you're one of us."

This time they threw their legs over in unison, and when they were both ready, he took a step forward like a cross country skier, the two of them rising to meet their saddles like forward pistons. They got down to the edge of the driveway and he began a leeward maneuver onto the empty street. The bow of the bike took the turn with a pleasing, graceful glide, but suddenly the stern felt sluggish and weighty. He could feel her swinging wide and responded by bearing down on the handlebars, but he knew they were going down again. Being clipped in meant abandoning ship was out of the question, and bracing, they pitched on to the pavement before it even occurred to him to call out a warning.

"Damn it," she said.

"It's okay," he told her. "We had to have our second spill at—"

"It's starting to hurt now!" She brushed gravel from her arms.

"Anything worth doing well will hurt when done wrong." He nodded, pleased. "I just made that up or possibly adapted it from the sort of thing written on inspirational posters. Either way, I believe it."

"Do I have to stay clipped into the thing?" She slapped the side of her own helmet in frustration. "The spills wouldn't be so bad if I could lift my feet off the pedals."

He righted the bike and leaned it against his hip. The sun was completely up now and he felt they needed to get going. "The problem is you aren't paying enough attention to me. If I lean left, you lean left. If I nudge right, you nudge right, no more or less than the way I do it. You have to be in synch with my every move. More really, you need to anticipate exactly what I'm going to do and do it with me. The better you get at it the better a tandem team we'll be."

"It's not so easy when all I have to look at is your back."

He had been refitting a fingerless glove but instead now develcroed it entirely and flung it dramatically to the pavement. "Plenty of other couples manage it!"

"Don't get so huffy, excuse the pun."

"I didn't hear one."

"Think bike manufacturers."

He retrieved the glove. "We're being silly" he said. "Let's just get going."

This time they were ready for the battle of angles after she seated herself and hunkered into position. They gripped tightly to their handlebars, shoulders loose, and while the bike wobbled under their disparate efforts, the center of balance shifting left then right then left, they both doggedly kept pedaling. They managed thirty feet straight, then turned gingerly out of their cul-de-sac.

He called back, "Are you pedaling?"

"I'm pedaling."

"What?"

"I'm pedaling."

"I'm asking you if you're pedaling."

"Yes, I'm pedaling! Yes yes!"

"It's hard to hear you with the wind up here," he tried twisting around as much as he dared. Didn't want to take his eye off the road. "But you are pedaling, right?"

She wondered how this exactly was going to bring them closer if they couldn't even talk. It was early and cold out, and even chillier on the bike, and she wanted to be at home with a cup of chamomile tea, a drink she'd recently discovered since learning from a magazine quiz that caffeine wasn't right for her personality type.

"Don't dead-weight me," he said. "I just need you to do enough to cover your own mass."

"I'm pedaling," she said quietly. "I'm pedaling." She tried to sit still, scanning the back of his event jersey, reading the names of all the sponsors of the Ogle County Ride around the Court House. Rock River Savings and Loan. Gatorade. Troix Souer d'Byron. Tratoria Breakers. Alfano's Pizzeria and Brew Pub. Supervalu Market, featuring organic produce and locally raised, sustainable meats.

It wasn't long before her back began to stiffen from the effort to not lean. It wasn't like riding her old Schwinn at all, no feelings of serendipity, just the effort required to be the guts of a machine; going along, getting along. It was possible to get used to it, but why should she? On one of their early dates they had gone on the paved trails through the northwest suburbs toward an arboretum. He had made sandwiches for them, alfalfa sprouts and American cheese with creamy mayonnaise which had all sort of melted and become distastefully warm and pale in his saddlebag during the ride. But it was sweet too and they talked about vacations and how her father's ideal holiday was to pitch a tent in some back woods and remain stationary, she and her brothers exploring the area until by the end of the week the wilderness was as familiar as their own block in Skokie. His summers were spent in short, frenzied bursts of movement, being ferried from one sight to the next, looking at the Grand Canyon only from the north rim, the sand arches of Wyoming through the window of a Volaré station wagon, the pine needles of the redwood forest as a green blur. "We had blisters on our ass by the end," he had laughed, "and anxiety dreams." She had laughed too and been under the impression that they were in agreement about her being luckier in terms of childhoods. His parents had eventually divorced, although not until he was in his thirties.

He reached back and handed her a Payday bar, and she felt brave enough to take it and even nibble a portion from the top.

"Can we stop and eat?" she yelled.

He took a showy swig from one of his bottles, swirled the cherry red drink around in his mouth, then tried to spit it through his front teeth like Bodie on the Wire, but it ended up spraying everywhere— partly from the effort of pedaling, but mostly because he didn't have any gaps between his teeth.

"No stopping to eat," he said, brushing the splatter off his shirt. "Got to learn to do it all on the bike."

"But I have trouble chewing when I'm gasping for air. Plus those energy snacks are so dry I'll need lots of water. It even says on the package to drink a bottle of water with each BoHydrate Bar."

"It's a challenge," he agreed. "Are you pedaling as hard as you can?"

The going was slower than he expected, but he had to admit

they were indeed riding in tandem. They were long past subdivisions and now the industrial parks off the expressway were safely in the distance, and they were just reaching the edge of the cornfields. The soil was dark and the corn was young and green. Farmhouses floated pleasantly in the distance, scenic vistas of farmland in decay, but as they pedaled on they reached areas where the corn was fuller and larger. Tops of silos stuck like archipelagos in corn oceans, and the corn yellowed and browned, and the houses dipped into the rising waves of ears and tassels, and soon the roofs and silos disappeared entirely. When the corn suddenly was gone they found themselves pedaling in a haze of dust left in the wake of distant threshers and combines. The crops changed to low, scrubby soy beans crowning golden in the late afternoon and beyond that the land emptied, and they pedaled along grey guard rails through a landscape of red clay and scattered, brown shrubs. The air was heavy with cow shit and motor fumes.

"Pound it out," he said supportively. "Go to your happy place. It's going to start getting challenging soon."

She thought about food. Real food. After a day spent working over carb bars like a docile ruminant, she was thinking of pot roast. A pot roast like her mother made. Hadn't seen food like that in years and years. God, if she could get another crack at her mother's pot roast she would eat whatever portion her mother put out for her, she wouldn't knife away the fat, wouldn't even purge later.

"They call this the magic hour," he said over his shoulder. "When the directors like to shoot scenes for movies. Pretty, isn't it, the light just now?"

"Fork tender," she called up.

His bike helmet bobbed approvingly. "I guess that captures something of the spirit."

"Bastante," she called. Then, "Finito. Whoa. Break time. Hon? Maybe we can just pause for a bit. Have dinner in a restaurant?"

"We never agreed on a stopping signal, did we?" he said.

"But let's do stop anyway. Hon?"

"Hang in there for a little while."

The sun went down in front of them, and he turned on their

headlamp and flickering reflectors. She thought to let her eyes rest for a just a second and closed them, and when she jerked them open they were in a woody place of foggy lowlands and soupy marshes. It was dark and cold, and headlights whooshed past her. It began to rain, enormous drops splattering off her arms and back.

"We need to stop," she called out. "Take shelter. Find food. Get near a fire and warm up."

"Hard to hear you up here. Clouds look pretty dark up ahead so we'll probably lose the moonlight."

They pedaled nearly blind into the ink, but when cars approached she could see the reflected road ribboning out in front of her. Occasionally the weight of the bike felt like he was carrying it all, and he assumed then she was taking little breaks and that was fine. He resisted the urge to call back, check in on her, because he knew he had to trust that she would still be there, and then at times his patience was rewarded as he could feel her stirring and pedaling hard for awhile before tapering off again. When the sun rose again behind them, the rain stopped and vapor came up from their limbs, and their bike helmets gave off steam like smokestacks.

"Maybe we can take a little breather this morning," she said hopefully. "See some scenery. Take a picture. Use a bathroom. Give our legs a little break. Hon?"

He wiggled his fingers to keep the blood flowing. "In a little bit," he said. "Maybe later. Let's keep going for now."

She became adept at rolling down her removable sleeves when it got cold, and then unzipping them once it began to warm up. She pulled down her leggings and hastily slapped sun screen against the accessible areas of her skin when the rotation of the pedal allowed her to reach. Now that they were in more mountainous terrain, when the sun disappeared behind a cloud or they found themselves in a particularly deep valley and it got cold again, she re-covered her skin with the leggings, only in an hour or so to find herself too warm and needing to re-remove the leggings and re-apply the sunscreen. She used lip balm on her face, and during one slightly dangerous moment, even came up off her seat and smeared a mentholated cream on as much of her bottom as she dared, savoring the sting when she took the greasy saddle again. Her shoes and socks remained soaked and her toes lost feeling and became heavy in her shoes.

"We're very near now," he said. "We'll be at Monarch Pass very soon. Epiphany anyone?"

After just a few miles straight up, the switchbacks began, the tandem stoically taking each directional flip. After the first few he would turn back and flash a victorious grin, but as they came with more frequency, the tandem got slower, and the nose of the bike seemed several hands higher than the back. At first she gamely nodded when he turned, but each turn caused more effort, until finally after one brutal flip he turned around to find the silver carbon frame of the bike stretched back like a demented trombone, her end of the tandem still making its way around the previous curve. He called back words of encouragement hoping they would reach her, but he couldn't slow down now, no matter how stretched and out of shape became the tandem. Sometimes he could feel the effort of her pumping and she would catch up and be right behind again. They made a game of it, with a burst of energy she would get alongside, until it seemed like the stoker might pass the captain. In this way they barely noticed the hardest part of the climb, when the air thinned and became frigid, and no matter how hard they pedaled it seemed like the top of the mountain would not come any closer. Snow came and accumulated on their arms and back. "Use your oxygen wisely," he said, knowing how funny that sounded.

The summit was just as he described, a painfully grand open space and their heads pounded from the strain of just being there. They slowed, listening to the thin air and the packed snow crunching softly under their wheels. She could hear her pulse throbbing inside the bike helmet against her temples.

"This is it," he said. "The summit! Where water changes direction. And now, are you ready to have the epiphany?"

"I need a break," she said.

He shook his head. "I promise we'll take a break over the edge, in Garfield. Or Poncha Springs or Salida. Or Kansas. Here we go. Honey? Here we go!"

He leaned into the final press until the earth tipped below and the tandem finally began moving all of its own momentum. In a rush of giddiness and fear the road seemed to drop them into the stratosphere. The back end tipped one way and he shifted to compensate. This isn't the time to lose your balance, he thought, unable now to speak.

But the descent was terrifying; his heart pounded and he wondered why he had bothered to take them on this journey in the first place. Think of all that could go wrong on a bike—he feathered the brakes, feathered hard, angling down and picking up speed. He wished he could tell her to lighten up if she could. Just be a little lighter. Then suddenly the familiar release of the fears just as he remembered it, like a veil being lifted he had said to himself last time and he had been right, that was exactly what it felt like. And now the feeling of freedom. They were really moving quickly, and now came that broomsticky feeling—he hoped she remembered his apt observation. They took a few turns and the bike was moving even faster, and there it was, the epiphany, as clear as the signs for the Runaway Truck Turnoffs to savor each moment as it comes, let go of yesterday's grudges and hurts; he wasn't mad anymore. The epiphany, again. This time for real! He feathered his brakes and rode down the mountain and his heart was full of glorious, cascading blue forgiveness. She would surely be feeling it too and though it was risky he wanted to see her expression, share just a second of epiphany with her, so he swiveled just slightly, took a quick look.

The stoker seat was empty. He was alone on the tandem, just he and only he, something so obvious it felt more like confirmation than revelation. Tears filled the corners of his eyes now and he forced himself not to weep, not at this speed. Lowering his head into the wind he rode the tandem down Monarch Pass all by himself.

The Tantric Butterfly

AFTER the failed vasectomy, after two weeks of swollen testicles and misery only to find the procedure had not worked, Todd remained a miserable but fertile Priapus. Sex became routinized, usually ending with him next to Erin, pumping against the loose flesh of her hip, finishing in her fist, then waiting for her to return with a washrag that seemed to get colder each time. Todd wasn't about to go through the procedure a second time, and since Erin was too young for a tubal they would have to settle for something else.

For Todd that meant hiring only girls at his shop, The Original Framers on East State. *A frame is just context*, was his standard patter with customers while filling work orders. *Difference between kitsch and high art is the context*, he'd wink, sliding the estimate across the counter for their perusal. *The Mona Lisa with a magnet on its back has as much value as the little league schedule it holds on the fridge. Girl at the register'll need a twenty percent deposit.*

Corrina was the employee-of-the-moment, whose big teeth and goofy grin Todd currently called to mind when spilling into his wife's fist, but before that it had been sober-faced Shelley, and before her two Christinas right in a row, one with a big chest and the other astounding dimples, especially when she pretended to pout about overtime or working through lunch. Had he been the same age as these girls Todd wouldn't have stood a chance, but the context was different now. Now he owned a business and when he put up a Help Wanted sign they came to him, dressed up and solicitous, trying to win his favor. Adjacent to the emergency exit, his office was really just a narrow walkway with a folding chair, which he offered to the applicants, leaving for himself a corner of his small desk on which he sat cross-legged, his knee practically in the girl's lap, leaning down to ask questions: *What drew you to the Original Framers? Are you planning on going to college? What are your best qualities?*

The ones he hired all showed something particular in the interview: sharp smiles suggestive of something even they might not be sure about. He wouldn't hire any slutty girls. That would be too obvious. No one who wore too much makeup or perfume. He liked a girl who seemed like she could control herself in a new situation and was maybe a little...adventurous? After all, Todd wasn't interested in forcing himself on anyone; he wanted the desire to be mutual. This was a lot trickier to engineer, and so far he had not been able to pull it off, a fact which only made the endgame that much clearer in his mind, that much sweeter in the abstract.

And yet, regardless of how promising the hirings were, Shelley or the Christinas, all the romances had amounted to the same thing, a fate the current Corrina was veering toward. One afternoon right when he got comfortable enough with Corrina to talk about non-framing things, the door chimes rang and there was Erin with one of his daughters.

"Thought we'd surprise you for lunch," she said sweetly. "And this must be the new cashier?"

Which meant another chance had come and gone. Erin began suggesting Corrina be allowed to baby-sit too, if she was interested, and then pretty soon Erin was taking Corrina out for lunches and leaving Todd alone in the store until it was understood that Corrina was now Erin's project instead of Todd's employee. Shelley had ended up engaged to a youth pastor at their church. The first Christina was going to a four-year college after Erin helped with writing the essay and the second Christina was doing missionary work. She sent pictures of herself in the homes of her hosts in Africa along with windy letters that Todd refused to read as a matter of principle. It was a short time before Todd came home one afternoon to find Corrina in his house playing with his daughters, wearing one of Erin's heavy cotton shirts and sporting the same short haircut as his wife. When Erin met him at the door she said, "Corrina has been here this afternoon helping me with the kids' home schooling. Isn't that nice of her? Would you mind giving her a drive home before dinner?" Something additional unspoken in Erin's eyes: *why not try to fuck her too?* And sure enough, in the car Corrina sat as far from him as possible and engaged him in a miserable recitation of all the cute things his daughters had done that afternoon. It was time to look for a new girl.

LATE afternoon in February the snow came more quickly than they predicted, and Todd was still a half mile from home when it happened: his car slid into its own universe—a nanosecond when the world fell away and there was nothing to be done but wait for the news. He ended up off the road, just slightly askew, encouraging enough that he spent a couple of tantalizing minutes rocking the Toyota back and forth, spinning his wheels, a nice industrial-age grind to match the lightweight information-age vehicle, until finally he could smell rubber. Bundled as best he could in his scarf and gloves, his chin tucked to his chest like a sleeping bird, Todd trudged the half mile home through the dreamy gauze of the snow storm, walking down the center of Cyprus Street where the drifts were lowest at just over his knees, seeing the dull glow of lamps and heat in the homes of smarter men and women who had gone home early as the radio recommended. A few other cars strewn onto lawns or pointing in odd directions told him he wasn't the only chump who had to abandon his vehicle, though rather than empathy, he felt sharp disdain for these idiots in the same predicament as he. There was even a strange car nosed into a drift near Todd's driveway, the rear of the vehicle still slung out onto the street. By the time he reached his own front porch, the oak door stiffly framed by tri-colored sidelights, he was too cold to take his keys out, so he pounded on the door with his gloved fist and waited for relief.

"Daddy, Daddy! Megan's here!" his youngest daughter cried as soon as he was let in.

The foyer was filled with boots and coats on a drying rack being used as a winter clothes hanger. He blew into his hands and nodded at Megan, though he was confused for a moment, unsure exactly who she was.

"Hey, man," he said gamely, stamping the snow off his pants and reaching for his soaked socks. "You cut your hair."

Megan looked curious. "Me? No."

"It was...or was it the long earrings?"

She flinched and laughed. "We haven't met before," she said with force.

Erin came to the entry way and kissed him. "Gosh, Todd. You must be freezing. You had to walk? This is Megan. Her car got stuck too."

"On your front lawn," Megan made a gesture with her palms out. "I'm really sorry if I damaged anything. I'll pay—"

Erin made a silly face. "Oh you will not! Tell her Todd. She's so worried."

The middle daughter danced wildly around their legs. "She can play piano and talk exactly like Mickey Mouse!"

"You're sweating, Todd," Erin ran her hand over his head.

"I had to walk from Lake Louise...." Todd was disoriented. He felt nervous and trapped in the presence of this woman in his home, but he was not sure why.

"I'm Todd," he shook her hand cautiously. Surely he knew her. A regular customer from the store?

"Megan," she said. "I've called my boyfriend to come get me, but he doesn't know. He thinks the roads are too snowy even with his four-wheel drive. I've never seen it this dark in the middle of the afternoon," the girl continued. Megan. She allowed herself to be pulled, one of Todd's daughters on each of her arms, into the living room, where she looked to be playing two board games with all three of the girls at once. Erin had the gas jets in the fireplace going and Todd took a moment to admire all the flush, square lines he had laboriously made with his contractor, rectangle living room, boxy loft with a railing like railroad tracks, the kitchen and foyer, the snow piling into cones on the window pains. It was all so familiar and sweet. Erin brought him a mug of tea and he sat in his recliner warming his fingers, trying not to stare at Megan. She was pretty and slim and had black hair in two pigtails which he recognized as the work of his oldest daughter. When

Megan addressed the kids her voice was low and husky, like a lounge singer. But then occasionally, when the youngest daughter made her laugh with a funny antic, she tossed her head back and made squeaky sounds.

It wasn't until he was listening to Megan play "Peter Peter Pumpkin Eater" on the piano—after his second mug of tea, her fifth hushed call to her boyfriend on her cell, her umpteenth apology for putting everyone out, the first crack of her facade when it didn't seem like she was so thrilled to be stuck with them—that he placed her. She was frowning at that moment sort of, curling her lip, eyes turned down coyly, when he suddenly knew.

"Butterfly," he whispered, startling himself. No one else had heard. But he knew that was right. This Megan in his house, she was the Tantric Butterfly.

Back when Todd first got home internet and began masturbating with the computer, he cruised the web for photos of naked celebrities or porn stars. The photos appeared slowly, dial-up access acting like the curtain that raises for tokens in peep joints. It was easier to go to the sites with smaller, stamp-sized pictures in series: usually 20 or so, with some sort of progress to the photos like stills from a sleazy movie: girl taking off her shirt, same girl taking off pants, girl sucking her own finger, girl bending over...and then an offer to see more with a credit card number. Theoretically these pictures might have done the trick except the lack of context became a distraction. Most of the series started right off with a girl in bed looking at the camera and Todd could never make the narrative work in his head: why would a girl be naked and posing in any room *he* might walk into? If the photographer had taken time, started the series with a girl on a bicycle, then the girl getting a flat tire, then the girl hitchhiking—provide a context—then start with the shots of her taking off her clothes in the truck or even in a bed that looked like it was in a cheap hotel...then the framing device would put her naked flesh into a fantasy, which itself would do at least half the work of the pornography.

Which is why Todd was able to spend several months with a mail order bride site using photos of destitute Russian women as onanistic fodder. The women usually weren't naked but some of them got pretty close, and what they lacked in nudity they more than made up for in narrative: these weren't airbrushed phonies indifferent to Todd's desires. The mail order brides were real, willing to become sexual slaves for a nicer lifestyle. This was titillating enough until the post-soviet drabness of the background furniture started to depress him, and Todd began casting his gaze at the online escort listings, a tawdry website originating from his own Rock River Valley with lists of hookers and rates and photos. These were more than just women, they were real professionals, with terms and prices—and they were on the same continent. He looked at their bodies and wondered endlessly about the nomenclature in their ads: *rub down with release* probably meant a hand job, *speaking Greek* had to be anal sex, *GFE* stood for 'girlfriend experience,' but what exactly did that mean? Dinner included? No condom and kissing? A call the next morning? And the ones that listed themselves as 'therapists' or 'healers' had terminology so arcane the names of the procedures themselves gave him a boner: *Egyptian reflexology, trigger point massage, ayurvedic aromatherapy, chakra bowl vibrations....* One ad promised an orgasm that would have the 'client' bursting into tears.

And now as though a direct answer to a fantasy, as preposterous as it seemed, the Tantric Butterfly had flitted to his doorstep in the middle of this snowstorm, and was at this very minute sitting on the couch talking to his wife.

"WE'RE putting dinner on the table, Todd!"

From the stairs landing Todd glanced into the delicate fishbowl of his kitchen, Erin and the Butterfly awkwardly working together, getting bowls of macaroni for the children and plastic cups filled with milk. The computer was in his basement office and he could hardly go there to verify his discovery, but on a whim, he announced he was going to get a sweatshirt from the hall closet, and when he was out of view of the kitchen, took the Butterfly's purse and stuffed it under his shirt.

"Be right back," he called taking the steps two at a time.

He locked the bedroom door and squatted on the floor, eyeing the Butterfly's red bag in front of him, calming his sudden wild breathing. He didn't know what he was looking for exactly. Surely she wouldn't have a business card that read Tantric Butterfly, sexual services—or maybe she would.

He unclasped the top. Wallet first off, next to that Vaseline which could be used as a lubricant, but in this small tube was probably for lip care, a small mirror, her cell phone now dead. Here was something: a baggie of beads on a small thread: this was interesting. What did she do with them? He tucked open the bag and stuck two fingers in, pushing around the sensuous beads. Probably some wild sex trick, like sticking them in some guy's anus and then yanking them like using a rip-cord, firing off an orgasm like a chainsaw. Todd's sphincter gave an involuntary pucker just at the thought. Jesus. It actually didn't sound that arousing, but one never knew what might become that one cherished fetish—the thing that always does the trick. He reluctantly put the bag of beads aside and pulled out the small paperback book on which it had been resting. Todd's heart thumped when he saw the cover: exotic, middle eastern writing, green and black, *Revelations of the Secrets of the Birds and Flowers*. He opened it, sure he would see all sorts of nasty drawings. She was the Butterfly after all, stick it in there, arch your back here.... Instead he found half the pages in Arabic, the English parts highlighted and marked up. *Be like the narcissus. Draw around myself the belt of obedience....* His blood rushed in his ears. *Hold myself as humbly as a slave*, next page, *the water-lily submits to its misfortune....* His eyes dropped to the bottom line, *at dawn I unfold my golden flower-cup and a thousand jealous hands descend on me....* He couldn't concentrate on any one passage for too long, and feeling sweaty, he tucked the book back into her purse. He was aroused beyond measure, although he still wasn't completely sure the book was dirty.

"Before your boyfriend comes," Todd heard himself saying after dinner. "Why don't we go out and see if we can push your car into the street?"

He and the Butterfly bundled up in the hall. It took some convincing for Erin to agree to let Todd and the Butterfly try to push the car out, especially since it was pretty clear that even if they could get it unstuck there wasn't anywhere she could drive until the streets were plowed. Still, he knew once this boyfriend of hers showed up he wasn't going to have any chance to make anything happen.

He pushed while she gunned the engine, and then they switched thinking that Todd could better rock it out of the snow. When they had both conceded the car wasn't going anywhere they rested in the front seat a moment, the Butterfly in Erin's rubber Christopher Robin boots and one of Todd's puffy down coats. She looked like a waif in her parent's clothing. She pointed the vents at herself while he blew into his palms.

She said, "Well, thanks for trying. I called my boyfriend but he's…"

Stuck too. She had told him several times. He understood why it was important for her now to mention a boyfriend here, with the two of them so close in such an intimate space.

"So," he said, "You're the Butterfly, aren't you?"

"Sorry?"

"I *know* it's you."

She reached for the door but he held her shoulder. "I won't say anything." He felt her shoulder go taut, saw the flash of fist, and knew that despite the way it looked on the web, this was no delicate flower, no flitting gossamer creature.

She said, "You don't know what you're talking about."

"I won't blow your cover."

"I don't have a cover," she told him. "I'm not trying to hide anything."

"I'm just curious, that's all. I've done some research online."

"Research?" she snorted. "That's what you call it?"

"I'm just curious, like it says on your website, or one of the other websites. My curiosity is leading me. How exactly do you perform a Tantra therapy session?"

"Tantra isn't performance." She had a very recognizable demeanor suddenly, of a salesman making a pitch, eye contact, something solicitous in her tone. "It's not something someone does to someone else. It's about opening up new channels of spirituality. Sexuality is a part of it, but a small part."

"What does it mean when someone gets his chakras rotated?"

She snorted again, amused. "Tires get rotated. You *balance* your chakras. Look Todd, if you're really ready to take the steps then send me an E-mail from my webpage which you're apparently already familiar with, and we'll make an appointment and do it properly."

"Wait, wait wait...." Todd's mind raced but he couldn't think of a way to make her want to stay in the car with him, want to do something to him right this very second. Wasn't she grateful for the food? Shelter?

"Todd," she said again. "My facilitation of your energy being released has to occur in an atmosphere of total relaxation and respect, not the front seat of my Civic. Also, I don't cheat on other women. That's not how it works. This has to be cleared through your spiritual partner, and I need to see waiver to that effect."

"Butterfly. My wife will *never* ever go along with this. And I can't come visit you. It's—"

She was resting her hand on his knee now and even through her mittens it made his leg tremble.

"Todd. Shhhh. If the gods will it you'll find a way to make it work. I don't need to know all the details. I can help you Todd, but not here. And not tonight. It has to be on the terms spelled out on the Spiritual Offerings page. That has to be it, for now."

"Butterfly—"

"My name is Megan." She took her hand off his leg and turned and was out of the car before he could say anything else.

He followed quickly stepping in the tracks she had already made, calling as loudly as he dared, "What are the beads for, Megan? What do you do with the beads?"

ERIN had set up a little sleeping area in the corner of the living room because Megan refused to "put them out" further, wouldn't take a kid's bed no matter how hard the kids cheered just at the suggestion of getting to spend the night on the floor in sleeping bags. When Todd found her again she was curled up on the recliner, the afghan up to her chin, pretending to be too tired to talk to his youngest child, who, undaunted, was trying to get Megan to play toy trucks with her.

"Adele," Todd said firmly from the doorway. "Leave our guest alone," he winked at the Butterfly, whose lips barely quivered like an unplugged appliance using its last bit of stored electricity. "It's night poetry time, Adele. Mom's waiting in your room."

Todd waited for the little girl to rush past before settling himself on the couch adjacent to the recliner. All the furniture was angled for optimal views of the television on the near wall, not for conversation, so Todd found himself having to lean over the arm rest to speak with Megan.

"The wife reads poetry to them every night. Tonight it's 'Thirteen Ways of Looking at a Blackbird.' Do you know it?"

Megan shook her head slightly, then turned it into a yawn and a stretch.

"No? The kids really love it. Let's see, 'It was evening all afternoon. It was snowing and then it was going to snow,'" his voice strained to its lowest timbre. "Kind of nice, kind of like today."

"Who wrote it?" she asked.

"Oh God, I don't know. A guy named Wallace. That's the first name, Wallace something. It's from a book of verse that Erin reads to the kids."

Erin's voice floated sweetly from the upstairs. *"Among twenty snowy mountains, the only thing moving was the eye of the blackbird."*

"It's a long poem," he muttered, not daring to look over at her face. "You could come sit by me on the couch, then reach over, put your hand on my leg like you did in the car, and we could talk about the weather or my job framing pictures, and then we could just be talking, and I would only look at your eyes, you have beautiful eyes you know, and then while we're talking just kind of run your hand slowly to my...Lingam."

"Make an appointment."

"A man and a woman are one. A man and a woman and a blackbird are one."

"I can't make an appointment because then it'll have just been something that I arranged." Todd fiddled with the piping on the couch, daring to only look at the Butterfly occasionally. "This has to happen serendipitously. That's how I always wanted it and here you are. Don't you ever role play?"

"What does that mean?"

"You know what it means. Do you and a customer ever...play games?"

She paused a moment before turning her head and taking him on directly. "If the client wants it. Yes."

"I want it."

"You're not a client. I don't want to discourage you, Todd, because actually I think you're the least spiritually centered person I've ever encountered and you could probably really benefit from squaring your chakras and putting your heart in balance. But you're going about it all wrong." Gesturing occasionally, she was clearly in full sales mode. "You have a business. How'd you get it? You spent money and worked for it. How about your house? Same thing. Work and money. Now you're hearing a call from the universe that it's time to open some new channels of experience. Heed the call. Maybe I'm here to inspire you to do this. Maybe that's why the universe brought me here on this day. But you have to achieve your spiritual centeredness yourself, and with the same tools a man achieves anything."

"Work and money."

A small smile now, a little treat for Todd getting it right. "Paying for our sessions isn't meant to shame you. It's meant to establish your power in the universe. It's meant to put us both in a relaxing and safe place. But only if you really want this," she opened her arms to demonstrate.

Todd swallowed. "Can I just tell you one of my fantasies? I have so many. But tonight, this is already pretty close to something I might imagine, you here...." He leaned closer and thought about trying to kiss her. She would understand. "Megan..."

"Todd!"

He jumped at the sound of Erin calling him from upstairs.

"The kids want you to get the clown hat and do the bedtime dance!"

Todd initiated that night. First he told Erin they needed to go to bed early so Megan wouldn't feel like she needed to stay up on their part, the poor girl had been cocooned on the recliner with an afghan over her head for an hour already, so Todd engaged the alarm system, checked the garage door locks and the back door. Then when Erin had finished in the bathroom, he put his hand in her panties the second she got into bed.

"Todd, Megan's right below us!"

It was marvelous that Erin thought they might make the Tantric Butterfly uncomfortable with whatever anemic bed-thumping they might generate, but not being able to tell Erin this he put his mouth on her ear and started to nuzzle.

"Todd! Is that why you were so keen to get me to drink wine at din~you really are ready. No pee-nee rub to get you in the mood?"

"Do you have to use that word? Try calling it my cock."

"Oh, gosh!"

Already logy from the syrupy Merlot, Erin was asleep minutes after the wifely hand-job, so Todd got his own washrag and used nice smelling soap around his privates just in case he got the Butterfly to use her mouth instead of just her vagina. Her pussy. Then he went to the railing and listened if she was up or stirring or watching TV or using the guest shower since Erin had provided her with several towels: bath, hand, and a wash rag, all of which the Butterfly had taken and stacked beside the recliner.

"Butterfly," he whispered, moving down the steps at a good clip.

She opened an eye and it was clear she hadn't been asleep. "My name is Megan."

He stayed at the foot of the stairs. "I'm just checking on you. I'm down here because I couldn't sleep and I'm making a sandwich. You can't sleep either, but you know a way that might make it easier for both of us to sleep. You call me over and I've made tea, which by the way is herbal and so no caffeine because we're both worried about sleep. You tell me you're grateful for letting me stay in your house and then point out the rise in my peejay pants. I'm embarrassed but you tell me not to be. In fact, you say, getting up off the chair, that you're kind of turned on by it."

"Are you brain damaged?"

"You ask me if you can touch it because you're a virgin, and your boyfriend is going to break up with you unless you get some experience, and I say, but my wife, she might—"

"You're all over the place, dude. Who's the aggressor, you or me? It keeps changing."

He was kneeling now at the base of her recliner, on his knees, hands on the armrest, looking at her face and the afghan. He screwed up his courage and took a breath. "You can use the beads," he whispered.

"Look, Todd. I was wrong when I said you were a good candidate for Goddess worship. You're not. You can't be a client of mine or any Tantra provider. A porn magazine is more where you're at."

"Girlie mags don't work for me. That kind of pornography is insulting, *Penthouse* with their fake breasts and airbrushed asses. And they Photoshop pissing now! Did you know that? As if everyone wants to get pissed on after sex. Who wants to be pissed on?" He suddenly looked ashamed. "But if you want to, you can. We could go to the tub to not make a mess and I could lie down in it and if you get enough to drink, not to be drunk, just to get enough fluids, you could just let a little bit out. A little squirt or two, right in my face."

"If I said yes, Todd, you would explode. Do you know that? You would evaporate. You would cease to be a human."

"Don't make me go back up there with nothing."

"Then try something, Todd. Use your powers of masculinity."

Todd leaned back. "I mean...really?"

She looked down at him from the chair, locked her eyes on his. "If this is a call from the universe, let's see how you answer it."

It took a moment, but finally he reached out, raising his right hand in front of his face slowly, so that her head was perfectly framed between his thumb and forefinger. He could close his hand and her face would disappear or he could just hold it like this, a perfect visual, but suddenly she was up, afghan in the air, and he was on the ground, his arm twisted behind, her knee in the small of his back, something sharp poking his neck.

"You see why you aren't going to get anything tonight?" she whispered in his ear. He tried to answer but took a mouthful of carpet. "These are my keys between my fingers and if I press hard enough your neck'll bleed in four places. And then I start making noise and we get Erin down here and suddenly you have a lot more problems than sexual frustration. Right?"

He tried to nod, moving just enough so that she got the message.

"When I get off you, you get up and walk back the fuck up those stairs, and you don't turn around once. Get it? You don't look back at me not one fucking time or I'll make you wish you never set eyes on my webpage. Got it?"

Todd found the instructions surprisingly easy to follow, his ardor for her pretty well slaked at the moment, and went up the stairs rapidly. He changed out of his sweaty clothing in the bathroom and very quietly stole across his bedroom and into his bed, where he took only a portion of the comforter to be sure and not shake the mattress. He closed his eyes.

"Still snowing?" Erin asked after a suitable pause. Neither of them expected Todd to actually answer.

The bed was all his in the morning when he woke, and he stretched across Erin's empty half, staking claim to her abandoned territory. Waking to an empty bed—there would be no greater pleasure in the day—he extended his limbs as far as he wished with impunity. The smell of pancakes and eggs wafted from downstairs and he changed out of his pajamas into sweat clothes. A plow worked the north end of Cypress street, making mounds of snow like cresting waves with its blade. The kids were watching TV and Todd walked into the kitchen. They were both at the kitchen island, under the hanging tea lights, Erin in her bathrobe, and Megan in some of Erin's pajama pants and Erin's long sleeve t-shirt that said Super-mom, which was a bit too large for her. Both had their heads down, huddled over something.

"Morning Sweetie," Erin said brightly.

Todd mumbled his response and got his mug from the drying rack and poured it half full with coffee.

"Help yourself to what's left of the griddle cakes, Todd. Megan made them for the kids. Any shape they wanted. She made a Dora and Thomas, and even a SpongeBob."

"SpongeBob was actually pretty easy," Megan laughed like a tinkling bell. "A couple left for you in the warmer, Todd, though they're just regular round kind. Hope that's okay."

"Todd doesn't like anything too exotic," Erin told her. She was distracted by what was between them on the counter. Beads. As Todd neared he saw the empty baggie and all the beads scattered, some alone, others on strings.

"See these, hun," Erin said to him. "Aren't they beautiful? Megan is a jewelry maker."

Megan waved it away. "It's a hobby. I'm a beginner."

"They're exquisite. Hey Todd, Valentine's is less than a week." Erin held up a turquoise strand under her ear.

"Those particular stones are from India. I really like them too. Please take it, Erin," Megan insisted. "It would make me so happy, you've been so kind."

"You know, Megan," Erin squared her mouth a moment. "You should really think about selling these."

"I have kind of toyed with the idea—"

"I could have a party with my church ladies. They would gobble these up. And you can get your own web-page with pictures and take orders and everything. You can sell anything on-line these days. Right Todd? Go get some pancakes and have more coffee. You look like a flattened tire!"

By midmorning, the plow had cleared all of Cyprus Street and Megan's boyfriend arrived in an SUV to pick her up. The children gathered at the door to hug goodbye. The oldest daughter had even made a poem and Megan clapped with delight after it was read. Todd watched the scene from a slight remove, several paces back by the boot-rack, pleased that his kids had lined up in such a way that the backs of their heads formed a triangle. Megan's boyfriend stood back too, leaning against the oak door and not saying much, a beefy guy with his arms crossed. He was named Skye, which was about what Todd would've guessed for the Butterfly's boyfriend.

"I owe you guys so much," Megan finally said to his wife.

"Nonsense," Erin told her. "You made a blizzard bearable, an adventure. And you're going to come back as soon as it thaws. We'll cook out and Todd can make his famous ribs for you. You come too, Skye."

"I love ribs." Skye's arms were still crossed but he was smiling pleasantly. Todd wondered how much he knew.

Erin picked her date book up from the hall bureau. "Then you have to come. Todd's ribs have won prizes."

"Oooh," Megan looked directly at him, impishly. "What's the secret?"

Todd grinned gamely, before realizing he was actually going to have to answer. "I just keep them in the oven is all. Most of the day, actually. I only use the grill to brown them."

"Use a rub or a sauce?" Skye asked earnestly. "Hey don't laugh, Megan." He pronounced it Meee-gan, and Todd felt jealous of their casual intimacy. "There's all sorts of barbecue debates on rub or sauce."

"I use both," Todd shrugged. "Dry rub before they go in the oven and I keep them in cider vinegar."

"It's so clever," Megan said.

Todd never felt more foolish. Skye had an electronic organizer in his pocket and he and Mee-gan found dates for both a cookout and a potential launch party for the jewelry business.

"You'll be making jewelry full time before you know it," Erin assured her. "You'll quit all your other jobs."

Erin was in a simple plaid sweater and pajama pants and fuzzy blue Ugg slippers. And as Todd watched her waving goodbye he thought suddenly that she was very pretty, his wife, a sweet upturned nose and high, cheery cheek bones. It was true that he had gotten very lucky with her.

Later in the afternoon Todd bundled himself and gassed up the snow blower. When he was edging the lip of the grass to make the snow bank flush with the curb, Todd remembered suddenly his first breast. Fifth grade, Maureen Blackwood, on the playground at school when someone dared her to let Todd touch her breasts, and she said okay so long as everyone else left them alone in the tire fort. His hand had hovered over her chest, respectfully leaving about an inch of space, pretending to squeeze them, saying loudly so the others could hear, *I'm feeling your boob, Maureen.* But she startled him by grabbing his hand and mashing it against her chest. He could feel the rubbery rise of flesh through her shirt, the fabric of the bra and the gumdrop nipple, and he wriggled to get free but Maureen kept him clamped firmly on her breast. "Squeeze it," she told him. "Do it. Hurry before they come back. What are you waiting for, Todd?"

He pushed the snow blower deep into the gash where Megan's car had been. By working it over furiously, smoothing away the snow that had gotten packed by her tires, extending out the snow bank from driveway to lawn, Todd managed to make it look nice again, as though no car had ever gotten stuck on his lawn in the first place

The Rate of Exchange

THEY tried at first living with the locals. Seven hundred *quetzals*—one hundred dollars American—bought Alex and Suzanne a room and three daily meals for an entire month with the Olivas family. They arrived at midnight and though the room was much more sparse than they had imagined—a soft mattress on the floor, a table and reading lamp, a few posters—they changed into their pajamas and brushed their teeth with bottled water and went to bed. Suzanne noticed some bites on her arm while dressing the next morning and casually asked the woman of the house, Señorita Olivas, what she thought they might be. The stout woman wiped her hands on her apron and took Suzanne's pale, bluish arm and pressed her thick fingers into the skin. "Could be the *wa-cha-ka* bugs." The señorita showed her teeth and made a face like a feral animal. She explained that the insects burrowed into an arm and stayed just under the skin and moved around at night and if one wanted to know for sure, one could put a little pen mark next to the bites to see if they moved. Instead Alex and Suzanne made arrangements for the remainder of their stay at the Hotel Santa Domingo, the four-star resort on the edge of town. They paid Señorita Olivas for the month which she took graciously, then pointed out that she and Suzanne looked to be about the same shoe size. Suzanne hastily slipped off her Madison Hikers and handed them to her before getting into the cab.

In the Santa Domingo they had a view of an interior courtyard containing a pond and bougainvillea bushes, and when Suzanne saw it for the first time she felt bathed in warm relief. Alex, however, remained glum and distant, the posture he had adopted upon hearing of his reassignment—the demotion, as he called it. Even in the Jacuzzi tub he brooded, and though Suzanne had a number of supportive things she was prepared to say—how she knew he would soon break the slump or how she would still love him no matter what happened—she remained silent, knowing full well that proclamations of unqualified support enraged him.

Alex Moss told people he was an ideas man, although he had for years actually been a money man. Ideas were money the way sugar was syrup, so it wasn't a lie exactly. His signature concept, the one that made his reputation with Nedderland Enterprises, was for a sport ski that warmed the wearer's feet using discreet solar panels in the boot: the ubiquitous "Nedderland Ski-Daddle." But over the last few years a certain abstraction had crept into his ideas: french-fry reservoirs under mini-van seats, TV remotes built into eye glasses that operated through corneal-movement; each was a little gem in his mind, but unworkable off paper. He had most recently spent several hundred hours developing a giant visquine sheet to cover refrigerators so photos would stick without magnets. His boss, Steve Nedderland, spent less than a minute listening to the pitch before pointing out that people liked refrigerator magnets.

It was then the move had been suggested. "Not as a punishment," Steve told him, forcing Alex to toast his new job over a pair of Plymouth gin gimlets he had prepared ahead of time. "But as a way of recharging your batteries. In our business you need to stay fresh, to move with the times or move over."

You mean move south, Alex had thought.

THE immersion school was a short walk from the hotel, down *Calle Santa Clara*, behind an imposing colonial wall of cracked stone. Nedderland had enrolled the Mosses for three weeks of classes—language and culture—to give Alex a place to start. Suzanne, he figured, could take classes for fun. The school itself was just an open space, a courtyard from some older building that had decayed and crumbled, leaving only the florid atrium. A large stone fountain had been erected in the center to cut the noise from the small worktables scattered around the garden. When it rained, as it did most afternoons, the students and tutors ran to the back wall and jostled for space under the single narrow awning that protected the coffee pot. The tutors, dark young men in sweaters and loafers, each shouldering a bag of brittle textbooks, stood at the entrance waiting to escort their students-of-the-week to designated tables.

Alex was paired with Rafael, a lean, angular man who bragged of his theater background, and who elaborately mimed his lessons. As soon as he and Alex began, sitting across from each other beside a small patch of stumpy green shrubs, Rafael opened his palms, making his hands perfectly flat. He then abruptly configured them as if holding a cup and saucer, one pinky out, then lifted the cup to his lips and blew across the invisible surface. Rafael took a quick, delicate sip before pointing to the invisible cup with his other hand.

"*Taza*," he said, loudly. "*Taza. Taza.*"

Alex repeated, "*Taza.* Cup? Cup is *taza?*"

"Now," Rafael said in English, dropping the stiffness of his performance. "Shall we get some coffee?"

Alex didn't mind the formal theatrics of the lesson so much, but he felt slightly rankled by Rafael's obvious advanced age. Rafael had to be in his early thirties, considerably older than most of the other tutors. As Alex followed him across the courtyard to the large coffee tureen beyond the fountain, he could see that the other tutors—like the students—were much younger, college aged.

Rafael handed Alex a half full mug. "Sugar-rr?" He trilled his Rs even when he spoke English. "Crr-rream?"

Alex shook his head and blew across the top. Rafael leaned against the wall and clasped both hands tightly around the mug.

"I have heard all about this new problem in America," Rafael said in clear English. "This organ harvesting that's going on in your country."

"Organ harvesting?"

"I've heard it's very *pope-you-lar* this practice of taking an orr-rrgan from a sleeping body. That you might be drinking in a bar..." He took a delicate sip of coffee to demonstrate. "And you might go home with a person you met there. You wake up in a tub of ice and have a scar or stitches," he ran his hand across his chest, "missing a kidney or liver."

"False. We call those urban legends."

"The man who told me this said it happened to his friend."

"I'm sure he did," Alex said, trying to be polite.

Rafael shrugged his shoulders. "Well," he said coldly, "I believe it."

Even more galling than being paired with such a credulous dinosaur was the realization that Suzanne's tutor, a thick-chested little guy, was probably the youngest in the school. The Director probably thought Suzanne was as young as these college students. Even now in their mid-thirties she was still carded at bars, while Alex, with his thinning hair and paunchy stomach, got his drinks without any comment. As Alex and Rafael walked back to their table Alex could see unmistakably that Suzanne was flirting, maybe even attempting seduction, leaning across the table, fingering the outline of her lips, staring intently at her tutor. Her top wasn't low cut or anything, but she was definitely pitching. Alex couldn't tell if the tutor was responding, but it was still irritating to see Suzanne working so diligently at it.

Suzanne had been adamant that they try a new restaurant every night, the less touristy the better. However, after the first day of class neither she nor Alex had enough energy to get past the hotel dining room.

"I think I hate my tutor," Suzanne said flatly. She had ordered something in Spanish, but her last vestige of adventurousness left once the dish appeared: a pile of small green peppers like gnome hats that she just knew were going to be too spicy.

"You don't hate anyone," Alex told her, chewing his steak.

"I hate Vidal," she informed him. "He's like a mean armadillo. His method, if you even want to call it that, is just drill the verbs, drill the nouns, drill, drill, drill. And when you don't know an answer, he stares. He stares and waits."

Suzanne prided herself on being able to put anyone at ease. She had once volunteered at a shelter for battered women where she worked the intake desk, asking tough questions of the clients about drug addiction or violence. If Suzanne detected even the slightest discomfort she would make some agreeable remark about the intrusiveness of the form and move on to the next question. But Vidal sat and pointedly waited for Suzanne's response, making her feel stupid. "He's relentless and he's mean."

"He's young," Alex told her, which made Suzanne think he had missed the point.

"I'm not getting anything out of this," she told him. "Are you learning anything?"

Alex pointed to his wine glass with his fork. "*Taza*," he said.

DURING next morning's lesson Rafael placed his hands over his face and opened them to reveal a broad smile. "*Feliz*," he said. "*Feliz. Feliz*."

Alex couldn't keep from looking over Rafael's shoulder into the vine-covered alcove where Suzanne and Vidal sat. Vidal looked like a squat little toad across from Suzanne. He sat implacably still while Suzanne was animated enough for both of them. Alex could never see his lips moving at all, never saw him nod or shake his head, and as the morning ground on, Suzanne began to slump in her chair.

"*Triste*," Rafael said running his index finger from the top to the bottom of his face like a rolling teardrop. "*Triste. Triste*."

When Alex didn't respond, Rafael finally turned to look over his shoulder. He sighed dramatically and shook his head.

"What?" Alex asked.

"You are worried about your wife?"

"Oh no. No no. She hates that guy."

"You are worried. Which is smart. Vidal takes what he wants. He is an," Rafael leaned closer to Alex, "*an-ee-mal*."

While Alex snorted, Rafael looked around to make sure no one could overhear. "He lived with an American woman in town. She was studying with a university doing…field rr-rresearch. On us. She lived with Vidal for a year. Two years. And when she left he was very altered. It was as if she took something of him back to America. Stole something inside, from his soul. Something important, *een-treen-sic*. Is that the right word?"

Alex shrugged. He was slightly irritated at the cornball dramatics but was unaccountably interested by the story. He looked across the courtyard and saw Vidal now alone at the table, staring off into space. Suzanne's chair was not pushed in.

QUITTING had been Suzanne's best idea in a long time. There were ways to support Alex other than taking classes with him. She could visit the sites of Antigua, poke around, make note of what might spark his creativity. In the afternoons she could retire to the hotel for massages or jogs on the rubberized track in the gym.

It was on one of these afternoons that Suzanne first met Maxwell Bather in the wide pool dug out of the actual ruins of the Santo Domingo monastery. She was alone apart from the man floating nearby on an inflatable raft in the shallow water.

"Like your *juipil?*" he called out. He was holding a martini on his stomach with both hands but he removed one to cup it over his mouth when he spoke.

Suzanne squinted at him. "My what?"

"*Juipil.* The Indian weaving you bought. The *camisa.* The shirt."

"Oh. The shirt." She had bought one that morning after a brief negotiation. As it happened, the woman's initial price was far lower than what Suzanne expected, but she felt obliged to ask for less because she had heard the locals got offended if you *didn't* try to bargain, though she couldn't imagine why this might be. The woman accepted her very first counter-offer with a disinterested nod and immediately folded the weaving into a plastic grocery bag. The encounter left Suzanne feeling a strange mix of emotions: pleased at having gotten it for less but afraid she had still overpaid since the woman had acquiesced so quickly, tempered by an overriding feeling of guilt that she had cheated an old woman who clearly needed the money.

"How did you know I bought a *juipil?*"

"Everyone does." He gave his martini glass a little shake and took a ceremonially brief sip. "But have you noticed"— his raft was spinning slowly and he needed to look over his shoulder slightly to maintain eye contact— "that all the traditional *juipils* you see in museums are bright and sort of...gaudy? Primary colors: reds and blues and yellows.

Yet the ones for sale on the street are all the colors of American living rooms. What color was yours?"

"I'm not even really sure." In fact Suzanne had walked past several vendors before finding a *juipil* that would match her bedroom: salmon and forest sage.

"The fear of course is that the Indians will stop weaving in their traditional colors altogether."

Suzanne nodded. "Maybe they could do both."

"Ah," he dropped one leg over the side of his raft and slid off without upending his martini. His legs were long and he reached Suzanne in a few steps. "A fellow Third-Wayer. Maxwell Bather. Pleasure to meet you. Been in country long? No? Have you tried *altol* yet? The traditional drink?"

He led Suzanne to the pool-side bar where they could sit and drink while still submerged. Suzanne didn't like meeting new people unless she knew about it ahead of time—at a party or after church— and she especially hated talking to someone for the first time in her swimsuit, but Maxwell was so at ease she didn't feel awkward at all. He was tall and his face gave off a warm heat under his wide rimmed Panama.

Maxwell chatted amiably about the *altol*. "Here in the hotel you can get it with a shot of Torani syrup," he informed her evenly. "Caramel is quite popular, although I think butter-rum complements the corn-base better. Tell me why you're here."

"My husband, Alex" —she had decided when Maxwell ordered the drink that she better get that out of the way quickly— "is down here looking for stuff to import. New ideas. Fresh things."

Maxwell got himself another martini and fiddled with the olives with his fingers. "There are lots of opportunities down here. We have an old joke in my business: How can the natives be so poor when they wear all this expensive Guatemalan clothing?"

Suzanne got the feeling Maxwell didn't actually think this was funny, so she didn't laugh. She liked his voice. Not the quality exactly, which was on the nasally side, but that he seemed unafraid to let you know he was smart instead of trying to hide it by being glib like most everyone else she knew. By the time Maxwell invited her and

Alex to travel into the countryside with him, she was sure it was an opportunity that should not be passed up.

SHE met Maxwell a few times during the week. They walked around the ruins of the city and he told her about the specific earthquakes and volcanic eruptions that had brought down each structure. They went to the Great Square and he explained how the masks were carved and how one could tell if a weaving was of a better quality than another. Suzanne was careful to mention these visits to Alex but to not provide too many details, nor to mention the traveling idea in the hopes that a more receptive mood might surface.

On the Friday after completing the first week of Spanish, Alex and Suzanne were walking to the hotel auditorium to see a dance revue, when Suzanne saw Maxwell by the lobby door. She recognized his figure even in silhouette under the intense setting sunlight. Adrenaline rippled through her hands and legs as she brought Alex over to meet him. They chatted for a moment about economic opportunities—Maxwell wished Alex luck with his venture and Alex thanked him and declared that it had been a pleasure meeting him— and it was done. Suzanne was surprised at how relieved she felt when it was over, and not in the least surprised that night when they were dressing for bed when Alex told her he thought Maxwell was a prissy idiot and he hoped never to see him again.

"He knows so much about the place," Suzanne snapped. The last thing she wanted to do was protest or defend Maxwell, but Alex's attitude was so deflating. "He's friendly and he could help you."

"An old man like that?" Alex called from the bathroom. "What could he tell me about business these days?"

"He's the same age as you. And I was going to suggest," Suzanne told him, feeling brave, "that if you really wanted to get some new ideas, you take a week off from your lessons and we travel the countryside with him."

Alex was furious at the suggestion. He was normally a peripatetic tooth brusher, walking around the house while vigorously working his teeth over, but now he deliberately stayed in the bathroom hunched over the sink. Suzanne didn't know it, but just that afternoon, as soon as his week with Rafael had ended, Alex had gone to the director of the school. The small man—the only person Alex knew in Antigua who always wore a suit—apologized profusely for Suzanne's experience. Alex waved it away and said it didn't matter and no, Suzanne wouldn't come back even for a week of lessons *gratis*. What mattered was that young Vidal be assigned as his tutor next week.

"I can't go," Alex told her firmly when he emerged from the bathroom. "I'm on the verge. Maybe a breakthrough, eminent."

She moved directly to her ace, the line she was saving for when all other rhetorical possibilities had been exhausted. "Maybe I'll go myself then," she said, as though it had suddenly occurred to her. "It's a good opportunity, I think. Just for a few days." She didn't want to appear too eager.

T HEY started at a natural hot spring in Xunil, up a mountain covered in fields of lettuce and onions. The lake was small, dug into a notch near the rim of a volcano so that the heated water ran from a fumarole deep in the mountain. The air was cold and the lake was in deep shadow this time of morning. Thick steam floated off the surface of the water. Suzanne and Maxwell paid three *quetzals* each to enter, and apart from a few Japanese men groaning loudly in the hot water, they had the lake to themselves. Despite her personal vow to reward Alex's trust with her loyalty, Suzanne found herself giddy with the pleasure of being so removed from the rest of the world. She let herself become shockingly flirty, letting her leg brush against Maxwell's, brazenly commenting on how snug his suit looked, playfully splashing until Maxwell took her arms and physically restrained her.

Maxwell had started flirting earlier, on the four-hour chicken-bus ride they had taken that morning, up a rutted clay road outside of Antigua. The bus had been painted in bright colors but inside it was still a familiar school bus, smelling of oil and funky green vinyl seats. The vigorous vibrations of the motor made Suzanne feel nostalgic. On a seat designed for two American kids, they squeezed tightly with a third adult, a grizzled Indian man who had smiled and promptly closed his eyes and fallen asleep. Maxwell leaned close to Suzanne and talked quietly into her ear.

"You see what he's wearing?" Maxwell asked. "You think he was a member of" —he surreptitiously looked at the Indian's windbreaker —"West Lafayette High School Pep Squad?"

"Unlikely."

"The Third Way is partially responsible for this."

"Max," she reached for the seat in front of her while the bus rocked and pitched, "Honestly: I'm not really clear on the Third Way."

"It's where Marx meets Keynes. We trade with them, but we try to be ecologically friendly. We sacrifice some profit for their betterment."

"I gave a woman my hiking shoes," Suzanne had told him.

"You're very giving. That's why I asked you on this trip."

A few moments later, after Suzanne had put her head against the window to feel the sun as it came up, Maxwell touched her face. Suzanne was startled but Maxwell continued to run his soft finger from her ear to her chin. "Your profile is extraordinary," he had told her. "Like a movie star's."

She now let her toes dig into the gravelly bottom of the lake and felt the intense heat of the stones on her feet. Maxwell explained to her the mystical properties of the sulphury water as ascribed by the *Popol Vuh*, the sacred book of the Quiche Maya. He told her that when the *conquistadores* had come from Spain, stepping off their boats like indifferent giants, they too had believed in the water's medicinal qualities.

He took her to the steep back wall of the volcano where the hot water trickled from the cracks and he told Suzanne to drink. He put his hand out to catch the flowing water and she pulled her hair from her face and bent down and drank, her lips brushing against the palm of his hand.

Later, in the sauna *mujeres*, Suzanne unwrapped her towel and lay across the wooden bench. She might have been even more forward and gotten away with it, she thought, maybe nipped lightly at the finger he had used to stroke her face. But, it was probably better nothing more had happened—she wasn't even sure she wanted to be unfaithful yet.

Daniel S. Libman

Alex's father had been a stern man. A spanker. If you didn't come as soon as you were called or if you had been caught using his good tools, he calmly informed you that later, before bedtime, you were expected to appear in the study for a paddling. Alex would spend the whole day in agonizing inbetweenness: not in pain yet, not in fear because the outcome was certain, not free because of what was looming ahead. It used to make him feel dizzy, as if his body were moving sideways even when he sat still. Alex had nearly forgotten it all, except that he was feeling it again now, in the school's courtyard sitting across from Vidal's icy, deploring gaze.

Vidal pointed to the surface of the table.

"*Pluma*," Alex said, gripping his chair with one hand to keep his equilibrium.

Alex had at first been determined to conquer Vidal's reserve, smiling warmly as they were introduced, even daring to place a hand on Vidal's shoulder. "I'm into sustainable trade," Alex had told him, detecting a slight jauntiness in his own voice before realizing with a jolt that he was unconsciously imitating Maxwell Bather. Vidal hadn't seemed impressed anyway, so Alex followed wordlessly into the small alcove.

"Oh, oh oh. Wait." Alex glanced at his note-cards but looked up quickly. "*Papel*, right? *Papel?*"

Vidal sat impassive, finger remaining over the table. Nothing registered on his face except a slight flaring of his nostrils.

Alex had only dared look away from Vidal once, a quick glance over his shoulder at Rafael who was slowly undulating his arms like a splendid bird for his new tutee. The *pajaro* lesson, thought Alex nostalgically. He flipped open his vocabulary note cards and paused for a moment, awestruck at the sight of his own trembling hands.

"*Mesa*." Alex held up the index card with his artless drawing of a table for proof.

Vidal pointed to his shoe.

In the agonizing silence Alex recalled a time with a particular girlfriend in college who also spanked him. She would make a list of the bad things he did on dates—not opening doors for her, looking surreptitiously at other women—and when they arrived back home she would insist that he take his discipline over her knee. He found he liked it, the feeling of handing over control. It was during one of these sessions that he saw suddenly a vision of a laser-tipped dartboard set, his first marketable idea and his entrée at Nedderland Enterprises.

"Leee...bro? *Libro.*"

Vidal kept his dark arm pointing down. Alex couldn't remember *shoe*, but it didn't matter. He looked in his cards. He looked at Vidal's thick arms and hands. *Mano,* he thought. *Brazo,* ask me something like that.

"I can't remember," Alex told him.

Vidal slapped the table with palm of his hand. The pop reverberated in the alcove and Alex closed his eyes. When things started drying up for him at work he had gone so far as to ask Suzanne to spank him like his old girlfriend had, something she'd performed without much vigor. He even gave her a leather corset and a shellacked paddle, making sure his approach was deliberately fun and jokey. But in fact Suzanne had gotten so upset just looking at the corset that he never mentioned it again. He shifted in his seat, hoping Vidal wouldn't notice his discomfort.

SUZANNE and Maxwell ate late lunch at an outdoor *comedor* sitting on stools around a mobile counter that clearly hadn't moved in years. Maxwell ordered for them in Spanish and they ate beans and warm tortillas and plantains. It was chilly up in the mountains and Suzanne was glad Maxwell had suggested she bring a heavier jacket. It was red with a padded lining and maybe a little flashy alongside the locals in their ratty second-hand American garments, but at least she was warm. Maxwell was in a short-sleeved shirt with buttons. Suzanne couldn't imagine how he kept from shivering.

After the meal Suzanne offered to haul Maxwell's pack on her back, insisting it wasn't too heavy and that she wanted to help out. Maxwell agreed because he was going to be carrying his black sample case separately; he said he had a good feeling about the day. Even after he removed it, a bulky sample case about the size of small filing cabinet, the backpack was still heavy and they spent a few minutes adjusting the belts and straps so that she could move comfortably under it.

With the afternoon sun behind them, they followed a low, winding dirt trail along the base of the foothills. The trees became more clustered but occasional improvised shanties appeared surrounded by modest vegetable patches.

"The folks in the mountain are poorer than those in the villages," he told her.

She had fallen into an easy habit of listening to his voice. It reminded her of the affable narrators for documentaries on cable television.

He shifted the sample case to his other hand and took a small, unimpressive camera from his pocket, which he hung around his neck.

"Now you look like a tourist," Suzanne told him.

"I don't mind. The tourists are the ones worried about looking like tourists. Nobody hates American tourists more than other American tourists."

"But you're not some silly little tourist. You're a businessman."

"Yes, but some business is better transacted by silly little tourists." He held the camera to his face and Suzanne turned to show profile.

The trees became more dense the higher they climbed. The fresh smells of the river disappeared now, replaced by a pervasive mustiness. It was much dimmer too, except for the occasional pillar of sun dramatically breaking through the canopy overhead.

Maxwell was quiet now, pausing to listen every couple of minutes, shifting his sample case from hand to hand. Suzanne watched him and found herself feeling slightly anxious. Even with that case of his, he was having a much easier time hiking than she was. If he did turn out to have some sort of dishonorable intentions towards her, she would be in real trouble. Even if she could somehow make it back to town—and she wasn't exactly sure where that was—she doubted she could communicate "sexual assault" in Spanish if it came to that. She could say *ayudame* if she had to. She practiced it in her mind, "*Ayudame! Ayudame!*" Had to make sure to pronounce the D as TH, accent on the "U." She felt suddenly concerned about the way she had been acting in the hot spring. Had she given him the wrong idea? Maybe she should say something to him.

"Hang a sec," Maxwell said suddenly and went behind Suzanne to take something out of the backpack. It was a can of Coke. Maxwell popped the top and took a slurp. Suzanne was about to ask for some but she something saw ahead through the trees: a woman moving quickly down the path toward them, carrying a large shallow basket in front of her. No, a girl. She had a cloth over the basket. Her cheeks were flushed when she reached them and her breath came in quick pants.

"*Para mi*," she said pointing to the can.

"Certainly, *para ti*," Maxwell said handing it to her. She grinned and immediately began drinking.

She was darling, Suzanne thought, with those chubby brown cheeks and long black hair. Not any more than 13 or 14. Her *juipil* was in traditional colors: blue and yellow. And her skirt was bright purple and covered in dirt and sweat.

"Drink up, my dear," Maxwell said. "The nice thing about finding these little villages off the beaten path is that the locals aren't jaded from all the tourism and are still excited to see strangers."

"What is your name?" Suzanne asked her. "Or, *como se llama...*"

The girl was swallowing and stopped. "Hello lady," she said. "My name is K'ek."

"Keh..."

Maxwell helped her. "K'ek. Actually it just means 'girl' in the Indian dialect up here: Quiche Mayan. They don't give names out to strangers."

Suzanne nodded. "They're afraid we're going to steal their souls or something?"

"Take a picture of me," K'ek said, pointing to Maxwell's camera. "One dollar."

"Oh, she's precious," Suzanne said, leaning closer. "What an adorable little girl you are."

Maxwell lifted his camera and slid open the lens cover. "Finish the drink, dear, and I'll take your picture. Get a dollar, Suzanne."

K'ek finished the drink and watched Maxwell. She didn't pose but stood looking forward, hands gripping the basket, waiting for him to take the picture.

Suzanne moved her hands from pocket to pocket. She had a ten and some twenties but that was too much to give to the girl. She and Maxwell were pretty isolated up here and this girl probably wouldn't do anything bad, but you never knew. She might run home with her twenty and someone would ask where she had gotten American money and she would say two tourists alone and defenseless walking up in the mountains and before you knew it... *ayudame*, she reminded herself. Have the word at the ready just in case. Of course there might be some smaller bills in her money pack hanging around her neck, hidden under her shirt. She had a wad of bills rubber-banded to her passport but that was for emergencies and she hadn't even told Maxwell about it. Of course he could be trusted, but still...

"Max, is there any money in the backpack? Because I don't know that I've got it."

Maxwell was leaning close to K'ek, running his fingers from her ear to her clavicle bone. He didn't answer Suzanne. K'ek flinched as Maxwell poked his middle finger near her thyroid, pressing his thumb quickly into her vocal fold. The basket wobbled in K'ek's grip.

Suzanne was taken aback that he was being so forward for a stupid picture. She had come to think of Maxwell as a serious, bookish individual that somehow she herself was drawing out; that when he had touched her face on the bus it was only because something about Suzanne had emboldened him to the point where he couldn't help but stroke her face. She was glad she hadn't told him about her hidden money.

"I don't have a dollar, Maxwell," she told him acidly.

"Oh?" He was distracted, carefully laying his briefcase in the dirt and opening it so K'ek couldn't see what was inside. He removed a blister pouch and tore it open and pulled out a washcloth.

"I'm going to put some makeup on you, K'ek. Like all the pretty movie stars in America, okay?"

He took the back of her head and pushed her face into the rag. The basket dropped to the dirt, spilling beans and peppers.

"What are you doing?" Suzanne's voice rose to a new pitch. K'ek's body went limp and Maxwell let her drop next to the basket. He folded the rag and threw it back into his case.

"I'm taking her head," he told Suzanne, pulling a long blade from his case. "It's nearly the exact specifications." He hunched over the body. "A little dark but that can be fixed."

Suzanne grabbed his arm. She felt rabid. "What are you talking about?" she shouted.

He shoved her and Suzanne fell on the backpack, flailing like an upside-down turtle. By the time she got to her hands and knees, Maxwell was sawing through the fleshy neck, and rivulets of fluid were dampening the ground around K'ek's body. Suzanne covered her eyes and a second later she was vomiting.

"The key with small heads," Maxwell told her calmly, "is to not shred the esophagus and to keep enough tracheal cartilage to make a good graft later. This one was put on order by a woman in New York. Part of a procedural package: gastric bypass, lypo for the thighs, I believe a breast augmentation, and finally a brand new, pre-adolescent top. Very expensive. The techs bleach the skin, a few minor alterations to the skull, switch the eyes; doesn't take long."

Suzanne got up to run, but the ground was uneven, her legs wobbled and she pitched forward. The backpack had thrown her off-balance. She could smell the blood coming off the girl, her insides, something rotting, she opened the clip across her chest and wriggled her shoulders but the pack would not slip off. She could run if she could get it off, get back to the town, and she frantically patted herself, trying to find some release or clips she had forgotten about.

"I tamp saline pouches into the mouth and neck cavities. It helps that K'ek just flushed carbonated sugar too. Means I don't have to worry about over-applying the desiccants."

On her knees, Suzanne felt a cold breeze. It was coming from Maxwell's case, like a refrigerator door left open. The inside was lined with thick eggshell foam, and on one side was a large ball of tightly wrapped cheesecloth, about the size of a basketball. The space next to it was empty.

She took a breath. He had left the knife on the ground near K'ek's shoulder. The thought of reaching for it made her gag. How was she going to explain this to the police? She thought of Vidal drilling vocabulary, *querpo, boca, nariz* —but what was head?

That was when she saw the legs coming toward them. *Ayudame*, she thought. Four legs; two people. Nice shoes and hiking pants. Americans. *Help*, she thought. It was lodged in her throat. She had to wait until she was sure they could hear but not close enough for Maxwell—

"Suzanne, I hate to be trite about this." He was standing over her, raising his shirt slightly to show a small holster on his belt. "This is the exact pistol the *secuestros* have been using for years." He was still speaking calmly, not threatening her, explaining, as if it were just another nugget she might find interesting. "If I end up shooting someone it's going to look like a botched kidnapping, as if one of the radicalized Indian groups did it."

He unzipped the top of the backpack and removed a native blanket to throw over K'ek, although the ground around her was still boggy and dark.

Suzanne kept her eyes on the approaching figures, willing them to notice the blood. She could see now that they were young and blonde, a boy and a girl, probably college-aged. The girl had a dark tan and short cropped hair. The boy was at least a foot taller than her and had spiked hair and dark sunglasses hanging around his neck. He smiled and nodded. His shoulders were covered by thick padded straps that held a mustard backpack so large it seemed to hover behind him like a full figured apparition.

"Hi," the boy said. "What a sweet day." He puffed his chest out and drew his elbows behind him and the pack dropped off, landing in the dirt with a heavy thud. "You okay?" he asked Suzanne, still on the ground.

Ayudame, she thought. *Run, get help....*

"What'cha got there?" the girl asked.

"Nothing to be concerned about," Maxwell told them.

The girl asked, "You harvesting heads?"

"Now why would you ask that?" Maxwell responded pleasantly.

The girl brazenly pulled the blanket off K'ek. Suzanne held her breath.

"Are you going to leave the arms and legs?" the girl asked.

"They're too small," Maxwell told her.

"No," the girl got excited and her voice rose at the ends of each sentence. "Because now they can pump 'em with hormones. Get the muscle tone later. Mind if we take them?"

The girl hacked into the arms with a hand axe, spattering blood everywhere. She was far less careful then Maxwell, twisting K'ek's shoulder a few times before yanking the arm out of the socket. The boy pulled K'ek's blood-soaked *juipil* over her neck.

Maxwell glowered. "Leave the *juipil*," he barked, incensed. "It's rude to take clothing."

"Leave this?" The boy held up the bloody fabric. "Haven't you heard of recycling?"

Maxwell sat in the grass near Suzanne. "This is a real problem in the industry." He spoke as if to lecture the kids but they weren't paying attention. "Any college kid with a passport can come down here and bring back a bushel of feet, a bouquet of arms, earn enough party money for a semester."

The girl picked up the basket and shook the remaining beans out. "The days of just using the head and throwing the rest away are over," she announced.

The boy added, "Wake up and smell the shade-grown, old man. Move with the times, or move over."

The backpack was already bulging with flesh, but the girl—grunting and making a comical, silent movie grimace—managed to get the zipper across the top even with the basket inside.

"You're flooding the market with donor parts," Maxwell said, furiously. Suzanne put her hand on his arm to try and calm him.

"Nice to meet you," the boy said, hoisting the pack onto his shoulders.

Maxwell refused to look at them as they continued on the path.

When they were alone Maxwell finished his work in silence, carefully wrapping K'ek's head in layers of cheesecloth and then plastic wrap, which he sealed using a hand-held heater. Suzanne watched him work. He was obviously upset. She had never seen him this quiet. He placed the head next to the other and carefully closed the clasps on his case and walked back down the way they had come. Suzanne put the backpack on again, tightened the belts and snapped the clips in place, and followed him back into town.

It was getting dark when they reached the village square and they sat on a low stone wall surrounding a church and waited for the bus to come. The sample case and backpack lay in the weedy grass at their feet. Maxwell was deliberately not looking at Suzanne. He was brooding, that same expression as Alex had when he was most discouraged.

She tried, "Those kids could have really learned something from you."

He didn't answer.

She rubbed his arm. His skin was cold and she wondered if it would be too irritatingly maternal to tell him to put on something warmer. She brushed the dust and dirt off the red sleeves of her jacket. A squalling came from the church behind them and they both turned to look. A bone-thin woman was sitting by the door trying to get her screaming baby to take a plastic bottle in its mouth. The baby was nude; the mother wore indigenous Mayan clothing.

"What a shame," Maxwell said at last.

"What?"

"In some of these villages the mortality rate among infants is nearly a hundred percent. And you know what's killing them? Diarrhea."

"Go on," she told him. His voice had a spark of something again. When Suzanne tried comforting Alex he just growled. But Maxwell seemed to be getting some of that debonair, confident quality about himself again.

"Their mothers feed them American formula and mix it with bad water—sewage and puddles. And the really pathetic part is they could breast-feed and give their kids a decent shot, but they don't. Big pharm has sold them a bunch of lies."

"It's terrible," Suzanne said agreeably.

Maxwell put his arm around her. "And it's cold and the poor woman has no jacket."

Suzanne tsked in sympathy. It was nearly dark now and she hoped the bus would arrive soon.

ALEX's third tutor was a much older man with grey hair: a pleasant, retired government administrator named René. René was easily distracted and Alex would catch him looking at the other tutors and nodding or winking, involved in some private joke. It didn't bother Alex that he might be the butt of these jokes. It didn't bother him particularly that Suzanne and Maxwell were now quite late in returning. And it only slightly bothered him that after two full weeks of struggling down here he still had not come up with a single idea that could even generously be described as "outside of the box." (The word *caja* suddenly sprung forth, bringing with it a quick spark of pleasure, in spite of his mood). The whole experience was beginning to fade around him even as he endured it. It must be what exiled politicians and revolutionaries felt like: banished, living with humiliation, walking numb while everything that mattered happened somewhere else.

It was a feast day in Guatemala and a contingent of students from the school went to the Great Square to watch the festivities. They marched down the narrow boulevards—each one paired with his tutor like little ducks—struggling to make conversation. Alex and René were the exception, neither making much effort.

Up ahead was Vidal and his new tutee, a jolly exuberant American boy. He and Vidal were about the same age and had an easy rapport. Alex watched as the boy said something to Vidal, who threw his head back and laughed. It was appalling to remember how hard both he and Suzanne had worked to win Vidal over, to triumph over his aloofness. Although maybe it wasn't too late. He could strike up a conversation with the American kid, ask him where he was from, then segue into a conversation with Vidal, not as a student but just as another one of the guys. It was a good plan, but as Alex was about to call out, René's foot caught on one of the cobblestones and he pitched forward. Alex quickly reached out to keep him from falling and the two men clawed at each other, teetering and rocking until Alex regained his balance and was able to steady both of them.

"*Ach, dios,*" René mumbled, releasing Alex from his grip. "*Gracias.*"

Alex looked up and saw the edge of the Great Square just as Vidal and the American disappeared into the crowd.

René walked Alex to an Indian woman squatting over a basket. He explained in simple Spanish that it was an honor and a tradition for a student to purchase an item of food, not unlike these flat tortillas, as a *regalo* for his teacher. Alex nodded and put up two fingers to the woman and gave both to René.

A large platform had been erected in front of the tall cathedral that dominated the square. With René chewing and following behind, Alex walked to get a better view. He stopped suddenly when he saw Suzanne a few feet ahead in the crowd. He could see her red jacket with the hood up, but when he called her name she didn't respond. Not until he had pushed his way through and actually put his hand on her shoulder did he realize it wasn't Suzanne, it was an Indian woman holding a baby. Alex removed his hand and apologized quickly. The jacket didn't even look like Suzanne's; it had a large rip as if someone had worn it while fighting and then sloppily stitched it back together. Suzanne would never wear something in that condition.

René took his arm. "Alex," he yelled, mouth still full of tortilla. "It begins."

A giant head was floating from the steeple door, a head the size of an enormous balloon, its hair made of long dark braids of rope. Another head followed with huge, pasty white cheeks, a sickening, almost predatory leer in the eyes, outsize lips protruding like tubes of blood. Under each giant head were the tiny legs and feet of the man holding it aloft.

"*Que es esto?*" Alex asked René.

"*Gigantica*," René explained. "The festival of the giants commemorating the arrival of the Spanish *Conquistadores* to Guatemala. They appeared like behemoths to the Indians. Every year the giant heads come out of the church and dance to commemorate the conquest."

And it suddenly came to Alex: American kids everywhere dancing at festivals under giant Guatemalan heads, organizing decorating contests at schools, marching in parades from Macy's to the Rose Bowl. Every kid in America working in teams or alone, each with their own giant Guatemalan head, kits sold and marketed under exclusive licensing agreement of Nedderland Enterprises, Alex Moss President Latin American Division. All inquiries through my personal assistant, Vidal. He scanned the crowd for the young tutor but couldn't see him. Didn't matter, he'd approach him after lunch with the idea. Surely Vidal would jump at the opportunity to quit teaching and come work for him; Alex would win him over yet. He could even hire a bunch of Vidal's friends. Surround himself with young blood. He couldn't wait to get on the phone and pitch it north.

New Pueblo, New Mexico

THE elastic bandage wrapped around Gloria Schindler's ankle made it impossible to wear her hiking boots, which meant she couldn't wear her khaki pants, and that meant she wasn't going to look the way she felt. For ceremonies on the reservations she liked to look the part of an explorer: open minded, youthfully exuberant, curious without being judgmental, always respectful. But the only thing that she could fit around the bandage was an open pair of her husband Buddy's sandals which made her feet look horrifyingly large and square. She had only taken a few steps away from the car, trying not to limp, seeing her yellowed toe-nails poking out from under her long skirt, before recognizing that on this day she was going to look mid-60s, frumpy, and woefully ordinary.

"I fell this morning with Hiking Club," Gloria explained as they walked. Buddy Schindler was in his navy windbreaker and jeans, and presented his arm so she could take hold of his elbow. It was a hot day, but chillier here on top of the mesas, and though Buddy's windbreaker was zipped to the quarter-mark, he was prepared to zip it half, even all the way up if need be.

"How did that happen?" Buddy asked.

"I said, I slipped this morning."

"How did it happen?"

Gloria knew he was actually asking how she could have prevented it from happening. It was a source of contention in the marriage that he spent too much time analyzing her mistakes. When they lived in Chicago she had begun a series of businesses: selling cosmetics and vitamins, buying property with liens on them for resale, even a mail-order bead business in the early 1990s when it seemed like everyone was making their own necklaces and earrings. Business would be fine for awhile until a boredom would set in, a certain weariness, an irritation with the activity, and things would fall apart. Even when she made money she struggled against this apathy until finally losing interest and quitting. That was when Buddy would step in with his officious, corporate manner and spin some explanation as to why she had failed: her marketing network was too incestuous, a competitor with deeper pockets had moved into the area, the booming economy was making people less interested in serving leftovers so they didn't need as many plastic containers.

"I just slipped on the hike," she said irritably. "I didn't step on a rock or loose dirt and my boot wasn't laced incorrectly; I was watching where I was going. I did everything right, but when I put my foot down...I slipped."

Even though Gloria was leaning on Buddy he managed to remain a pace behind her, a mild protest at the way the day was going. Gloria had her own theory about her failures anyway, a vague, unformed idea that her problems were rooted elsewhere, in some realm that no one had ever told her about. Failure was organic to the suburban Chicago landscape in which she had spent her whole life. It was the reason she had wanted to move to New Mexico, to an open, unknowable landscape, rather than remaining in the same groove.

They followed the sounds of drumming, walking between the haphazardly parked cars. Buddy let his eyes scan bumper stickers, reading whatever caught his attention: *My Other Car's a Mule. Free Leonard Peltier. Got Peyote?* Some stickers had their edges scraped off indicating that a driver had changed his opinion or the car had been sold to someone who preferred a different radio station. Gloria concerned herself with not grimacing on each step.

It wasn't so much the slip that bothered her. That had been a mere accident which could have happened to anybody. In fact, when she had lost her footing and cried, "Whoo-oopsie!" in a sort of funny way, a couple of the women nearest her had reached out to help, and in that way of finding yourself surrounded by people whose company you enjoy and in front of whom it's okay to err, she found the whole thing a fairly pleasant experience. But just after righting herself, she saw Donna Markham's lips twisted in amusement, and Gloria felt herself suddenly humiliated. Donna had said, "You need to be careful," as though she were speaking to a child. As though Gloria didn't know that she needed to be careful. Gloria knew when she was being made fun of.

In just six weeks since moving in to New Pueblo, Donna Markham had already joined the Garden Club and she was a member of the Arts Group and she was in Woman's Financial Club, which Buddy had only recently relented on and given Gloria the requisite 1,000 dollar check to join. She had even brazenly shown up to Book Club 2, the club that Gloria herself had founded. It baffled Gloria that all the other women seemed to like Donna or at least, up this point, were disinclined to talk behind her back. Gloria had tried a few little opening lines. *Can anyone tell me why the Markhams have three kivas in their kitchen....Is anyone else worried about the amount of peroxide she's using on her head*, but so far these remarks had been met with shrugged shoulders or awkward silence, so Gloria was lying low, taking notes, waiting for an opening.

The ceremonial park was just another expanse of dirt, but surrounded by a series of low wooden homes that stretched to form a long rectangle. There were no trees or bushes, but several basketball hoops had been erected along the edges, despite the lack of pavement. The drummers were at the far end of the park—two men, each beating a pair of kettle drums with a steady, unornamented beat, with faces impassive and serious like airline pilots. The crowd was sparse and Gloria settled on a spot near an Indian family in jean jackets and cowboy hats.

Two separate groups of costumed children moved in the open space. The group closest to the drummers was dressed in white gowns and had multicolored feathers on their arms like birds. They circled each other, arms straight out like wings, their moccasined feet remaining more or less in rhythm with the drummers. The dancers across the rectangle, closer to Buddy and Gloria, were in brown leather and had antlers on their heads like deer. Each one was stooped over, leaning on two walking sticks like ski poles, which extended their arms so the children resembled four legged animals. They too were keeping the beat, but not in unison, and Gloria, who'd played the clarinet in junior high marching band, kept thinking, *left, left,* as she watched their feet, wishing it didn't bother her.

Buddy suddenly took a step in front of her and lowered his head. "Let's get out of here," he said, and took her arm.

"What's wrong with you? You're being rude," she hissed, moving her head so that she could see around him. Buddy silently took his place beside her but kept his body at a strange angle, with his face turned so that it seemed he was looking at the basketball hoops instead of the dancers. He zipped his windbreaker as high as it would go.

Everyone began ringing bells. The deer shook their walking sticks, which had bells on the ends, and the birds began to flutter their feathered arms revealing bells sewn into the sleeves. The spectators too began ringing bells and though Gloria didn't have one of her own, she felt a sudden euphoria at being in the center of all this authentic spiritual outpouring, and she began to smile without being aware that she was smiling, and it was while she was smiling, scanning the crowd and the dancers, that she saw them.

Across the way, sitting in folding, cloth director's chairs and looking—Gloria was sure—like the photo in whatever catalogue they had ordered them from, in smart jackets and dark sunglasses, were the god damned Markhams. Donna had red lipstick on her thin lips and an expression of superior boredom. And there was Bill Markham, sitting stiffly in his chair holding a wooden cane across his lap so that even if someone wanted to stand next to the Markhams they couldn't. As Gloria watched in horror, Donna stuck her fingers in her ears to drown out the ringing bells.

The birds broke from their stations and ran down the rectangle towards the deer. The deer stood firm. The birds ran around the deer, passing just in front of where the Markhams were sitting and for one painful moment Gloria was sure they were going to try to include Donna in their ceremony. Not that it would have surprised Gloria at this point; the Markhams were everywhere, and everyone was fascinated with them.

Even Buddy, who normally couldn't care less about anything that happened with "the gals," as he derisively called Gloria's friends, was very interested when the Welcoming Club made their traditional outreach to the new neighbors. He had sat in rapt attention when Gloria had described the day.

"Get this," she had told him upon her return. "Bill has an enclosed greenhouse and a roof-top patio with a 360 degree view. Both the mesas and the Sandias." Gloria had shrugged as if to say, what can you do? The Schindlers only had a long-view at the very edge of their driveway, where one could see the Sandia Mountains between two of the homes across the street. They had wanted to live somewhere where the Markhams now were, but they had settled instead for a lower-priced subdivision where the lots were cheaper because they abutted the arroyo, a deep cataract that snaked through New Pueblo and collected the flood water when it rained. Nothing could be built in the arroyo, so the Schindlers, like all the other neighbors, had to construct their homes on the usable half of the property.

"Did you talk much to...?" Buddy had asked, raising his eyebrows.

"Donna? No, actually she seems a little snotty to me."

"You think she's snotty?" Buddy repeated.

"I get a weird feeling around her. She seems, if you'll excuse the term, a tad Midwestern."

At that, Buddy had nodded, "I didn't like them either." Which had delighted Gloria since they so rarely agreed on people.

The deer began swinging their staffs at the birds as though to defend their turf. The birds began running randomly around individual deer, ducking and gliding to avoid the staffs. Gloria remained fixed on the Markhams. She heard Buddy's voice in her head in his analytical mode: *When did you start to dislike it here?* The very afternoon the Markhams arrived. *Could you have done something to prevent that?*

She could have. The New Pueblan Realty office had originally asked Gloria to give a tour when the Markhams arrived. Gloria was the realty's office favorite guide because she spoke enthusiastically about the landscape and never made snide remarks about how tough it was to get good service in restaurants or how the drivers didn't slide into the intersection when making a left turn. Had Gloria been on hand for the tour she would have noted those undesirable Midwestern aspects of the Markhams, the East Bank Club T-shirt and the fact that Donna twanged her A's pronouncing "cash" as "kee-yash" and "dint" for "didn't." She could have discouraged them from looking for houses in New Pueblo. But the Garden Club had been given pre-opening passes to see the Georgia O'Keeffe museum in Santa Fe that day, and Gloria had been looking forward to it for weeks. She decided to ask someone to give the tour for her. She had asked Buddy.

BILL Markham was a lousy traveler, but a studied one. He prided himself on knowing exactly when to take his pill so that he would sleep soundly on any flight he took; and he knew which dosage to take for each flight: .25 mgs for Chicago to New York, .5 Chicago to California, 1.5 plus a glass of white wine for Chicago to London. This was why on the morning of the scheduled tour of New Pueblo when he awoke to find his heart slightly racing and his bowel movement suspiciously light considering the previous night's steak fajita, he decided to spend the afternoon in the hotel bed and let Donna make the appointments by herself. Donna was an enthusiastic person in general, and never more so then when she traveled. She often found herself swept away with the spirit of adventure on vacations. She sampled foods that at home she wouldn't put in the garbage without sealing it off in plastic grocery bags tied shut at the handles. She had conversations with people to whom she normally would not give her spare change. In fact, Donna and Bill had met just a few years back at a resort in the Bahamas, and got so close that when she returned to Chicago she found herself getting married for the third time, something she had sworn—literally, one hand on the family Bible—that she would never do.

As soon as Donna stepped out of her rental, Buddy figured her for late 40s possibly even early 50s. Out here, where Buddy and Gloria, both approaching 65 and generally the youngest at any of the events they attended, seeing someone like Donna was fairly novel. And it wasn't just her age, it was her entire bearing; she was plump and robust and healthy. She had large breasts, and the way she was dressed actually revealed cleavage, a rare sight around New Pueblo, where the women dressed in outfits—long sleeves, collars, hats with wide brims—chosen to keep as much skin as possible protected from the sun.

Buddy didn't object to giving the tour, especially when he heard the Markhams were from Chicago. He took pleasure in being envied. There were views here that any Midwesterner would be impressed by. He felt as if the landscape was somehow his own accomplishment: the Sandias towering over New Pueblo, the mesas on view from his deck. The contact-high made his palms sweat. He pulled the clingy plastic wrap off the plate of crackers, cheese, and cactus jelly that Gloria had left for him in the fridge.

"So, moving to New Mexico?" he asked. There was something ugly about her face. Maybe it was the way her nose ended unnaturally with those knobby bits like a chicken leg. It was her torso that Buddy was drawn to; the straps over her meaty shoulders, the way her sunglasses hung snugly between her breasts.

"Possibly," Donna answered. "We're just looking, for now." Donna took one cracker and ate it dry. She had just lost 15 pounds, on her way to her goal of 25. And even though she wasn't quite finished, she felt light and attractive. "My husband has just retired. Do you know Fermilab?"

Buddy nodded.

"From Fermilab. He's going to do some consulting at Los Alamos—"

"Consulting, then." Buddy interrupted. "Because you don't seem old enough to have a husband who's retired."

Donna considered for a second telling him about the age difference between herself and Bill, but she could sense Buddy's interest in her, and decided to be mysterious. She shrugged her shoulders and ran her hand though her hair. At home the muggy Chicago climate added weight to each strand, but here in the desert her hair was full and voluminous. She hadn't felt this good in years.

Donna followed Buddy past shelves displaying meticulously arranged objects. "This is called a dream catcher," Buddy said. "And these are kachina dolls and this gourd here was painted by Jose Riviera who is the main gourd artist out here. He lives in Old Pueblo which isn't too far." The Schindlers had left all their Chicago furnishings and decorations behind. Gone were the black and white photos of stern-faced immigrants that Gloria claimed repressed her. In their place now were Navajo rugs, folk art renderings of buffalo hunts, great kokopellis forged in copper and painted green and turquoise.

Buddy opened the door to his office. He still audited documents for his old firm, Chicago Masticates and Creosote Corporation, the Midwest's largest manufacturer of chewing gum and pine tar. When he had started with the company the goal was to get a corner office in the heart of the industrial park. But now the most desirable jobs were the ones you could do at home with a modem. Buddy was proud of where he had ended up and still started every fax and e-mail with a little braggadocio: *Hey Steve, 80 degrees here. Thought about your proposal, in my home office, looking out my window at the juniper tree, and it occurred to me that we might require a whole new submission to the regulators...*

"Now this looks like a comfortable chair," Donna told him, sensing that he was waiting for a comment.

Buddy glowed. The chair was what he was most proud of. It was leather and had a high back and spun just like chairs in movies. Whenever Gloria would enter the office Buddy spun around and.... surprise! Buddy Schindler is starring in this movie! He was only sorry that none of the girls from the secretary pool could see him in it.

He led Donna through the patio door and around the juniper tree, and then over the cobblestone walkway to the back of the house where Gloria had her garden.

"My wife is growing tomato plants out here," Buddy gestured to where a soaker hose hissed into a patch of black dirt where three droopy plants stood. Gloria had erected cylindrical cages for the vines to cling to and though there was some growth, none of the plants were tall enough to require the support of the cage.

"It's a neat idea," Donna said politely. "Out here in the desert."

"Yes. It's almost impossible for these Midwestern crops to take root here." Buddy shrugged his shoulders. "It's nearly....absurd." He gave a little laugh to cover the momentary flash of disloyalty he felt.

Donna immediately took hold of his arm, a little gesture of intimacy and comfort.

"Shall we see the rest of our humble little community?" he asked formally. Donna nodded. They walked awkwardly a few steps until she released his arm, but even then he stayed in her immediate orbit and their hands brushed against each other every few steps. He had almost forgotten how much fun a Chicago girl could be.

They started in his Jeep down Sage Hill Drive, then took Pine Nut Road, which went up into the foothills of the Sandia mountains. The homes began to get larger and more spread out. Each one was tastefully designed, all adobe style, matching the color of the earth so well they seemed to have risen right up from it. Buddy felt that some of the houses up here were ostentatious and not nearly as cozy as his own, but he held his acerbic comments to himself since he didn't want to sound too critical or snobby. Plus, you never knew with whom the Markhams might align themselves if they moved in. He didn't want anything to get back to anybody.

"The Sandias are now right in front of us," he told her. "You know why they call them that? How they got their name?"

She looked at him and shook her head sweetly.

"Because just at sunset, just as the sun is about to drop into the horizon, the mountains turn pink. Just like pink sand."

"Pink sand?"

"Like in fish tanks," Buddy said. "That's why they're called the Sandias, for this pink sand effect."

The road ahead of them was hazy in the heat, but it was cool inside the car. Donna tilted all the vents in the center of the dash so the AC would blow at her. She held her arms in the current and her skin became prickly and the soft white hairs of her forearms straightened and stood. She tried to imagine herself living out in the middle of a desert in a gigantic home. She worried about boredom, about being left alone by Bill for long stretches. She wondered idly if Buddy's company would be the sort that could keep her sufficiently entertained.

"What goes on here in the evenings?" Donna asked, still inspecting her arms.

"Oh, there's lots of social life around here," Buddy told her. "Our Garden club is popular, all the gal—the women—belong to it. And there's lots of little side groups, like the Picante Cooking Club and the Chamber Music Society. I'm in the Orion Belt Guild which is the astronomy group for the guys; husbands of wives in the Garden Club."

"All men?" she asked, trying Buddy on for size.

"Mostly," he told her. "It's not restricted or anything, it's just the wives aren't that interested. They are when there's an event, like a meteor shower, or that lunar eclipse a few months back. Then the wives come."

"Bet that loosens the belt some." Donna said. She wasn't sure herself what she meant but she hoped he could pick up her intention by the tone of her voice.

"Bet you could loosen a belt or two," he said. "A girl like you could pull those belts right off, I bet."

She used an expression which she kept near the top of her arsenal; a slight turning of her cheek in parody of chaste shock, then a barely noticeably pursing of her lower lip to suggest playful sexual interest. She had been using this stock expression regularly ever since coming across it accidentally in the 12th grade when a teacher had suggested she go on an overnight trip with the debate team and he had become so quickly unglued, tripping over his own words to say that he hadn't meant anything untoward and that she had misunderstood. Still, it had been a few years since she'd used it, and she worried that at some point she'd reach the age when it was more comical than seductive. She could see by the way Buddy shifted in his seat that it had the desired effect.

Buddy looked forward again but was thinking of Donna's sunglasses, which remained in the groove of her breasts despite the glare on the road. He felt the same giddiness now that he did back in Chicago whenever he got a new secretary and he would begin to see how far he could take things. You never knew when harmless office banter might lead to after-work drinks on Rush Street or even a weekend business trip.... Maybe Donna could be part of his New Pueblo landscape. He could come over afternoons when the husband was at Los Alamos, and she could invent things for Buddy to do, like fix the swamp cooler, for example. Maybe Donna had forgotten to put the cover on the hot tub and a mouse had gotten in and drowned. He could come over, reach into the tub and hold the mouse by the tail. She would cover her eyes. My hero, she might coyly say....

BUDDY was looking only at the reservation ground now. He felt nauseated. The frenetic tumult in front of him, feathered dancers running madly beside antlered dancers, bells, whistles, stomping feet, bellowing, kettle drummers banging furiously now; it wasn't helping him quell his anxiety. He looked across the dirt to see if he could get some sort of reading on her. Donna was facing forward and might have been looking at him, he couldn't tell because of her dark glasses. He nodded to her, a little infinitesimal movement which, if she saw it, she would understand. But just as he did, a group of feathered dancers ran in front of him and Buddy could only see flashes of her face between the arms and legs of jumping men. Buddy felt a sudden desire to run, to flee before he was swallowed up in the chaos.

The drumming ceased suddenly and the dancers immediately stopped moving. The entire world had stopped, arms in the air mid shake, legs frozen mid step. Even the spectators were deathly still. Buddy was looking directly at Donna, and when he looked away he felt as if he was the only one moving.

Gloria cocked an eye at him then brought her hands together to be ready to applaud, should that be what the others did. But instead, after a few beats of silence, the crowd began to murmur. The dancers slid out of position and began to move naturally, reshuffling the groups and talking to each other casually. Donna Markham stood up and extended a hand to Bill, who planted his cane and let her guide him out of the lawn chair.

Gloria took hold of Buddy's arm and stepped in the direction of their car. Buddy steadied her wordlessly, since it seemed like she was just as anxious to leave as he was. When they were back among the cars, a swarm of children ran past. They were still wearing their costumes, birds and deer, and they jingled and clomped in a joyful blur. Gloria followed the children with her eyes and watched as they gathered around a man dressed as Ronald McDonald, who was handing out coloring books and little slips of pink paper. The clown was constantly shifting, wincing under his grease paint, moving his head back and forth to keep from getting impaled on antlers. He was handing out merchandise just as fast as he could, but birds and deer continued arriving until the clown was all but buried under the raucous children.

Gloria mumbled. "That's appalling. Just a sec...." She made an effort not to limp—wishing for a moment that she had one of the deer's walking sticks or even Bill Markham's cane—and approached a woman sitting behind a card table selling bags of pinion nuts and small, paper cups of lemonade.

"Excuse me," Gloria said leaning down to the woman. "I'm Gloria Schindler, a member of the New Pueblo Regional Historical Interest Society. Actually, I'm—" she made a self effacing grimace— "an officer of the club. Anyway, I was just wondering what the, well-" she gestured towards Ronald McDonald with her head. "What's the significance of having him here?"

The woman repeated, "Significance?"

"Yes," she said, and when the woman said nothing further, Gloria asked, "Why is Ronald McDonald here? Why are you allowing that?"

"The kids like him," the woman answered flatly.

Buddy already had the RoadWaster idling impatiently as she stepped up and buckled herself in. "You'll never believe it," Gloria said waving one of the pink slips she had found on the ground. Buddy answered by backing the car slowly out of the space and on to the dirt road. "They're going to build a McDonald's out here. Not in the park but on the main road. I guess it'll be part of a new gas station too. Out here. It'll ruin the way of life here. Can't they just stay away?"

"Why don't they kick him off?" Buddy asked.

She considered the question and answered, "The kids like him."

Buddy laughed. He made his voice stiff and deep and syncopated like movie Indians. "Hmm," he grunted. "Me like Ronald. Him funny. Him trickster clown."

For a moment Gloria could only think about how unlucky she was.

No matter how much she changed herself, how much she grew, she was still stuck with him—a little piece of her past that was unalterably Midwestern. Buddy was a little like Donna Markham in that way. And here all Gloria had ever wanted was to be swallowed up by New Mexico so that she herself would be a part of the landscape. She carried that ideal in everything she did, the way she dressed, the way her house looked, the food she ate; even the club she founded, Book Club 2. It was different from Book Club by relying less on Oprah's books and more on those that had relevance to the landscape. She required every other book to be written by a regional writer: Scott Momoday, Tony Hillerman, Barbara Kingsolver.... For every Wally Lamb there would be a Marmon Silko. For every *1000 Acres*, there would be a *Bless Me, Ultima*.

But the memory of that creation no longer gave her any pleasure. As soon as she thought of Book Club 2, she thought of Donna Markham, and how Donna Markham was now a member of that club and, in her very first meeting, when she should have been quiet and deferential, she instead insisted they read one of her books. As if that wasn't boorish enough, the book she had wanted was something by John Cheever! The antithesis of New Mexico. A book that was not just off topic, but offensively inappropriate to boot.

Gloria crossed her legs as best she could in the car and massaged her ankle through the bandage. Donna Markham. Donna was pure Midwest, she was the kind of person who said "Oriental" instead of "Asian," and she didn't even say "Oriental," she said "Ory-enal." Gloria decided not to speak to Shelly anymore because she had seen Shelly having lunch with Donna at the New Pueblo Café. And she wouldn't speak to either Duck sister, not Sandy and not Nancy, because Sandy Duck had brought Donna to Book Club 2 and Nancy Duck had sponsored her appointment into the New Pueblo Mahjong Society. Nellie Strinberg had seconded the Cheever book, which according to the bylaws of Book Club 2 meant that they had to read it. What was wrong with everyone? Just a week before, at a Wild Flower Club meeting where the members were weeding the little gardens in the medians, Gloria wore a *"Sanitary Tortilla Factory"* shirt, and Donna wore a shirt that said *"Carson's Ribs."* Gloria felt like yelling,

"Don't you see? She doesn't get it!" But if any of the other weeders had noticed the irony, no one had commented on it to Gloria.

Once Buddy had exhausted all the good views from the road he drove Donna back to the house. The tray of crackers on the counter still had the cling wrap bunched over half the plate from when he had lifted it. Earlier when he had originally offered them to Donna they had both been tentative, polite. But now Donna reached for the plate without being offered and picked up three crackers and began chewing on one.

Buddy took out the pitcher of margarita mix and ice and poured her a large glass in a San Felipe Casino tumbler. He got up close when he handed it to her and warned her it was strong. She took this as a challenge and began drinking it down without pause. She got halfway through the cup before putting the glass down and wiping her mouth with the back of her hand. She shivered.

Buddy said, "The best way to drink that is in the hot tub. Now you're talking New Pueblo lifestyle."

"And me without my swimsuit." She took a big gulp of margarita while Buddy tried to figure out what to offer her next. "Of course, I could borrow one of your wife's."

"I don't think you would fit," Buddy told her.

"I'm getting used to wearing clothes that are too big...." Donna said, thinking of her diet.

Since Donna was actually considerably heavier than Gloria, Buddy could only think of one option. "You could have a shirt of mine," he said.

Buddy made sure that Donna got the view of the mesas, his spot, and held her hand as she stepped into the tub. She had one of his off-white button-down work-shirts which cloaked her sufficiently and still reached about mid-thigh. He was certain she was naked underneath, though it was possible she had left her panties on. The shirt was a lot less sexy somehow, it revealed nothing on top, and her legs were chunky and not at all as appealing as the rest of her.

"Hot," Donna declared settling in. "This is a beautiful view," she said raising her voice to be heard over the motor of the jets. She kept her arms pressed into the shirt to keep it from billowing.

Buddy hated where he sat with its view of the back of the Fishman's house and their hot tub and their little section of the arroyo, but he tried to focus on Donna. She looked better now that the frenetic white water hid her lower half. It occurred to him again that there was something ugly about her face, a certain repulsiveness, and for an instant he wished she would go away. He kept his legs at an angle so that they wouldn't brush against her.

"If we moved here," she said contorting her body so she could reach her glass on the deck and keep her other arm holding down her shirt, "I'd need to get good sun block. I've had some skin cancer on the back of my neck, little skin tags. It tends to recur so I would really need to watch out for that."

"They sell skin block at all the drug stores," he said, in his helpful voice. "In bottles."

She nodded, looking past him at the expansive sky and the dark red mesas.

"I've had a bout with cancer myself," Buddy continued, suddenly needing to keep the conversation going. "Ten years ago."

"Same thing? Skin cancer?" she asked.

"Nooo...." He waved away the rest of the answer as though it was too painful to even think about, though in reality he was just embarrassed saying "colon."

"You know what this reminds me of?" Donna asked. "Do you know that story by John Cheever about the guy who swims in all his neighbor's pools?"

"I think so, yes." Buddy said. "And he could listen to his neighbor's private conversations, right?"

"No. That's a different story. They made a movie about this one. I'm looking down this valley here and I'm seeing all these hot tubs."

Buddy turned and looked. On the edge of both sides of the arroyo were hot tubs, a long chain of winking blue water like a string of Christmas lights.

"This guy in the movie," Donna shouted, then paused until Buddy turned and faced her again. "He swam from one pool to the next. Burt Lancaster was in the movie. He played the swimmer. I can't remember what it was called. Lake of Pools or something."

"It sounds vaguely familiar, that story. And he had a big radio with him, right?" Buddy asked.

She smiled sweetly at him. The conversation was boring her. She brushed her toe against his leg, and though neither one acknowledged that it happened, Donna could see that Buddy was getting agitated.

"This is the arroyo," Buddy said quickly looking away from her. "You called it a valley. But actually this arroyo goes through all of New Pueblo and it's supposed to fill up in the event of a rainstorm. Although it hasn't happened since we've been here."

"Guess you can't build in it, then," Donna said.

"That's true. But actually my property extends into the arroyo. Over the edge here and all the way down and then for another fifty feet or so till just about the other side. It's part of our lot even though I can't do anything with it."

Donna had positioned her ankle against his calf to see what he would do. He was grinning a little so far but still ignoring it.

"I'm glad we own part of the arroyo, though. It's like owning a piece of the landscape. It's almost better than just having some great view that you can't buy.... Um...if you're getting tired of holding that shirt down I can turn the jets off. Or you could just take it off, the shirt."

She thought it was bold of him. But she could be bolder. She crossed her arms and pulled the shirt over her head let it drop on to the deck. She slid down, slouching in the water so that her breasts hovered, but her paunch and the patch of wrinkly skin just under it were still hidden by the white water. She let her feet land in his lap and wiggled them a little.

"All adults here," said Buddy in a consoling way, as if she had just committed some horrible faux-pas.

"Are we?" Donna smiled. She was glad that she had spent the time to have her teeth chemically whitened.

Conscious of her view, of the solid mesas behind him, Buddy stood up. He paused for a second, unsure what to do, but Donna raised her arms out of the tub and dug her fingers into the waistband. She yanked his bathing suit enough to lower it to his thighs. The nylon scrim on the inside was bunched up and stuck inside his buttocks like tissue sticking out of the top of a box, so he shuffled his legs back and forth to help her lower his suit more quickly. He let it get as low as his knees, under the water level, before sliding one leg out and then moving forward to put his knees on either side of her so that his penis was between her breasts. And though it wasn't at all what Donna was expecting—she had figured him more for the sloppy, open-mouthed kiss, then breaking it off claiming to feel too guilty type—she squeezed her breasts together with her forearms to accommodate him.

Buddy had always assumed that people only coupled like this in porno movies, but he was surprised how good it felt. Not just the rutting, but the whole scene. Adultery felt good again, and being outdoors felt good; the hot tub and dry air, it was all somehow very sporty. This was the sort of thing he and his fellow managers would brag about on Mondays, and he only regretted there was no one in New Mexico with whom he could share his good fortune. Maybe an E-mail: *Hey Steve, just got done tit fucking a stranger in my hot tub and I wanted to run the new specs by you before the meeting with regulatory....*

She leaned forward slightly to give him a better groove in which to travel and she opened her eyes as wide as possible, which she knew men liked. She had done this particular act so many times it was second nature. Buddy felt himself moving forward now, almost hovering over the pool, the whirls and rumbling of the jets, the white water churning all around him, the pretty blonde not his wife, leaning forward and looking up at him, two fists clenched and arms pressed against the sides of her breasts just for him, and now the woman, not his wife, showing him the tip of her tongue—like a little ridge of pinkish-red chewing gum—and letting it rest on her upper lip. He was sorry he had given her the good view because seeing the mesas now would make this the absolute perfect moment. He turned his neck slightly but he could only see the arroyo. He wanted something bigger, something beyond his property. He wanted to see the mesas. He twisted a little more, nudging Donna a little...if she could just slide an inch or two...

He had no idea what hit him, but he felt a sharp contact with his shin and the bench of the tub and then he was under the water, flailing around. He might have twisted his heel, or slipped on the bottom of the tub, or maybe his legs wobbled from the strain, fatigue, heat stroke perhaps. When he managed to get up the water was roiling and splashing every few seconds over the sides of the tub. The left side of his head was throbbing, and when he got himself seated again he saw that Donna's chin was pressed toward her chest, her nostrils and eyes opened wide in disgust.

"You need to be careful," Donna shouted, rapidly flicking the water away.

He was breathing hard and felt queasy in his stomach. He thought for a moment that he might get up and finish, but he couldn't seem to stand.

"I didn't want to get my hair wet."

Buddy didn't respond. Something was wrapped around his right foot. He couldn't figure out what until he pulled it off and saw that it was his bathing suit, and even then he couldn't figure out why he wasn't wearing it.

"Do you want a refill?" he asked, noticing her cup was tipped over.

"I need a shower," Donna said, rising out of the pool.

He turned off the jets and listened as her wet feet slapped across the deck. When he was sure she couldn't see, he stood and pulled his suit up.

It occurred to him that he might join her in the shower, the stall was wide enough for two and even had twin shower heads. But the idea made his hands shake. He decided instead to dress and make a glass of iced tea for her. The shaking only subsided once he heard the water being shut off, which meant proving himself was no longer an option.

When she returned she took the drink and said thanks, as though nothing had happened, which encouraged Buddy enormously.

"My wife will be home soon," he told her.

Donna said, "I really have to be going. But I'm sure we'll meet in good time."

His body went cold: she didn't get it! She thought he was asking her to stay when really he was asking her to leave faster. He felt a creeping horror: a repulsion you feel when realizing somebody you thought was just like you turns out to be completely alien.

At her car, she gave him a kiss on the cheek and said, "Thank you for the tour. Oh, look at that," she pointed to the Sandias behind Buddy. "Pink sand."

Buddy turned to look. "No," he told her. His own voice sounded strange to him. "That's not it. Because of that little cloud cover over there, the sun isn't as bright as it should be for the effect. The conditions have to be perfect."

Although he wanted her to leave he felt the full pinkness of the Sandias might somehow redeem the afternoon and she might leave thinking everything had gone as it was supposed to. But she hadn't waited. She had just gotten in her car and driven off.

And now, half a year later, as Buddy drove home from the reservation, just exiting 25 at Bernalillo and heading into the foothills towards New Pueblo, adobe houses beginning to dot the landscape, Gloria sitting quietly next to him rubbing her ankle, there was the exact effect, the whole range of the Sandias radiating a perfect bright pink.

"Now, that's pink sand," he said out loud.

"What is?" Gloria asked.

"The Sandia mountains, here in the sunset. It's perfect right now. That's why they call it Sandia, for this pink sand effect that we're getting now."

"No," she said. "It means watermelon."

"What?" Buddy asked.

Gloria said, "Sandia is Spanish for watermelon. It looks like a watermelon in the sunset. Not pink sand." She saw an opportunity to get some gossipy satisfaction. "You know who else said that same stupid thing about pink sand?" Gloria was quiet for a moment, and then she stopped talking altogether, poked momentarily by an idea, an absurd random thought, an icy cold finger stabbing at her from across the empty desert.

GLORIA stopped in the driveway and looked back at the Sandias. The sun was almost gone and the mountains were now dark and purple.

A little ribbon of lights winked off in the distance; the town of Old Pueblo at the base of the Sandias. She thought about Old Pueblo, about how it had just been known simply as "Pueblo" for over 300 years but became unofficially "Old" when New Pueblo had been developed in the 1970s.

You can't control the way the landscape shifts around you. You live in Pueblo and then suddenly you're in Old Pueblo. You join Book Club and one day, without anyone consulting you, there appears a Book Club 2. You move to the outskirts of a development and soon you're in the middle of it. Just when you think you you've got your hands on the desert, it lurches away. Even a marriage...it wasn't like selling beads or buying property. A marriage could be a perfect success, no mistakes, no errors, but in the aggregate you find you still have not turned a profit, and no amount of analysis in the world will ever explain why.

She felt disappointed at how recognizable everything in her house was. The dolls, the objects, the rugs; she could recall purchasing each and every one of them. The more Southwest she acquired, the more she collected, the more regional authors she read, the faster the landscape receded into the horizon. She used to be able to walk down the street to lose herself. Now she couldn't even do it on an Indian reservation in the mesas.

She walked, stiff and tired, into the bedroom. It was early, but Buddy followed her and together they pulled the bedspread off their bed and silently folded it against itself as though it were a flag returned from war, and then draped it at the foot of the bed. They dressed in their night clothes and lay down.

Gloria thought of her property from above, a mental tally to help her relax, from street to yard: the sloped driveway, the low clay wall, the garage, the soft-edged adobe house, the patio and rock garden, the tomato plants, the gas grill and the hanging chairs, the juniper trees and the barrel cacti, the cobblestone path, the deck and the hot tub; the world she had created. When she reached the hot tub she started again from the driveway, picturing it exactly the way she had made it.

The Kiss

SHE was engaged, but not to him.

He asked for a date, to the theater, because he knew that her fiancé was out of town. She agreed because they had known each other for years. They had worked side by side with the animals, feeding them, taking care of them, cleaning the cages, and they had a good time together even though they were at work. He was funny; she was smart and pretty. He was kind of fat and had yellow teeth, but you didn't notice them after a couple of minutes.

"I'll go because Richard is out of town, and I bet it would be interesting to see a play with you," she answered. "I've never seen one before, a real play, and so you'll be able to point stuff out that I might miss otherwise: themes in the writing, or maybe acting techniques."

He picked her up at her sister's house where she was staying. She got in his car.

"You look very nice," he said. Her hair was more fluffed up than at work and her nails had been painted red. She thanked him and smiled. He had said she looked very nice before, in fact lots of times. He was saying it about once a week at work, although now tonight, with her hair and nails fixed up, and sitting in his car, she looked particularly nice to him.

After the date, on the way home, he asked, "What did you think of the play?"

"It was strange," she answered. "They really socked it to the status quo, I guess. Although not as much as I expected."

"I think the primary target was the mainstream theater

establishment," he said. "And since you've never seen a serious play before, you probably missed some of the subtle jabs, like all those references to cattle calls."

"Maybe that was it. It seems a little silly to get so angry just because people like plays with music in them."

"They call those types of plays musicals," he told her.

"I know. And I know what a cattle call is too."

He pulled into her sister's driveway and let the car idle.

"It should be interesting to read the reviews tomorrow," she said. He shut the car off and faced her. They were both quiet for a moment, although she was smiling.

"Thank you for coming," he said.

"Thanks for inviting me. I'm glad I finally saw a real play."

More silence. He turned the ignition key one click, and found a classical music station. His heart was pounding and his hands were getting moist. He was afraid he was being too obvious, but she made no moves to leave the car.

"Also, the beer was good," she said.

They had walked to a bar near the theater after the play and each had tried a different imported beer. They had sipped from both glasses comparing the flavors.

"It was a good idea to try new beer," he agreed. He was watching her lips very closely now. They were painted the exact same red as her nails, and in the dark car, they seemed to be hovering in front of her face. His own lips felt very dry but he figured it was because of the pressure of what was happening and that they were actually— probably—moist enough; either way he sure wasn't about to let her see him licking them.

"I should probably go inside now. I've seen my sister peek out the window more than once already, and I don't want to give her the wrong impression."

"Okay. I understand. But before you go..."

"What?"

"I want to kiss you goodnight," he said.

"You do?"

He was watching her very closely and he noted that she hadn't flinched or made a face or done anything to indicate offense.

"I think we should, I mean, I know you're engaged and everything but it seems—"

"The engagement isn't the issue," she said. "I was wondering if that's appropriate to this evening. A kiss, I mean."

"I think so. Yes, definitely. And not just the evening, but also the way we are at work. Always together, people calling us Frick and Frack, sometimes bickering like an old married couple about the animals. And all the while we're aware of how it sounds and looks to other people and don't care."

"More than don't care, I think we enjoy giving off the impression that we're closer to each other than to any of them. It sets us apart. It gives them something to gossip about: the way we're a team and have fun together, even when we're cleaning tanks."

"Absolutely. And I don't think I could be as close to anyone at work, or maybe anywhere else, other than you."

"Me too. And if it wasn't for my fiancé, I would say that I'm closer to you than anyone."

"Right. And if we didn't work together, we might be dating right now."

"I don't know about that. I like you because I've gotten to know you so well at work. If we had just met... You don't exactly look like my type. No offense!"

"None taken. And of course I understand completely. Your fiancé is very handsome, not at all like me."

"No, I think you're handsome, just in an entirely different way then the men I date. Dated. Also you're smart, and that's not a put down of my fiancé. He's smart too, but not like you are, and that's something I wouldn't have found out about if I had met you in a bar, the way I met my fiancé."

"Well, despite it all," he said, "I really want to kiss you goodnight. I don't want to sleep with you, or feel your breasts, or have you do anything that would make you feel strange about me Monday at work. But I really want to kiss you right now, just for a little bit."

"You don't want to feel my breasts because they're small, and the way you say, 'kiss you a little bit,' makes me think that you want to have a long passionate kiss with our tongues, which wasn't exactly what I had in mind when I was considering letting you kiss me."

"Wait a minute, hold it up a sec. I do want to feel your breasts, of course I do. Size doesn't matter. It's true they're on the small side of average, but you're skinny and that makes them look bigger. Also, when you wear that beige T-shirt, with the unicorn and the clouds, your breasts are just about all I can think of. I'm just saying, for our purposes right now, a kiss is all we ought to do to consummate the evening, and to a certain extent, the friendship."

"Consummate?" she asked.

"Bad choice of words. I would love to feel your breasts, even with my mouth a little if you wanted, but a kiss is what I really have on my mind. And about my tongue, I can guarantee that I won't use it, unless our lips linger naturally on each other, and it goes into your mouth on its own. My tongue, I mean. You can do the same."

"Use my tongue?"

"Only if that's the natural progression. As for now I just want to give you a sweet kiss goodnight."

"So you're just going to lean in and kiss me nicely. You aren't going to move your lips up and down and possibly start to bite my lower or upper lip? You seem like the kind of guy who would kiss like that."

"I wouldn't, although in truth, I do like to kiss like that. But since you ask, I promise not to. Not at first. Not if it doesn't happen on its own. You know, I may not look like it, but a lot of the women I've kissed have told me I'm good at it. One woman said I was the best kisser she had ever had. I get some repeat business."

She snorted. "I don't have trouble believing that at all. Although now that you say it, I'm a little concerned that I won't be up to your standards. My lips are kind of thin and no one's ever commented on my ability. You have nice full lips. It may be a disappointment to kiss me."

"That's silly. I can tell we'd be perfect for each other. And I don't mean that in a scary way, like I think about you all the time. I do think about you more than I would just a regular friend, but I know you have a fiancé and all; I'm trying to get beyond it. But believe me, I do want to sleep with you and fondle your breasts, and your buttocks too. Only, I guess I think it's kind of pointless with the positions in life that we're in."

"Agreed. So the right thing would have been to not go out tonight, and not even discuss doing anything outside of work, because my biggest fear, even bigger than messing things up with my fiancé, is that things will get messed up between you and me at work."

"Exactly!" he said. "We have a great working relationship and we have to be careful of it. I'd hate my job if you weren't around."

"And I feel exactly the same way. I'm very glad you said that."

"Still," he said. "We've come all this way and I want to give you a goodnight kiss before we call it a night."

"If it happens, you said it'll be sweet and respectful, and on the lips, without too much slobbering on each other's faces?"

"Absolutely."

"And what about your hands?"

"I'll put my right hand on your arm above your elbow like this, and I'll place my left hand on your left shoulder." He unbuckled his seat belt, moved over to her, and arranged his hands just as he described. She allowed herself to be moved to accommodate the new position.

"I guess that'll be okay," she said. "But make sure your hands stay that way. If things get a little passionate during the kiss I don't want any roaming."

"Okay. But what if I squeeze you little bit, while still keeping my hands where they are?"

"That might be nice," she said. "Especially on my shoulder. I've got a knot. And what about my hands?"

As she shifted, he felt her breath on his nose, but just for a second. She rested her palms on his hips, thumbs hooked over his belt, fingers digging gently into his paunch. They had never been this physically close before and he found it difficult to swallow normally. He was sure she could hear his saliva moving up and down his throat, and he wished his own hands weren't sweating.

"It is okay if I hold onto your sides during the kiss, right?" she asked.

"It's okay, but your hands so close to my stomach reminds me of how overweight I am." He was happy to be talking, and hiding the sounds of his heavy swallowing. "How about if you put your hands on my back more, and that way, we would be closer too."

She did. "That was a good idea," she said. "I can tell already that those other girls were right and you really know what goes into a good kiss."

He smiled. She was smiling too. Her face was distorted this close up, and if he didn't know it was her, that normally from a distance she was attractive, he would have been repulsed. She was looking too, and he thought that maybe she was examining him with this new perspective and finding him even more hideous. He hoped she understood the way one's vision distorts at close range as well as he did.

He cleared his throat again but didn't move. They sat like that for a few seconds, looking at each other's faces, considering, listening, taking inventories. They waited for something to happen.

"I think I might go in now," she finally said.

"No kiss?" he asked.

"Not just now. Are you mad?"

"No, I'm not mad. And on Monday, everything will be the same with us."

"Good. And thank you for the play again."

"My pleasure again."

She moved around, pulling her purse up to her shoulder and reached for the door.

"I think about you also," she said. "Not a crazy amount, but slightly more than I would a regular platonic friend."

"Goodnight," he said.

He made sure she got in the house safely before backing out onto the street.

Just Like Spain

FIRST time it happened he was in the condo hallway, just after bolting the door behind him, and pocketing the keys. It usually smelled like soup in his building this time of night, something heavy, onions or cabbage. Even though he was alone in the hall he took a big showy sniff.

"Spain," he said. His nostrils flexed and twitched theatrically. If someone opened the door he wanted to be seen sniffing and twisting his neck around comically so that he might suddenly notice the neighbor and say, "What is that? Do you smell that? You know what it reminds me of?"

He took off down the steps and into the early winter darkness where his wife, Carol, was waiting for him in the passenger seat of the running and heated car. Stuart continued to think about Spain even as he pulled into the Friday night traffic.

"I'm thinking about Spain," he told Carol.

"Oh?"

"The way the light is now, kind of purplish as though it were midnight even though it isn't. That's how all the nights were in Spain."

"All the time?"

"When I was there. And the traffic was like this too, in Madrid on the big streets. I was only there once, Madrid. Mostly I lived in a little village called San... San Fernando? San Francisco? I can't remember anymore. Isn't that funny? Going on ten years already. That's wild, that I was there and now I'm not even sure of the name. Can we turn the radio to an oldies station? I only listened to oldies in Spain because that's all they played on the radio station from an American military base. Okay, now concentrate on finding a space. Concentrate. Don't just wish for it."

He found a tight spot a few blocks down and managed to squeeze in. Carol waited as Stuart inspected the inch of space between the cars in front and back and then came around to take her arm.

"You know," he said. "This is the same temperature it was every day I was in Spain."

She nodded.

"It was just like this. Dry and cold and a little breeze," he sniffed. "I swear I can feel the Mediterranean. That's weird how everything's reminding me of it. The light too, just like Spain. This exact shade of yellow on all the streets, the same eerie kind of soft shadows. Like a cubist painting, I think. I didn't see any while I was there but Picasso was born there or maybe just lived there when he got rich. Also, that weird guy, what do you call him? With all the melting watches and whachamacallem? He lived there."

The restaurant was crowded. They stood in a throng at the bar and waited. She flipped through a free neighborhood newspaper that had been discarded by the door. He worked on a bowl of salsa, scooping large portions of it with triangle chips, using only the ones with bent corners. He started to laugh.

"You know what honey? Honey? Honey? Honey?"

She looked up from the paper with a blank expression.

"The first time I tried to use Spanish on the Metro—that's what they call the subway in Spain—I asked for, ha ha ha, ten old ladies instead of ten trips. See the words in Spanish are real similar; *viajes* and *viajas*. I can't remember which is which anymore but oh boy, did I get some funny looks."

When they were seated, he noticed that all the tables were close together. He chuckled and was about to say that this too reminded him of Spain: tables so close you could be dining with strangers, but he decided against it.

Carol ordered a fried vegetable plate as an appetizer and he asked for another rum and Coke. When the appetizer came they ate off the serving platter, not bothering to use the little plates.

When it was all gone, she said, "I love sweet potatoes."

And he said, "Did we eat sweet potatoes?"

"No. But the dish... Not the dish, I mean the food. All those fried veggies. The last time I had something like that it had sweet potatoes."

The main courses came and the waiter warned them that the bottoms of the plates were hot. They both nodded. A basket of warm French bread was put on the table and as soon as the waiter left, Stuart pulled a fistful of bread off the loaf for himself.

"Look at this! This is so Spanish!"

He waved the plug in front of her face and she followed with her eyeballs.

"This feels Spanish! A loaf of French bread, the polite waiter, the cramped tables." He couldn't resist adding that last one.

"In Spain you say *Garçon* when you mean the waiter but actually, it means literally boy, not waiter," he told her.

She nodded and took some bread herself. When her mouth was full she said, "That's actually French."

When the last of the food was gone he checked his watch. The movie didn't start for another half hour; they were right on schedule. This pleased him immensely. He waved his arm and caught the waiter's attention and made a writing motion with his hand and wrist.

"Ha ha ha," he laughed. "This is too much. I know this is going to sound hard to believe, but I just asked for the bill the same way I always did in Spain." He shook his head. "Maybe I'm in Spain," He told her.

"Where am I then?" she asked.

"Spain! Spain too. Spain, with me."

The movie was lousy, a silly romance that they both couldn't stand. Stuart stayed with it because the female lead reminded him of another actress he really liked.

On the way out he walked by the concession stand.

"No Toblerone," he pointed out. "That's what they eat in movie theaters in—"

She cut him off. "Maybe we could travel somewhere," she said pushing on the glass door.

He answered quickly, "It's a good idea. We haven't been anywhere since the retreat in Maine and that was like five years ago already. Time really flies. I can't believe it's been ten years since I went to Spain."

"We can go somewhere romantic. I wonder if I still have my passport."

"Mine's expired I think." He unlocked the passenger door. "I only used it the once."

The bedroom felt stuffy. He cracked the window and she reciprocated by laying the comforter over the blanket. They got in bed and pulled the covers up. He turned off the light.

"I don't know that we can go anywhere for too long, about this vacation idea," he said. "I can't get more than a week off and probably not more than a long weekend, like a Thursday and Friday with a Saturday and Sunday in the middle. We couldn't go too far, not that we could anyway with that time constraint, but money too."

She shifted on her side, moving her shoulders back and forth to get comfortable.

"It's too bad we can't just up and go like I did when I graduated college and went to Spain."

"Sweetheart," she said. "Can you get me a glass of water?"

He got up and went to the kitchen, filled a glass under the tap and put an ice cube in it. He snuck a sip on the way back to the bedroom.

"Thank you," she said and took a few loud gulps. He could hear the water sloshing into her stomach as he got back into bed.

"Ahhh.... Here." She handed him the empty glass, which he put on the night stand.

"Don't just leave it here," she said. "Take it back to the sink, please. And rinse it out and put in the dishwasher."

He got up and rinsed the glass but left it in the sink.

When he walked back in the bedroom and got under the covers she said, "Hey. Do you want to?"

"Do you?"

"Why not," she answered. "Movie, dinner? Why not?"

"Okay."

"Do we have anything?" she asked.

He sighed. "We do...." His voice trailed off.

"But I won't put one on," she finished for him. She made her voice more nasally to mimic him, "Can't feel a thing."

"You won't take anymore, quote, hormones, end-quote," he said.

"I don't like when my breasts get sensitive," she reminded him. "Plus I get too crabby. That's okay," she said. "Just spoon me and we'll go to sleep."

He patted her shoulder.

"Spoon me," she told him.

He pressed his knee into the back of her knee.

"Spoon me," she said. "All the way."

He hugged her and smelled her hair and closed his eyes.

"That's nice," she told him. "Thank you."

"*De nada*," he answered.

Her breathing got heavier. Stuart listened. He thought about the bull fighting ring, the one he had visited in Madrid. He pictured himself in the center, bowing low to the cheering crowd in the stands. The Queen was watching from the royal box, many rows up. The great bull charged and Stuart sank his steel deep between the shoulders of the beast. The bull stumbled and fell, and when it was too weak to struggle Stuart rushed in and cut off its ear.

Following tradition, he took the beret off his head and solemnly approached the front row. He handed his beret to a spectator, who passed it up to another, so that eventually it would reach the queen. Stuart watched his beret ascend the crowd slowly, waiting for the applause to die down, for the adulation of the crowd to subside and for the long awaited moment, sweet acknowledgment from the queen.

Lemons

THE desk called and said a Vickie LaFaye was coming up to his room. Miller was expecting someone, not a Vickie LaFaye, although she was as good a choice as anyone, just odd for being female. And since she was a Hot Lobster management trainee, this Vickie LaFaye would be young and bubbly and have an outgoing personality. Miller knew for a fact that the corporation didn't hire any other kind—it was in the job description. He unwrapped a plastic cup so he could take a drink of tap water from the bathroom sink.

Normally he audited in the restaurants themselves, usually in tiny break rooms, sitting on a folding chair, highlighting numbers next to waiters hastily smoking between orders. But they hadn't been ready for him at the Columbus outlet on High Street so he agreed to wait at the hotel. He had been worried about killing time anyway—nothing good on TV tonight and he'd seen all the cable movies this month— before getting on the road to make the next day's audit, and then the one after that.

He wasn't crazy about auditing, but the numbers themselves he liked. He learned secrets from the numbers. He knew which cities ate more chicken than seafood, which cities had big drinkers; he could even tell you which city consumed the most desserts and which ones ate more salads. Miller loved secrets. As a kid he read and reread a book that he found in the library. It was full of all sorts of information like how credit card numbers were assigned, and what the symbols on currency were all about, and what the initiation rituals were for private organizations like the Shriners and Freemasons.

Miller inspected the water through the smoked plastic. Little flecks of white and brown spun harmlessly in invisible eddies. All she'd be doing is delivering the box of documents and waiting for him to crunch the numbers and a woman could surely do that as well as a man. But the thought of one of these young women up here made him nervous. He had let the tap run but the water was still only tepid. The bucket of ice was a few feet from him on the counter, but Miller continued sipping. He wished he'd thought ahead of time to order a beer. Now it was too late. To a man he might have been able to say, I'll get us a few cold ones, or Let's go the lounge so we and do this over a pitcher. But to suggest this to someone named *Vickie LaFaye*...

There was a knock at the door and Miller caught himself wishing he wasn't wearing a tee-shirt; something button-down would have looked more professional. At least his tan slacks still looked pressed.

He saw the box first. It was open at the top, and the flaps were folded down to make handles. A strip of brown packing tape ran vertically across the front for no apparent reason. Vickie LaFaye was small. The box obscured most of her body, and even though she was hunched over it, she kept her head up and smiled at him.

"Hey," she said. Her hair was black and long, and she had large hoop earrings that swung against her cheeks as she swayed to keep her balance. She grunted, and the box seemed to teeter and sink, but a knee appeared out from under her dress and she righted the box against her leg. Miller put his hands out to steady the box and was looking into the top of her dress before he could stop himself.

"I got it," he said. It weighed a good 15 pounds and the folders were loose inside and slid back and forth. Vickie stood and fussed with her outfit, a wrinkled yellow sun dress, alternately tugging at the waist and realigning the straps on her shoulders. He was relieved to see that she was not dressed professionally either.

"So you're the famous Miller?" she said. Her voice was low. "I saw your presentation at The Future Feeders Leaders Conference in Orlando last month. Do you remember? The thing with the new restaurant design?"

Hot Lobster often tapped Miller to give humorous presentations to the store managers, or "the troops," as the bigwigs called them.

Last time Miller had presented a fictitious new design for Hot Lobster restaurants. He had told the gathering that the corporation was doing away with the decades old "on the dock" motif with its upside-down boat kegs for tables and rusted blubber pikes on the walls. Instead, he'd suggested a "contemporary coast guard look." All the walkways were going to be narrowed and ceilings lowered so that even the tiniest patrons would have to stoop deeply to get to their tables. And best of all, Miller had described to howls of laughter, each new store would be built on a motorized platform so the restaurants would tip back and forth—sometimes rocking quite violently—to replicate sea travel.

"We're still talking about it on the news group. Do you ever check it out? Alt dot hotlob dot trainee?"

"Eh..." Miller did check it almost religiously, and even though it happened less and less, he felt a little ping of pride whenever someone made a reference to it. "No," he told her. "But I should look sometime. This way."

He led her through his small business suite, past the bed and the TV, and over to the table. He had already set up his laptop. He put the box of folders at the foot of his chair, as Vickie dropped inelegantly into hers. She let out a big breath of air. She seemed completely relaxed somehow—just the sort of person Hot Lobster loved hiring for management. Maybe he could feel her out about getting some beer after all.

Miller too had possessed that bouncy Hot Lobster personality when he was Vickie's age, although he had planned for a career in dentistry. He had only worked weekends at a Hot Lobster near the Inner Harbor of Baltimore. First he had been a prep chef, mixing giant vats of crab stuffing and baking the cheddar biscuits from the bloated mixer sacks that corporate sent. He eventually got on to the floor and hosted, welcoming guests, setting up booster chairs, pointing out the daily specials on the menu. He fell for a co-worker, a brown-haired, smart-alecky girl from Towson. She was a bartender and he'd pursued her relentlessly, even coercing her to dump a current boyfriend who wasn't in the restaurant business and so had a different schedule than the two of them. She had become pregnant the same week Miller learned of his acceptance into dental school.

Back then Miller's manager was a middle aged man with soft skin and a huge stomach from decades of eating buttery dinner rolls and big bowls of chowder from the kitchen. He smelled of drawn butter and grease. Even though Miller himself often smelled like that, there was something about being in such a confined space with this man that had made him uneasy. The manager told Miller that it was time for him to reevaluate. Miller couldn't support a child, the manager pointed out, let alone a wife, on the earnings of a dental school student. The manager fished a thermofaxed notice from his desk that featured a lobster dressed like uncle Sam, pointing with one claw. *If you're a go-getter, Hot Lobster wants you.*

"Funny dentists are a dime a dozen, Miller," the manager had told him, resting a hand on his shoulder. "Mine's got pictures of the Three Stooges up in his waiting room and a giant rusty drill that he pretends he's going to use on you."

Miller found himself agreeing. Dentistry had always been more his mother's dream anyway, he had told himself.

Vickie pulled the fabric of her dress away from her stomach to fan herself. The yellow reminded Miller of the chemically ripened lemons he used to slice when he tended bar. He was constantly nicking his flesh with the paring knife and the citric juices burned his cuticles. He spent more time on that chore than even cleaning the glasses or mixing drinks, because customers loved seeing a bright lemon wedge perched atop a glass of free ice water. It was a way of getting something for nothing, a cheapness of the general public that grated Miller's sense of righteousness. If you wanted a drink with flavor in it, order a soda. And if you only wanted water, fine. But asking for a lemon—it was like complaining about a gift.

Vickie took handfuls of her dress with both hands and flapped the fabric like a pair of wings. She looked directly at him. Miller knew he was being challenged to notice—to make a comment, or ask what she was doing.

"When's take-off?" Miller asked, obligingly.

"Hot out there," she answered him. She stuck her tongue out and panted like a dog and when Miller knit his brow in confusion, she curled her fingers like paws and gave a little "Yip!"

"Can I get you a bowl of water?" Miller asked.

"Yeah right," she said, dropping her hands. "Something tepid with dog spit please. Kidding. Actually, I wouldn't mind a drink."

Mention the beer, Miller thought. "If you want water or something, there are some cups and ice in the bathroom. Or, tell you what, if you'd rather—"

"Water's fine," she said, standing. He watched her walk to the bathroom. He thought for a second that if his wife could see her, Vickie LaFaye, a girl this young dressed like that, in Miller's room alone with him, she would divorce him in a second. But, he reminded himself, that was only a phantom fear. Their divorce had been final now for three months.

He opened his laptop and tilted the screen so he could see it better. The sun was just beginning to set and he needed to adjust the angle several times before the glare disappeared. Reaching into the box, he removed the first random folder he found: Chicken. He wanted to look busy when she returned, not too eager to talk to her.

He kept his head down and brushed his highlighter lightly over the totals. *Chicken Fingers, Chicken Tenders, Chicken Wings both Wild and Mild.* He entered a few numbers into his spreadsheet while she settled back into her seat.

When he allowed himself a look at her, she gave a quick, "How ya doing over there" wave, and Miller nodded back, hoping his grin didn't look too dopey.

"Nice view," she said, gesturing towards the shopping mall across the street with her chin. "What were they thinking when they designed these hotels? These," and she put her fingers up to quote, "business suites. What sort of a sadist would put a conference table next to a bed?"

"Yeah," Miller said. "Right. And cable TV."

"The hardest part about any business meeting is staying awake," she told him. "They expect you to just talk numbers and not—you know? It's like, I'll get those figures for you right after I take a little nap?"

"Or a swim, right?" Miller said. "How about we finish the meeting in the hot tub?"

"Sounds good," Vickie said laughing.

Miller felt a jolt of embarrassment. But she couldn't think him that crude. After all, they had just met. She must know he was kidding.

He looked down at the spreadsheet and saw rows of numbers on the page. It had been a long time since he'd had a conversation with anyone, let alone someone who gave him a little ping—a sexual charge that he knew would amount to nothing—but a feeling he liked anyway.

When she shifted in her chair he allowed himself a surreptitious glance, a quick flick of the eyes. Vickie was facing the window, head back a little, neck elongated and throat rippling. Miller guessed she was fingering the ice cubes with her tongue, maybe separating them or selecting a small one to keep in her mouth. Her sleeveless dress was puckered and he saw a glint of side-breast cushioned in light yellow cotton, and maybe a peek of an areola but he wasn't sure and he looked away very quickly before he could verify. For sure though, she wasn't wearing a bra. He suddenly was aware of the utter absurdity of his situation. She was at least 15 years younger than he, and she was pretty, and even though he was funny and he'd be nice to her if something started up—he always treated everyone nicely—and even though they were alone and enjoying each other's company, and for chrissakes there was even a god damned bed just a few feet away from them, nothing would happen. Even so, he couldn't make himself work on the numbers anymore.

"LaFaye," he said looking up from the page.

"Here," she said, like roll-call in grammar school.

Miller liked the fact that she could handle a non sequitur with such aplomb. "Is that French?" he asked. "Your name?"

"No," she said. "I don't think so. *Vickie*," she said, as if trying her name for the first time. "I think LaFaye may be French."

"Well that's what I meant," Miller said. "Your last name."

"I'm kidding. I suppose it might be French, I don't know. Probably at some point on my family tree? I have a grandfather from Versailles, Ohio, but that's on my mother's side and his last name is Berman."

Miller was feeling that little ping at regular intervals now, like the sonar of a submarine. He remembered now a secret he had recently heard on the radio: that the famous French reputation for snootiness was a trumped-up myth, perpetuated by Americans who just didn't know how to interact with locals when traveling in Europe. Americans walk around grinning and being overly friendly, and the French take that as a sign of mental slowness. The French respond more positively to a somber tone and something the radio called, "eye-flirting." Miller wasn't quite sure what eye-flirting was, but this was just the sort of little secret he liked, something to tuck away in his pocket to use at a later date—should he ever find himself in France.

"Tell me how you got stuck here tonight. You low man on the totem pole over there or what?" Miller asked her. "Some job, take the files over to old man Miller—what, do they hate you over there?"

"Old man, right." She rolled her eyes.

Oh my God! Miller's mind raced. He had no idea what to do, so he quickly furled his brow seductively. *This is eye-flirting*, he thought.

"Anyway," Vickie said swallowing loud enough for Miller to hear. It gave him a machine gun volley of pings in his chest. "Anyway, I'm honored to be in the presence of such a famous man."

"Who, me?"

"Everyone talks about you. Miller's the guy who makes you laugh even during an audit. The guy who wrote the infamous dessert list. It's hi-larious!"

He stared at her as hard as he could, and through a little squint in for good measure. "That thing?" he said. "People still remember that thing?"

Miller knew people still remembered the dessert list. He saw copies tacked to bulletin boards all over the country, on yellowed facsimile paper, peeking out from behind new uniform regulations or the latest edict from corporate. Inspired by Hot Lobster's ever changing dessert menu, updated by an outside consultant every three months to be "dynamic," Miller wrote his own list, a sophomoric parody, one afternoon on the road. He invented items like: *Apple Underside-a delicious gooey caramel concoction, sinfully delicious, and served piping hot directly into your ass.* It had cracked up his boss when he showed it to him, made the gang at the water cooler laugh, and was faxed to store managers all over the country, who universally clucked their tongues and said, "Bet Miller wrote this." One manager told Miller he was so funny he could even make a root canal fun. Miller was surprised at the stab of pain he felt to be reminded of his aborted dental career.

"Stick the cake right in your ass," Vickie told him, pumping her small fist in the air. "Right on, bro."

And it occurred to him with a jolt that she liked him. He had power here. Vickie LaFaye, young Vickie LaFaye was impressed with him. With Miller. He sent a blast of intense eye flirt across the table.

"I'm only kidding man," Vickie said suddenly.

Miller's expression dropped. "What? What's wrong?"

"About sticking it—"

"No, no," Miller said talking over her. "I know you were quoting the list. My dessert list," he couldn't help reminding her.

"I thought you were...got offended," she waved away the rest of her sentence and then covered her eyes with her hand.

Miller's pinging stopped and was replaced by a wave of embarrassment, a feeling he was much more familiar with. He shook his head in embarrassment.

"I'm an idiot," he said, shaking his head.

"What do you mean?" she asked.

He decided to just come clean. He knew he could say anything— even the truth—so so long as he made it funny.

"I was flirting with you," Miller told her.

And he was ready to continue, to tell her it was just something he knew, that the French responded to eye-flirting, that he made some insane connection because her last name was French. And then he was going to go for the laughs by playing up how pathetic he was—separated from his wife and isolated because of the traveling and lonely—but he stopped short. Vickie had turned away slightly and lowered her eyes.

Miller felt a surge of power and confidence. She liked him. He could do whatever he wanted. He stood up abruptly and stretched casually, as if he had been sitting for hours. His t-shirt came untucked and he didn't bother tucking it back or hiding his naval when it popped out. "I'm going to use the rest room," he told her, rolling his shoulders back and forth. "When I come back, I don't expect you to be wearing any clothes."

The building lurched but Miller managed to land his foot with a loud clomp. Even though his feet felt like they were in oversized clown shoes, he managed to walk clumsily past the bed and shut the door without falling.

He looked at his own face in the mirror and tried to decide what he had done. What had been her reaction? He couldn't remember a change of expression. He guessed that, despite his best efforts, he had looked away while making the lewd suggestion and so hadn't seen any betrayed emotion, surprise or offense or abject horror.... She hadn't made any noise or at least nothing he could hear over his sudden gasping shortness of breath. He was careful not to speak out loud since she was so close and could hear, but in the mirror he mouthed to himself, *I can't believe you did that.*

He tried to pee but couldn't get the urine through his hard penis. He ran the tap to cold—hadn't done this since high school—and then brushed both his wrists under the pillar of water, a little secret he had learned in adolescence, until his erection dissipated. It flagged enough for him to piss through. He felt much better having the noise of the tap and so kept it running. He gave a little cough now, mostly because he knew he could and she wouldn't be able to hear him. It gave him a feeling of control, and so he coughed again. He took a deep breath and smelled her perfume—or was it deodorant—still lingering from when she had come in for water. Miller looked at his own cup, the one he had been drinking from when she knocked, and he felt an almost nostalgic feeling of warmth for that old cup. He wished he could just be drinking warm water from it again and not have to deal with whatever was happening right now outside the bathroom door.

He noticed a few drops on his tan slacks. It was probably splatter from the sink, but it looked suspicious, sloppy. Now he'd have to wait at least until those evaporated.... Back when he had been serving, all the waiters and bartenders wore an apron that tied around the waist. Miller had always liked the fact that it hid pee stains too, because when you were waiting tables or tending bar you were always in a rush

Daniel S. Libman

and so had to use the bathroom on the run and things got messy. He remembered thinking that half the time he had been working on his wife, trying to get her to go out with him, he had pee stains on his pants hidden only by his apron. How different his life might have been if that repulsive fact had ever become known.

Miller slapped the faucet with the palm of his hand and when the silence washed back, he wondered again how he had gotten into such a ridiculously absurd predicament. She would be dressed when he came out, he knew that. The state of her dress was the least of his problems. Should he ignore that he made the suggestion or make some joke.... What could that joke be? *My your skin looks awfully yellow, like your sun dress*—my God, how cornball. Maybe the best way to end this was to just admit that he had been rude. To say that he had been attracted to her but he was over it now, and he was very sorry, very sorry—got to stress that. He knew that the secret to speaking sincerely was to do it with your palms out, fingers splayed apart slightly—he shouldn't be flirting with a girl this young, who could react any number of ways, scream, hit him, call the police. For all he knew she had already walked out.

He gained control of his thoughts. He decided that she had to understand that it was all a joke. Miller had himself convinced of this—he had only been kidding when he asked her to take her clothing off. He mouthed his excuse, palms forward, to the mirror. *Who could possibly be serious about such an hilariously unusual suggestion? Miller's a clown, ask anyone at Hot Lobster. The funny dessert list guy. That wasn't a pass, it was a punch line: Take your clothes off?*

It suddenly felt like ages since he had hidden in the bathroom. He checked quickly that the urine stains were satisfactorily faded. His heart pounded. Hand on the doorknob, he began a silent laugh, so that when he opened the door and turned left to face her, she would think he was in the middle of an enormous guffaw. He threw open the door and took a big quick step, like an actor walking on to a stage from the wings.

He was confused at first by what he saw. It was dark in the room now, which didn't seem possible since it had been fairly light before, too bright even—had he been in the bathroom that long? But then he realized: the curtains. She had drawn the curtains across the window. And she was still there in the same chair with her back to him, in the giant oversized vinyl chair, her bare shoulders and neck coming out over the top.

Miller paused at the sight. He cast his eyes around the room furiously for a clue as to what was going on. And there it was, at the base of the chair, the dress—hurriedly discarded—with a cone of fabric billowing up like meringue. It looked as if she had dropped it, then changed her mind and picked it up, before finally deciding to leave it on the floor.

Miller continued to walk and looked down at her body in the chair. Her legs were crossed and her hands were folded discreetly in her lap. He stepped over the box of documents, still at the foot of his chair, and sat. Vickie's breasts pointed at him, capped with brown nipples like children's band aids.

She stared at him now, a slight grin, her eyes black and fixed on him; was that a challenge or eye flirting? Miller had no idea. She leaned back, and exhaled lightly, slowly. It was the loudest sound Miller had ever heard in his life.

He cast his eyes down at the paper work and then back up. He noticed now the two hoops still dangling from her lobes. He could make a joke about that, and that could be his opening line. *And what about those earrings? I told you to take everything off.* But had he? What was the language he used—how in the hell had he gotten into this predicament? He put his hand on the file and drummed his fingers. He could grab her—but that would mean standing up again and he had just sat down. Why had he sat down? This was ridiculous. He reached down for another file.

"Let's see...beverages." He told her, looking up from the file as he set it carefully in front of him.

Her smirk dropped away for just a second and her eyes shifted left. He knew he had surprised her.

She leaned forward, brought her elbow to the table, and rested her face on her hand. She lowered her eyelids but kept her gaze fixed on him. What ever the game was, she was still playing.

"*Okay,*" he mumbled like before. He streaked his highlighter across the page. "*Lobster Lager, Lobster Lite, Ice Lobster*. She shifted in her chair, but Miller pretended not to notice. The ping was gone, replaced by fear pecking like a little bird at the lining of his stomach. This was another feeling he was comfortable with.

When he first decided to drop dental school and make a career out of Hot Lobster, he concentrated on the orderliness of his job to stave off that pecking. He took everything seriously. He learned all the little secrets of the restaurant trade. He learned food presentation techniques and restaurant atmospherics.

He had done well and was now Deputy Chief Auditor in the field. When he was told of his promotion, his director, a toned young man in a suit who loved to talk about his exercise regimes, took him out for a steak lunch. "We're giving you this position because the jobbers love you already, Miller. We don't want them intimidated, and you make them laugh."

"People laugh at Mr. Toole," Miller pointed out. He was Hot Lobster's CEO.

"Naw," his boss told him with a wave. "People laugh at those cornball jokes because they're nervous. Like when the president makes some glib remark and the reporters start slapping each other's knees. It's different for you Miller. You're actually funny. No one's afraid of you." It was now his job to monitor the big picture numbers, to make sure the side salads weren't going out with too much dressing or too many shavings of carrots. Even when they brought in the shallower bowls, the servers had a tendency to heap on the greens. "We aren't Ponderosa," Miller would say to the managers whose lettuce numbers were out of whack with corporate goals. Everyone listened to him and no one got mad. The managers knew Miller thought what he was suggesting was absurd. After all, you were only talking about a penny's worth of lettuce, but at the same time they understood his advice needed heeding. He very rarely encountered the same problem twice. As for the customers, he never felt guilty for nickel and diming them in that manner. He had spent too long waiting on tables not to know that they did it back to the restaurant whenever possible, asking for the free bread rolls as an appetizer, or wanting ice water as their beverage—with a lemon. Miller knew what that lemon was—a little something for nothing, a poke in your eye, an aggressive act of pleasure in the face of tight corporate cost controls.

"*Yeah, yeah, yeah,*" he murmured, streaking the pages yellow. As he reached the end of the page he allowed himself a glance at Vickie. Her eyes were on him but seemed distant, like she was daydreaming—her lower lip now curled slightly under her teeth. She breathed and the row of knots in her sternum rippled under her skin.

He reached for his shirt sleeves to roll them, just so he had something to do while looking at her, but he came up with his bare arms. He forgot he was only wearing the t-shirt. He pulled his shirt away from his chest and then let it fall back as if he were nonchalantly fanning himself.

Poor Vickie, she had none of the sartorial crutches for nervous energy, she couldn't even fan herself with her clothes. She was totally vulnerable and Miller felt miserable for having put her in such an awkward situation. Maybe he could just lunge across the table and they could do it in her chair. If he wanted her, he needed to act now. He had to transition away from the paperwork and towards Vickie's body. He decided to do it, and ignoring the pecking in his stomach, he slid the paperwork awkwardly aside.

"You know," he said. "You don't need to take these.... I, eh, I could just drop them off tomorrow on my way out of town...."

"Fine," she said standing quickly, her bare stomach scraping the table, and Miller blinked and saw for just a second her pudenda and the small tuft of blonde hair.

"We could—" he began, but stopped short.

She was dressing. She pulled her dress up from the ground and slid the shoulder straps into place with her thumbs. Miller watched her, watched her arms and legs and the flurry of lemon yellow fabric and was more aroused than he had been all evening. He ran through his options; apologize, stand up and make a joke, grab her, tell her he loved her.... She turned and slipped her shoes on.

More than anything, more than even sleeping with her, he wanted Vickie to ask what was wrong. He wanted to tell her about his divorce, and how he had wanted to be a dentist, and about how his kids were good kids even though he had been such a nervous father, that he'd so doggedly wooed his wife, and even now, years later, he wasn't sure if she really loved him or just got trapped. He wanted to tell her how hard he had worked to get where he was, in be in his stupid job making sure people didn't get too much dressing on their side salads, and how hard he had worked at home to raise his children, and that there were no free lunches for him, no lemon wedges on water glasses for Miller. He could do any of those things so long as she said something first. He could still pull this off, but he needed Vickie to give some set up so he could deliver the punch line. If she would just accuse him of something, insult his libido, his sexuality, anything—just something so that he could hit himself in the face with the pie. He was choking on the joke, whatever joke it would end up being, as she walked out and closed the door without another word.

THE hotel's lounge was small and dark, and Miller slumped on the stool and signaled for the barman who was down at the other end talking to two women. The bartender was leaning forward earnestly telling a story. The women—middle aged maybe, maybe older, but not bad looking, Miler noted—were both smoking and the one closest to him was unconsciously pulling at her ear lobe. He knew from an article on the secrets of body language that both the women were interested in the bartender, especially the one fiddling with her ear. And the bartender was playing it cool. He knew what was going on; he knew how to handle it

Miller reached for the small wooden bowl that had a layering of popcorn on the bottom. They were mostly old maids but there were still some attractive fluffy pieces, and he located a full kernel and tossed it in his mouth. He noticed from a tentative test chew that the kernel was stale, and so he maneuvered it to his tongue where it could dissolve in his saliva of its own accord.

When he tended bar at the Hot Lobster he always had plenty of salty popcorn which he served in wax lined paper boats. Miller knew the routine. Customers ordered a beer, then slid a boat of popcorn towards themselves. At first the popcorn is a novelty. You look down at the yellowy mass and pick at it slowly, choosing the kernels that looked best, the fat yellow puffy ones. But—and he had observed time and time again—the patrons would stop paying attention to the popcorn, start staring off into space, and begin to shove the corn into their mouths faster and faster.

He had read a little secret about movies and popcorn, that the real money in the movie business was at the concession stand and not on the screen. Once in a movie theater Miller turned himself backward during a bright scene to test this piece of knowledge. He had observed the hordes behind him unconsciously shoveling handfuls of the stuff into their huge faces, loads at a time, hands like steam shovels digging into bushel sized bags and scooping out grosses of it, kernels rolling down their bodies, jaws set on autopilot pulverizing and grinding like machines. Miller never let himself get carried away in frenzied pleasure like that.

Another thing about popcorn, Miller thought, getting angrier, it was just supposed to be a snack, a god dammed treat—something to do with your hands while making small talk. But they took advantage, people, they made meals of it! The idea that you could come to a bar at happy hour and eat ears and ears and get away with it—something for nothing—dinner and beer for the price of a beer. He was different than those people. More in control, better.

The bartender was ignoring him. Didn't he see Miller just sitting here like an idiot? Why didn't he come over and get his drink order? It was starting to get humiliating. When Miller tended bar he would never have humiliated someone like this. Miller brought more spit to his mouth and let the stale kernel dissolve on his tongue before fingering the bowl again for another.

Ovarian Dancer

"I'm not Marcia," Molly said to the nurse holding the specimen cup. It was the second time she had corrected someone in the surgery pavilion and I could tell the mistake was making her edgy. Marcia was in the next staging room, a woman roughly the same age, height, and build as my wife, also with shoulder-length hair and eyeglasses from the current season—probably bought at the same store. Stacked together, these coincidences might have gone unnoticed at a lunch or dinner meeting, but at the South Loop Surgi-Center, at 6:00 a.m. with both women in gowns being prepped for surgery, having a doppelganger in the next room was disconcerting. As soon as the harried nurse disappeared behind the rolling shower curtain, Molly gripped my wrist. "They can't tell us apart."

"They can too," I tried to soothe, tugging the gown so it covered more of her shoulders. "It's just the similarity of the names throwing them off. Molly and Marcia."

"Why'd they put us at the same time? As if I don't have enough to worry about."

Normally Molly was even-tempered, a middle-school math teacher unflappable even in the face of egregious student behavior problems, but the strain of the past several weeks had pushed her to the limits of her even-keeledness: the strange bloating in her stomach, the clinical speed with which her doctor responded, a flurry of ultra-sounds, cat scans, magnetic imaging procedures, the numbing jolt of having her file transferred from gynecology to oncology.

"Just my luck," she muttered from the bed. "The two of us...."

Actually, several people were having operations at the Surgi-Center that morning. Molly and I had sat with them in the family waiting room, all of us signing forms we had barely scanned. Four different patients were called at the same time, each assigned a room in which to prep and meet surgical teams. In truth, Marcia hadn't seemed any more pleased than Molly to have a look-alike amongst the patients. Her husband—the man she sat with, whom I assumed was her husband—sat stiffly in a dark overcoat and a wide-brimmed hat, staring into space. He had an air of irritation and disinterest and hadn't accompanied Marcia into the prep room, as I had Molly. The last I saw of him he had taken it upon himself to fiddle with the knob of a hanging television, apparently trying to get a different station, despite several signs specifically forbidding anyone from doing so.

Surveying the job I had done folding her clothes, Molly was startled by a trio of gowned women rushing the curtain who immediately busied themselves in the small cubical, one opening the sides of the bed, the second setting up a hypodermic needle and rubber tubing, while the third, a mousy woman with dark hair covering most of her eyes, ticked items off an official-looking clipboard.

"Mmmmm..." she paused.

"Molly," I finished, trying to keep it light.

"Molly," the mousy nurse said happily. She was one of the ones who had already made the Marcia mistake. "This is Pattie, your caretaker nurse who will be with you from surgery to post-op until you're released, and this is Sharza, your anesthesiologist."

Sharza, a pale-skinned woman wearing jewelry visible through her gowns, winked as she pressed a needle into the bluish vein now prominent in Molly's arm. The mousy nurse continued from behind her clipboard. "Since your procedure is laparoscopic, you'll be able to leave sometime this afternoon. Is your husband coming back or waiting?"

"Waiting," I called, standing back to give everyone else more room.

"That's a good man," Sharza interjected. She began ripping pieces of cloth tape and affixing the tube to Molly's arm.

The mousy nurse kept her eyes on the clipboard, making little hash marks as she spoke. "For the next two weeks Molly will need to be on pain killers, no driving and no heavy lifting for a month."

Sharza joked, "You'll need to wait on her hand and foot for six months!"

"Six months," Molly repeated dreamily.

"Business as usual then," was my line, but no one laughed.

"No showers for 48 hours after the procedure," the nurse added another check. Then she looked up sheepishly, "And I have to say this because it's on the list," her face colored and she raised the clipboard to just under her eyes. "No sexual activity for two weeks."

"For either of us?"

Molly ignored my joke, but the nurse lowered her clipboard enough to glare.

"That's very important," Sharza said, inspecting her work by slightly tugging the tube a few times. "I think that should be the rule when you get married, too. No sex for two weeks after the wedding ceremony." She gave the tube a last pull and Molly grimaced.

"Dr. Lowe is ready, so unless you have any other questions..."

"I think we're fine," I said.

Molly said, "I've asked this before, but I won't be different, right?"

"What do you mean?" Pattie the caretaker nurse now stepped forward. Her rough voice was intimidating and Molly didn't elaborate, but I knew that much of Molly's concerns regarding the procedure had to do with sameness: would she emerge from surgery somehow altered? It was something she had mentioned right after getting the news of the tumor and then again just the night before. "It's an organ they're taking," Molly had cried one evening, giving in to her growing panic. "It's not a haircut. This is something intrinsic."

"Mother Nature always provides us with a replacement," Sharza smiled reassuringly. A small blue stone on a ring in her eyebrow winked under the lights. "If you lose a kidney, the other one will do the work. That's why you have two ovaries and he," she pointed with her thumb like a hitchhiker, "has two testicles. Nature always provides us a way to replace what we lose."

The fluid in the tube changed from clear to a milky white and

Sharza indicated I was to leave the room.

SEVERAL more patients had come into the Surgi-Center and now the Family Waiting room was filled with an uneasy crowd of concerned and murmuring supporters. I positioned myself near the standing ashtray so I could smoke, something I had given up awhile back but allowed myself during this day of waiting. I was also able to monitor the Status Board, a large, flat-screen TV with the full docket of all procedures being performed in the pavilion. One could follow all the cases at the Surgi-Center from prep, to operation, to post-op, and finally dispatch.

"Just like at the airport," one of the older men muttered, nearly awestruck in front of this pixilated God.

"Except you don't want to see *Departed*." It was as far as I dared go with a joke. While Molly's case was reasonably straightforward, the tumor already thought to be benign, this man might be waiting for more dramatic news. *It's more complicated than we thought,* I had already heard one doctor tell a family with practiced coldness. *Let's talk in the consultation room*: the exact thing a waiter didn't want to hear. *No surprises,* is what we all longed for from our doctors. *It was actually easier than I had hoped. To be honest with you, the whole thing was sort of fun!*

Later, as I was grading papers my seventh-grade biology students had written on catalysts, I was astonished to see Marcia come out. Because all the cases on the Status Board were coded for privacy, I could only track Molly through her case number: 9782644. Despite that, I had occasionally wondered what happened to Marcia, and now here she was, without medical accompaniment, while Molly was still listed as being 'in surgery.' Marcia cast about the waiting room, presumably for the man she came with, looking something like an immigrant stepping off a packed steamship after a miserable crossing. Her eyes were now ringed dark and her skin looked sallow. Carrying her own duffle bag low to the ground, she walked slowly, feet shuffling, soles barely coming up off the ground, to the same cluster of chairs she had been in earlier filling out forms. Seemingly resigned to being alone and having to wait, she gingerly lowered herself into a chair and after a few moments of shifting, dropped her chin to her chest. I thought of offering to get her a bottle of water or something, but she soon closed her eyes. I occupied myself by checking once again the smudged windows of the vending machines, wishing the tuna sandwiches and cans of Dinty Moore had miraculously turned into something edible.

THE day went by slowly for me, and eventually I stopped hoping each doctor who emerged was coming to give me news, instead settling all my emotional energy on being jealous of families who were being visited. Late in the afternoon, as I unwrapped my second package of Bedouin Unfiltered, the dull routine of waiting was interrupted by several Emergency Technicians running in from the outside and into the operations room, causing a ripple through the waiting room the way a distant wolf howl might in a chicken coop. One particularly fidgety man walked to the reception desk.

"Has something happened back there?" he demanded. "Why all the commotion?"

I pitied him for his lack of faith in the system and was also irritated on behalf of the receptionist attempting to calm him down. *Perfectly normal, sir.... Please take your seat....*

But even my laissez-faire attitude was stretched to the limits as Molly's stay in the post-op column stretched into its seventh hour and I was still without an update from any medical personnel. Taking a desultory route from the ashtray, I approached the reception desk as though I was wandering around and simply had found myself standing in front of her, and then—only to make conversation—asked, "I'm wondering about my wife, Molly. Number 9782644. I was told she'd be in surgery for an hour, post-op another hour, then someone would come get me to visit with her in recovery. It's nearly dinner time and I haven't heard a thing."

The receptionist smiled soothingly, "The doctors always underestimate the time these things take sir," she typed a few things into her computer and I watched the flicker of information dance on her glasses—the same sort as Molly's and Marcia's, with ironically over-sized frames like B-movie nerds. The receptionist paused, pursed her lips while scanning a screen in front of her, then hit a button and scanned another screen. I watched her as she silently read one screen after another, her eyes darting back and forth tightly across the lines of information. Finally she looked up, almost surprised to see me standing in front of her. "Everything's perfectly normal," she said mechanically, and cleared her throat once. "I'm sure the doctor will be out shortly."

Back near the ashtray Marcia was asleep in her chair, head lolled to one side, chest heaving under the heavy overcoat, her hand still gripping her dark valise so tightly I could see veins popping around her knuckles. I was distressed to find I was out of cigarettes.

"Mr. Libman?" Dr. Lowe was standing somberly at the door to and cocked his head toward the consultation room. My legs felt numb but I walked steadily. Dr. Lowe had two manila folders both stuffed with papers, and he positioned them in front of his chair. He smiled amiably, mindlessly fiddling with the tractor feed on the side of some documents as I took the seat. His face changed when I sat across from him, reminding me of a lion tamer who suddenly loses his nerve. His lips twitched into a narrow, dry smile.

"Everything went just as I thought it would. A best-case scenario type of situation for this sort of thing." Dr. Lowe spoke quickly, only looking up at me at the ends of sentences, as if my presence were a mere formality and he might be giving this victory speech to the table and chairs anyway. "We biopsied the mass immediately, freeze-dried segments of it, and saw nothing at all indicating a malignancy. Exactly what I thought. And your wife has successfully voided, so she's free to go."

"Voided?"

His face immediately softened. "Ha ha ha. I forget to not use medical terminology around non-professionals. Your wife made wee-wee. And with the laparoscopic procedure that means she's free to..." Noisily he cleared his throat and wiped his lips against the back of his hand, drawing a thick pen from his breast pocket, which he now began drumming against the top file. "Anyway, I've written a script for some pain killers should she need any. Either way, no driving for two weeks, no heavy lifting for four weeks, no sexual activity until the scars heal, and if you'll sign here, you and Marcia can go home now."

"Marcia!" I started. "My wife is Molly."

Dr. Lowe put the pen down. "Marcia," he said. His eyes were kind and blue. I remember she had told me after her first meeting that she didn't like to see a male gynecologist but that Dr. Lowe had put her at ease right away even though he was young, another strike against him as far as I was concerned. "Marcia is ready for you to take her home. Here are her papers." He was pitching his voice loudly now, as if others were listening. "Her medical histories that she gave me from her regular doctor. You can take them home with you and go over them if you want. Marcia is a great...patient." He nodded and smiled tightly. "You'll take her home now. Go ahead and sign this top sheet and I'm going to release Marcia into your care."

Dr. Lowe handed me the pen.

A nurse I didn't recognize was helping Marcia adjust her overcoat around her shoulders as I approached with her personal file under my arm. When I got near I marveled at the change from when I had seen her in the morning. Her eyes were puffier and it looked as though she had been crying; her cheeks piebald and her lips dry and crackly, perhaps from having been asleep and breathing through her mouth.

"Here he is to take you home now, Marcia," the receptionist said in a chirpy voice. "Take good care of her, Mr. Libman. Wait on her hand and foot for at least a month."

"Six months," I corrected, and we both chuckled.

Marcia struggled not to lean against me as I walked her to the car, and seemed relieved to find the comforter and the pillow for the ride home. I closed the passenger door and walked around, pausing to watch Marcia cover herself with the comforter. She sniffed at the pillow once, wrinkled her nose, then closed her eyes.

In the house Marcia crossed her arms more tightly, letting her eyes wander over the photographs hanging in our foyer, and the easy chair and couch in the living room. I offered to take the coat but she cinched her arms tighter, squinting at our paintings, stepping heavily past the dining room table still piled with the week's laundry, the writing desk with the bills and the calculator, the little liquor cabinet with the upside-down martini and margarita glasses hanging from above. I put her suitcase on the couch for the time-being. Marcia walked slowly around our kitchen, brushing her hand along the stove top and the counters, eyeing the fixtures and the table top, before stopping in the center and looking at me through her heavy lids and droopy hair.

"I could make an omelet for us, for dinner," she finally offered.

"You need to take it easy," I reminded her. "The surgery."

She seemed unsure of herself, tracing again the place on her coat where the organ been removed. "But that *is* what you're always like," I said helpfully. "Never worrying about yourself, just trying to keep things moving."

She took that as a cue to shrug off her coat and get the frying pan, which she located after opening three cabinets. She cracked five brown eggs into a mixing bowl. By the time I was done hanging my own coat she had the butter melted and was using the spatula to swirl the beaten eggs around, her lower jaw chattering, I assumed against the pain of effort.

"Why don't you sit and let me finish?"

She didn't answer and only spoke when finally telling me to set the table, which I did under her careful watch, plates and silverware and cups, and we ate in silence, the scrape of her fork against the plate and my nervous habit of chair-tipping causing a squeak or two on the linoleum. She took two of the pain killers even though it was a bit earlier than the doctor had advised, and she let me take her to the bathroom and undress her in the dry tub, using a washrag to wash off the iodine stains on her legs and thighs, washing her legs and breasts, being very careful to avoid the incisions, both of which were covered almost whimsically with a crisscross of clear adhesive tape, one on each side of her navel.

I left her to change into pajamas and listened at the bedroom door to the sounds of drawers being opened, hangers clacking against one another in the closet. Approaching carefully, I got in on my side of the bed while Marcia watched, then she lowered herself into the other.

"Good night, Marcia...." I said, the words sounding funny in my mouth, but only for a second. The heavy cotton of her robe shifted like melting fudge and Marcia put a hand on my thigh and then to my surprise, through the fly in my pajamas. "You shouldn't do that," I told her. "No sexual activity for two weeks. And you need your sleep."

"I'll just do this," she said thickly, continuing to rub me. "I'll just do this and then we'll both go to sleep. It'll be relaxing."

The digital clock read 9:56 p.m. which made it much earlier than we usually went to bed, but it had been such a long day, the drive in to the Surgi-Center at 5:00 a.m., all that waiting and pacing and smoking. I hadn't eaten anything until that omelet and now I let myself sink under the blankets, into my pajamas, into the glide of Marcia's hand, not worrying about all of tomorrow's horrors—the recovery and the waiting on her on hand and foot—my whole world narrowing to just her hand and my pajamas, in my house, relaxing in bed with my wife.

Sentimental Values

...tHREE bicycles, a set of ladder-back chairs that the Amish could have made but didn't, braided rugs, a musty barbell with enough weights to go to 90 pounds, hummingbird feeder, pencil holder with two pencils so it wouldn't be mistaken for a paperweight, a paperweight, sandwich baggy containing fabric swatches, polystyrene trays from grocery store steaks priced FREE which Eric decided was the most absurd item in the entire garage but in fact was the first to be taken....

Eric and Millie had driven to her family's farm to help with a garage sale, though he would rather have been doing farm work—tossing hay or wrangling cattle, two chores he had previously done. Actually he hadn't *tossed* hay bales but had been positioned at a remove to monitor that none dropped over the side as the men stacked them on a flatbed. And wrangling cattle for Eric had consisted of driving into the pasture with water to refill jugs for the regular farmhands—at least that time he had been on the four-wheeler, which was sort of manly. Working his way up to more physical chores was his strategy, showing his father in-law earnestness and ambition until he got asked to do something more challenging. It had been the same at Shoe Village where he had started on the sales floor and moved to assistant manager before having his potential recognized and being promoted to corporate.

...swimmer's goggles, keychain with a plastic rum bottle, comb and brush set unopened, two stacking broiler pans, waffle iron in the original box, older waffle iron—more used—much cheaper—no box, bag of pipe cleaners, set of five state quarters in a display priced at a dollar, lawn chairs with most of the

cushions intact...

The garage was attached to the house in a grove of evergreens and had the damp, cheerless feel of a room always in shadow. Eric found himself blowing into his palms and wiggling his fingers despite the overhead door being open and the 70ish temperature. Sorting musty piles of clothing and arranging used coloring books didn't stop him from keeping a longing eye on the farmers down the hill. When Millie returned with a box of clanging, mismatched Pyrex cookware he felt sufficiently piqued to confront her.

"Why are you selling the earrings my mother gave you?" He gestured to the far table although he had no idea where the jewelry had ended up. "We weren't even engaged then and she didn't have to buy you anything. Whether you liked them or not or wore them, it was from the heart and now here it is on the table. And for only a buck?"

Millie raised an eyebrow. "Are you mad that we're selling them or that we aren't charging enough?" She blew at the hair that often gathered in the corner of her mouth, although this time it was only habit as she had recently gotten a radically short haircut after a lifetime of hair to her waist.

"Someone *gave* that to you. Where I come from you don't sell a gift, it's white trashy, excuse the expression, because I'm not saying your family *is* white trash. Like you say, they've been to Ireland and read a lot, although I noticed on the shelves it's mostly Dick Francis."

She didn't change her expression. He felt more cautious around her since the haircut. Her face was severe now, and something about seeing her ears made him nervous. He didn't mind the new look exactly, but it was still sort of like being around a new person.

"I'm only kidding," he said finally. "But I saw my wool coat on the rack here, and I never said you could sell my wool coat."

"It has a tear—"

"But I never said you could sell it! It isn't even ours, that coat, it's mine. And 75 cents? Come on!"

"I told her to make it three bucks. Would three bucks make you feel better?"

Millie's mother entered the garage with another mound of clothes and Eric's heart thumped for a moment. Natty never liked to see anyone idle—she had never watched a moment of television unless she was also folding laundry or paying the bills. She smiled pleasantly, chilling Eric further. Her entire wardrobe consisted of sweaters with teddy bears and blouses with blocks and alphabet patterns, though she had been retired from teaching kindergarten for years.

"Say, Natty. I was just running this by Millie, that I might be, you know, more useful, out there, giving Abe a hand with some of his action items out in the field."

Natty smiled as though he had just said something *adorable*. "Well, Eric. I do have special job just for you! Would you be interested in driving the truck?"

HE didn't know which was worse, the patronizing or how good she was at manipulating him. He really was excited to be driving the truck. No suburbanite SUV pickup, this baby had a diesel engine and cow shit caked in the tire tread. Eric needed the side mirror just to hoist himself up to the runner. He maintained a speed of about ten miles per hour because that was the cautious, deliberate way Abe and the others drove in the pasture, and also because he was only going across the gravel road to Millie's grandmother's, a distance that took less than five minutes to walk.

He parked next to the stone walkway, leaving the keys in the ignition and the door unlocked the way they did it out here. A stentorian books-on-tape narrator boomed from the open windows. Confident, Eric opened the door and walked in without knocking.

"It's Eric, Grandma," he called. The foyer had florid, tactile papering cured for decades with nicotine. Eric hopped courteously over the braided area rug in case his shoes had picked up mud from the fields, although having not been in the fields he knew this was not likely. "I'm here for the chair!"

The living room smelled vaguely of box elder bugs and was nearly bare, although the carpeting had divots and deep indentations where furniture once stood. All that remained was the easy chair, an ottoman, and an end table with a massive portable stereo with so many switches and knobs it might have been removed from the cockpit of an airliner. Two enormous speakers the size of serving platters hung over the edges of the end-table on which it had been awkwardly placed. Grandma's face was immobile, head listing toward the sound.

"Hello, hello!" he shouted gamely, waving toward her.

Her eyes were small and misty and she smiled amiably toward Eric. Grandma was massive but gentle in bearing, the way a grizzly bear might be illustrated in a children's book. Millie once told Eric that in her prime Grandma could catch fish in the creek and had them gutted and fried by dinner. Now she was blind and spent the day listening to books-on-tape. She fumbled a few of the knobs before finding the one that would stop the cassette from running.

"Natty told me you were coming, Eric. But I must say, I don't think I want the chair sold. I only have a piano bench left, and I certainly can't sit on that all day. Do you think the chair is as bad looking as Natty says?"

The chair looked fine to Eric. "Do you know what happens to me if I don't come back with that chair? Have you ever crossed Natty?" He used the self-consciously comical tone he adopted with his own grandparents, though Millie's Grandma didn't seem to find it half as amusing, if she noticed at all. "It's listed in the ad: comfortable chair. Someone's supposed to go down to Kewanee and get you a new one."

"But I like this chair. I've been sitting on it for years and it's very comfortable and just the right height. They sold my tape player last time. I begged them not to. It had a play button and review and go-forward, and they brought me this one for Christmas and I can't get it to work a lot." The machine had CD, DAT, and MP3 capabilities and often in Granny's fumblings she would press something that rendered cassettes inoperable and she would have to call Natty to readjust the settings.

"I have a routine, Eric. See, I sit here and I can reach my tea like this, and I can turn my tapes over when I need to. It's frustrating to have to get used to something new, Eric. They took my Fiesta teapot yesterday and now I have to pour my tea right out of the kettle. I suppose it's not such a big deal to most folks."

She had been slowly rising on her cane while she spoke, and as soon as Eric saw light under her, he pulled the chair out and made his way out the door. Natty had been right. It was much lighter than it looked, not a recliner fortunately, though he didn't like the musty smell when angling it through the door. He got it in the bed of the truck, across the road, and into the garage next to a chest of drawers going for five bucks, on which was the Fiesta teapot, marked fifty cents.

Natty was waiting with an unsheathed sharpie, her mouth soberly drawn shut.

"What do you think we should ask for it?" she said.

Eric sized it up. "Twenty?"

Natty didn't respond. On a strip of masking tape she wrote, "Seldom Used – $8."

EVERYBODY went to bed early, Natty so she could continue pricing in the morning, Millie's father Abe because he got up at dawn and always fell asleep during the 9:00 pm news despite its stupefying volume. But Eric was surprised when even Millie announced she was going to bed. She had come out of the bathroom in her adolescent nightclothes and the still startling short hair and he hadn't quite recognized her. "Are those your glasses from high school?"

"I lost track of my regular pair somewhere."

"Out there? What if someone tries to buy them?" He sidled up and placed his hand suggestively into her robe. "Stars are really bright tonight. Might be fun to go for a moonwalk."

She gave his arm a polite squeeze and then closed the door to the bedroom.

"I'll come in later," he said through the door. "I'll try not to wake you."

He took a bottle of beer and walked out to the porch. At first he sat alone on the swing listening to the prehistorically large insects flutter against the screens, and when that started to feel oppressive he walked in his bare feet across the wide open lawn. Below the house, he could see the darkened barn and a scattering of oddly shaped farm machinery looming like watchful supplicants. One of the cows bellowed low and long and another trumpeted a response in the distance. He wondered if there was a problem...should he wake Abe?

He was about to turn back up the hill when it stopped. A real man would have taken some kind of action without running to get someone else. Watching the men throw hay bales had been inspiring; no one asked what to do or where to stand or where to pile the hay. A shoe store, on the other hand, was all noise and confusion. He walked gingerly now on the pebbles near the barn and thought of all the commotion of his life—nothing happened in the corporation without snacks and clipboards, people asking redundant questions, clarifications, additional signatures, a great diffusion of responsibility. It wasn't like that out here—if a man saw a cow having trouble giving birth, he reached in and pulled the calf out.

Eric leapt forward suddenly like a pitcher on the mound and hurled his beer bottle into the sky and listened for the shattering glass. He waited, ear cocked, to hear the crash, but the sound never came.

... AIR popcorn popper marked "Works," plastic owl keychain, three boxes of curlers, unopened nail polish, two sunglasses, blank Aloha From Hawaii postcard, single ping pong paddle with several loose balls, mugs, coffee pots (three of these), wristwatch with flexi-metal band, several decks of playing cards, porcelain rabbit...

By the time Eric took his position behind the shoebox, the door had already been lifted and the garage was full of browsers.

"Experienced garage-salers all know to come before the posted start time," Natty explained.

He glanced into the shoe box and scanned "the bank." Natty had rubber banded several dollar bills and had organized piles of coins into sandwich baggies. The box itself was angled to cover writing on the table:

PROPERTY OF RED CHIEF METHODIST
–PLEASE RETURN WIPED!

Cars were scattered along the driveway and several customers milled around the tables, picking through the match books and dinner plates and Lego sets. A quorum of women were gathered near the front of the garage, heads bent, murmuring as if in prayer. Between them hanging from a bicycle hook and fluttering in the breeze was something new. It only took Eric a second to realize what the women were clustered under.

"Excuse me," he muttered to Natty and went back into the kitchen where Millie was sitting over a bowl of oatmeal in her bathrobe. The newspaper was folded on the table facing away from her.

"Your mother put your wedding dress out there. She's trying to sell it. Enough's enough now, you better get out and talk to her."

"I put it there."

Eric blanched. "You did?"

Millie reached to push hair behind her ear but came up empty.

"But...." He waved his arms dramatically as if just completing a long manifesto. "It's your *wedding dress!*"

"What better opportunity to be rid of so much clutter," she answered calmly. "What are we saving it for? Our daughter's wedding? That old chestnut? Maybe we won't even have a daughter, maybe no kids at all. We've been going how long now without using anything?"

A large woman appeared suddenly in the kitchen window, making the cat, resting on a cushion in the bay window, jump suddenly. The woman squinted and pressed her face into the glass.

"Is it here?" came the muffled question.

"There," Eric pointed, shouting. "The garage!"

"Mother was right," Millie reached for the pen on her father's half finished Soduku. "I listed the size as eight on the tag, but can you change it for me to a 10?" Her gaze went to the window and the women shuffling from their cars. "Or 12."

THREE flat-bed trucks moved over the horizon, coming from the fields, piled high with hay. Eric watched all morning through the garage door as the men loaded more and more bales on a conveyor belt taking the hay to the second floor of the barn. He was interrupted occasionally to make change for a 25 cent spoon, or to politely nod at random comments about the weather. He had to negotiate only one sale—a cotton wall-hanging with an embroidered dragon—to a woman who had asked, "What would you take for the ory-enal?" He took two dollars.

Customers never failed to approach the wedding dress, touching the long sleeves or running a hand down the buttons on the back. Eric remembered his own first sight of Millie, stepping toward him down the banquette hall aisle, Abe at her side. Eric had assumed he would carry Millie in that dress into the honeymoon suite. Of course that hadn't actually happened; by the time they got to the hotel she was in regular clothes anyway. He hadn't thought about it since, but now watching the gown being groped and pawed by these thrifty vultures, he wished he had been more romantic that night, wished he had whisked Millie off her feet and over the threshold to a bed covered in rose petals, or something like that.

Occasionally Millie herself would come out of the house in her bathrobe and shoot the dress a petulant eye-roll, like an adolescent embarrassed to be seen in public with her parents. "You still here?" she'd say, and fuss with the lace on the veil or square the shoulders evenly against the cloth hanger.

"More'n three hundred dollars new and all I'm asking is eighty," Eric could hear her muttering. "I'll be God damned to go down to fifty. God damned."

At lunch the dress did go down to fifty dollars, and an hour later thirty. Eric stayed at the shoebox. A number of items he sold surprised him: his solar powered calculator which he assumed was in his briefcase, a paisley tie that was still one of his favorites. At one point he found himself making change for his travel coffee mug —the one he had used yesterday on the drive down to the farm, but with Millie occupied there was no one to whom he could complain. Despite some interest from the customers, some cooing and fabric petting, no offers had been tendered on the wedding dress. Eric tried to cheer Millie during one of her inspections by reminding her there was still another whole day of the sale, and when that didn't work, he told her she looked nice.

She had answered flatly, "I'm going to assume you're kidding."

In the late afternoon when the stream of cars was about dry, Abe's truck appeared in the driveway. Eric was afraid he was going to walk around and inspect the sale, and the thought of sitting behind the shoebox during it gave him stomach pains. But instead the old man rolled the window down and leaned out.

"Natty! Let me take the boy a quick second."

Eric climbed into the passenger seat and pulled his seatbelt across his chest without hearing her response. Abe was in bib-overalls with a red bandana tied around his neck and not wearing a seatbelt; Eric felt now the strap might actually cut him in two.

They drove silently to the dirt road across from the driveway toward the barnyard. Abe finally asked, "How's the sale going?"

"Good." Eric knew to keep his answers short and unambiguous.

"I've got to..." Abe paused now for no apparent reason, other than he was making a slow turn around the barnyard in the truck, and the silence was excruciating for Eric who literally clenched his lower lip between his teeth to keep from ending the sentence. *Round up some cattle? Start digging a trench and need me to stake the route with you?*

"Tend some bottle calves. You'd be saving me time by filling the feeder bins."

They walked into the barn and Abe gestured with his chin to the sacks of grain. "Bout two scoops worth in each."

Eric walked to the sacks and put his hand on one.

"Abe? Abe? Abe?"

Abe finally turned.

"Do I use any bag, or do some expire first?"

"Any bag."

"Okay. Level scoops or heaping?"

"Heaping?"

"I don't want to over-feed the cows."

"Can't."

"So... just the two scoops of each bag, don't level it. Now where... is there some kind of starter string? You know, to get them open?"

Abe sucked his teeth once. "Tell you what, son. Switch with me a quick second." He handed Eric two bottles of warm milk, capped with oversized rubber nipples. He showed Eric how to stand by the baby calves and hold the bottles upside down over a wood gate into the pen. The calves—orphans, their mother dead from the strain of delivering twins—came running unsteadily, tripping over themselves, crashing into the gate, until finally latching onto the nipples and sucking from them frantically.

Out of the corner of his eye Eric watched Abe roughly splitting open sacks with a knife, spilling grain all over the ground, then hauling them up on his shoulder and dumping them imprecisely into two long troughs. Eric knew he would have worried about smoothing the pile so it was even, but Abe had just let it mound up as it poured, letting quite a bit spill over the sides, which of course, the cows would just eat anyway. Meanwhile the baby calves were drooling and struggling on those nipples, forcing Eric to hang tightly to the bottles in an undignified manner. One calf gave a sudden strong pull, yanking a bottle out of Eric's hand and when he tried to grab it, the other bottle got loose as well.

"Hey guys!" he yelled. "Guys! Cool it!"

Both calves attacked the milk with their heads, and in a frenzy of hot saliva and drool, the bottles were lost under all the straw and muck. The larger one smashed a bottle with his hoof and chewed the nipple free. Sweet milk pooled into the straw and both calves began to anxiously slurp at the ground.

"That's okay, boy," Abe yelled. "Go in and get it,"

Eric tugged on the gate but it was firmly locked. "How do you get this thing open?"

The gate jerked suddenly as Abe climbed over the top. "Yah!" he shouted and kicked the first calf back and grabbed the bottles which he handed back to Eric.

"Should I refill them?"

"Naw," Abe answered, climbing back over.

THE sky was purplish now, the last piece of sun dropping red behind the trees. The silence was only broken by the drone of the motor and random shots of static from the CB. Eric willed himself to not feel humiliated as he scratched the sticky milk drying on his arms. Abe pulled up slowly and waited for Eric to hop out by the garage before driving on. He opened the garage partway and hunched under, blinking to get used to the gloom. The tables looked pretty bare;

Natty had done all right. Looming near the far wall were several fresh boxes, the staggered inventory Natty had held back for the second day. Deciding to finally make himself useful, Eric opened the first box and removed something heavy: a kerosene lamp that he could put on the middle table with appliances.

But it wasn't *a* kerosene lamp, he realized catching the final rays of sun on the metal shade. This was *his* kerosene lamp, the one he bought for camping with his buddies in college. It had been resting on a crushed baseball cap, his Unocal work cap, still smelling vividly of hair grease from years of working behind the register. How had Millie gotten this stuff? Also in the box were old Mad magazines and his pocket knife and a little emergency penlight.

Eric put each item back in the box and closed the flaps. This stuff was his, and this stuff he was going to keep. Steadying the box against his chest, he leaned into the storm door and pushed. Cautiously he scanned the dark yard for a place to hide the box; opening his car trunk would require going into the house for keys where he would have to answer questions. He walked down the driveway, instead, looking over his shoulder occasionally to be sure no one was looking. The moon was still too low in the sky for much light and the crickets and frogs were quiet. At the mailbox Eric rested just long enough to catch his breath and rub his now throbbing lower back.

Inside the barn Eric powered the electric lights, scattering several barn cats and two frenzied, low flying bats. The air was thick with dust. He carried the box to the straw-filled pen where the two orphaned calves were sleeping, curled in one corner, their legs tangled around each other.

"Hello boys," Eric said grandly. "If indeed you are boys." He opened the gate easily now, wondering why he'd had such a problem doing that in Abe's presence. One of the calves raised its head only when Eric launched into a vigorous sneezing jag while scooping up armloads of straw from the ground to cover his box.

"Sorry." Eric waited until the calf closed its eyes again. "Actually," he whispered, "you better hope you're girls. You don't even want to know what happens to boys around here."

Eric had once passed out cups of lemonade to the farmhands

while they worked cattle, and he had seen a long line of calves jammed into a breaking-pen. "Steer," a farmhand would yell after pinning the legs of a screeching animal, and then, after two sickeningly moist slices, the severed testicles were tossed into a bucket. Eric was sorry now that he had deprived these two orphaned calves of their miserable little allotment of milk. And he was suddenly sorry he had taken Grandma's chair as well, and he wondered if it had sold. He uncovered his box again and took his penlight.

Eric sprinted toward the garage. No one was looking out the window which gave him hope that he might actually be able to get the chair down the driveway before anyone looked for him. He shifted his weight against the storm door to be sure it wouldn't squeak. The garage was dark now so Eric took out his penlight and twisted on the beam.

His heart lurched when his light caught the figure hanging.

But no, it wasn't a person dangling from the ceiling, but Millie's wedding dress dangling like an apparition, bodice sagging, shoulders slumped in defeat, the handwritten sales tag pinned to the belt. "Eighteen dollars," Eric read with the small beam, and under that, "Any offer considered."

The shoebox was still on the cash table and he hastily stuffed a twenty into the proper baggie and took two singles in change. Then using the white stepstool (unsold at three dollars) he lowered the dress and gently gathered it up in his arms and walked through the doorway.

HE couldn't keep it exposed, of course, but Eric wanted to see the dress one last time, so he hung it from the rusted milk pulley and let it hang freely in the middle of the pen. As he worked the satin and lace, one of the calves woke and stretched its legs, emitting small peeping sounds. When he finished, Eric sat back on the barn floor, scrutinizing the dress from a distance. Even under the dim barn lights the wedding gown shimmered, and the veil swayed slightly in the stilted air. Suddenly a calf stumbled into him like a drunken masher, running its bumpy tongue against Eric's face and biting his hair.

"Come on, man..." Eric pushed it away. The calf jumped back, bawling so loudly the other calf jerked and stood slowly on its own spindly legs. Eric hugged his knees to his chest as the calves edged nearer and nearer to the bottom of the wedding dress, brushing against the gown. The smaller one began chewing the lace and soon they were both standing on the hem, tearing hungrily into the fabric in search of something to sustain them.

Best Man

BOZE was best man based on time spent. He hadn't seen William—the groom—in years, but drove from Chicago to Bucks County, Pennsylvania to be a good sport. The turnpike had disoriented him. The road clung perilously to the sides of mountains, thick mashed-potato clouds hovered just over the car, and stanchion wielding men in orange work-vests floated in the periphery of his vision. It didn't seem possible that one could leave the pleasantly sedating Midwestern grid and in the very same day be navigating mettle-testing twists and turns, passing through long tunnels in utter darkness. When the 17 hour drive was over, he felt unnerved and anxious. But his figuring of the mileage had been impeccable; he turned into the gravel driveway of the estate just as the rehearsal dinner was scheduled to begin.

The estate was in a wooded hillside adjacent to the Delaware river, on a plateau of pine and fir trees. The main house, which served as the Inn, was a red bricked Georgian with a gabled roof, and when Boze was shown his room he was pleased to find a large suite all for himself. The walls were cranberry red and arrayed with creepy, oval-framed tin-plates of sober men and women. The room also had a couch, a coffee table, two reading lamps, and the largest bed Boze had ever seen outside of a museum. It was king-sized with posts and a canopy, and reeked of carnal possibilities.

"Do you need a fold-away, or is it just the two of you?" the innkeeper asked when she showed Boze his room.

"Actually, just me. My wife didn't come. She was going to...but..." Boze was looking at the bed. His bed at home was a queen-sized mattress that he and his wife kept on the floor. Palatine, Illinois was another planet.

As soon as she left he took his shoes off and jumped sideways onto the bed. At six feet and 220 pounds, Boze was used to beds creaking with metal fatigue at the slightest movement, but this bed made no noise and supported him effortlessly. He got up, combed his bright red hair—parted to the left—and made sure his undershirt was tucked into his slacks. His argyle sweater was purposely untucked and hung loosely around his middle. The cotton's brown coloring softened the spatter of freckles on his pumpkin-shaped face. He left his car keys on the coffee table and took his room key and went down the stairs and across the yard.

He stepped lightly. Having a different key in his pocket, a different weight and bulge against his leg, made him feel hopeful about the possibilities of the weekend. A group of teenagers, tuxedoed and taffetaed to the nines, were coming towards him, and even though he smiled and nodded, they decreased their level of merriment as they walked past. Boze was used to this: something about his face or body shape made people suspect that he was a cop. Strippers never hustled him and no one ever tried to sell him drugs in the park, though he often wished very badly for either. Boze assumed the kids were going to prom. While she ran his credit card through the reader, the innkeeper had mentioned that a local high school had rented the main dining room for the night.

"Prom right under my room?" Boze had asked. "I can rent my room to couples. Bet I could pay for my whole trip that way."

The woman hadn't laughed.

The rehearsal dinner was being done in what the innkeeper called 'the barn out back,' a squat building with stone walls. It was actually a small banquet hall with a wooden dance floor and a bar, although you could still see the rafters and beams in the ceiling.

"I bet this is where Billy Joel and Christy Brinkley got married," Boze said to William after shaking his hand. "Here or somewhere just like it."

"Why are you thinking about them?" William asked.

"I don't know. East coast. They're the first classy East-coast couple that came to mind. I know they're long divorced and so I don't mean it as any kind of slur or omen on your marriage."

William was in a smart black suit and silver bow tie. He was a few inches shorter than Boze, but thin and muscular, with black hair and brown eyes. His face had always been gaunt, but somehow complemented his surprisingly bushy sideburns that he had been cultivating since early college. Only William could have gotten away with those mutton chops and been popular too.

"The room okay?"

"Adequate. Just kidding. Soo-poyb! But when I called and told you I was coming alone, I assumed you would change me to a single."

"I wanted you to have that room. I think it's the best they've got. I hope it's not too expensive."

"No," Boze said. "In fact I'm renting it by the hour to the prom kids so I might make a profit."

The barn was crowded already. Noisy conversation bounced off the stones and rippled back.

"I thought I heard Boze." Marla, the bride, slid over and gave Boze a hug. He had only met her a few times before this, and none of them recently. "I'm so, so glad you could come," she said giving both hands a squeeze. She had grown her hair to her shoulders and looked 20 pounds thinner than when he last saw her. Her skin had a drippy, uneven tan, as if it had been splattered on her like a patina. "Room big enough?" she asked.

"It'll do. Kidding. It's eeee-mense! But you should have changed me to a smaller one since I'm alone."

"William insisted you get that room. It's the only one with a couch and a bed like that and he was adamant that his best man have it. Let me introduce you around."

The room crackled. Conversational rings formed and shuffled and reformed. Boze turned left and Marla introduced him to stepfathers and stepmothers. Boze turned right and William introduced cousins and uncles. The group pressed in close, and even though the chatting was amiable and light, the voices and words didn't always match the lips and faces in front of him.

He flashed back to the morning: the turnpike between New

Stanton and Breezewood. He had been driving slowly because of the fog. One of the workers—beige coveralls, hard hat, bright orange vest—stood on the side of the road waving traffic forward in the direction it was already going. It seemed funny as he passed by, this guy standing there alone as if he had been spit up by the mountain, pointlessly directing the cars down the only road available, but as Boze continued to watch in the rearview mirror, the slow robotic beckoning of the arm started to creep him out.

The same vague intestinal eeriness hung inside the barn. All the people were variations on the same theme: compact faces, pronounced lips, long eye-lashes waving like wheat when blinked. Two small women with the same face, the same black hair and big eyes, reached out to him, and he shook both hands.

"You're the best man," one of them said.

Boze held up a deferential palm. "Well...I'm good," he said. "Maybe not the best..."

Both of the girls laughed identically—mouths open and heads back—lots of noise at first then a rapid intake of air.

"I've met you before," the one on the right said. "This is Debby. I'm Jenny."

Boze puckered his forehead and pushed his lips out.

The other woman, Debby, said, "We're William's stepsisters."

"Okay," Boze said. "That's right. We did meet once, when William's mom married your dad. That was high school, and William and I were already not hanging out as much; he had his marching band friends and I had, you know, the television."

"We went skiing together," Jenny said. "You and William and me, and we got snowed in and sang songs—David Bowie and Boom Town Rats—to pass the time."

"No. Not me. I've never been skiing and I don't really know those groups, although I remember when William was into David Bowie. Oh boy. He wore eyeliner, William did, and I think that's when he started growing the uh..." He tapped his own sideburns, little stumps shaved evenly at the mid-points of his ears.

"Are you sure? I remember so clearly. You don't remember the Jiffy popcorn disaster—"

"Believe me. But I did go to your parent's—your dad and William's mom's—wedding. It was on a military base. Your dad's some muckity-muck in the Army—"

"Air Force. He's on leave but still active. He's got a part in a movie playing a Colonel. That's a stretch, right? Got cast by a director to play a hard-ass because one of the producers was in the Force and remembered him."

"And plus he's *sooo* handsome," the other sister told him.

The girls turned their necks to look at their father who was in another crowd. Boze could see over most of the heads and had a clear shot of the Colonel, who was the only other person as tall as Boze. Boze tried to catch his eye, but the Colonel was looking down intently; his face was hard and his gaze never wavered, giving full attention to whomever was speaking.

They're leaving on their honeymoon the morning after the wedding? Boze scanned the tops of heads and heard another snatch of conversation: *...the food here got a wonderful write up....* The conversations swirled from an unidentified center, each group getting ideas from phrases they heard around them, each ring linked smoothly to the one adjacent. Jenny said to Debby and Boze, "I wonder where they're going on their honeymoon."

And Debby said to Jenny and Boze, "The food here is supposed to be great. I wonder what they're serving tomorrow."

And Boze said to Debby and Jenny, "I wonder what they're serving tonight," and all three of them laughed.

A heavy man, sporting a wrinkled, bloated version of Debby and Jenny's face turned and said, "We're having turkey."

Boze wondered, turkey today or turkey tomorrow, but when he shifted his foot slightly he found he was standing in another group composed of William and three women.

"Where did you say you were going on honeymoon?" one of the women asked William.

"You're the best man," the heavy man from the original group said. Boze was covalently bonded to both groups.

"Well....I'm good," he said. Both groups laughed.

"Australia." William said. "Elizabeth, Amy, Kathleen, this is

Boze, my best man." Then to Boze—who had shifted his body and disconnected from the first group—William said, "I was just saying that Marla has family in Australia and so we're going to spend some time with them. Do it on the cheap. They're meeting us at the airport."

"I bet they're going to...put another shrimp on the barby," Boze said.

The closest woman, an attractive blonde, put her hand on Boze's arm. "I never understand why the best man isn't the one getting married."

Boze didn't know who she was since he hadn't been paying attention to any of the introductions. She didn't look like anyone else in the room, yet still seemed very familiar—blonde hair with yellow highlights, large blue eyes, round face with thick lips and a smart, surgically altered nose—the prototype William girlfriend. Boze felt a thump in his stomach for all the women he had known who looked like her, all the adolescent crushes, the desires he couldn't prosecute, one after the other; creaky doors swinging in the necropolis of his wet dreams, all with this woman's face atop this body—except that this one had her hand on his arm.

"I've met you before," she said. "William took me to Palatine one spring break and we went out for coffee with you. Then we drove up and down Lake Shore Drive and you pointed out the Frank Lloyd Wright home because I was studying design." She was fiddling with the zipper of a light spring jacket as she talked.

"Gee. I don't remember. I don't think it was me. I don't know any Frank Lloyd Wright houses on Lake Shore Drive, or anywhere else, so it couldn't have been me. You're..." They faced each other, effecting a perfect mitotic split from William and the rest of the group.

"I'm Elizabeth. I could have sworn it was you who drove us around. And then I remember William telling me that his friend Boze got married. But you're not..."

"I am. Married." He held up the appropriate hand and she looked at the finger with the ring. He felt bad saying it and worse for feeling bad. He was used to losing girls because they were turned off by his looks or by his personality, but no one yet had been turned off because of his marital status.

"Is she here?"

"My wife? No. She doesn't like to drive, gets nauseous. Got a thing with her eyes and can't read in a car. Blah blah blah," he said. It wasn't exactly the reason his wife hadn't come. The real reason was she just hadn't wanted to. And Boze didn't force her because he hadn't especially wanted her to go either. "So, you're an ex of William's?" he asked. "You're just his type."

"No, we never dated. We were always just friends. We're like brother and sister." She beamed and moved closer. "Isn't it strange, him marrying her. She doesn't seem his type at all...."

Conversations ebbed and flowed, but Boze and Elizabeth stood firm. She took his arm when the crowd drifted—slightly but noticeably—towards the buffet table. The estate workers tonged clumps of mesclun salad drenched in raspberry vinaigrette, dispensed lumpy biscuits, and sliced turkey and roast beef from under heat lamps. Boze took a beer in a green bottle while Elizabeth said she'd stick with water since she would have to drive back to her hotel in New Hope and the roads were dark and winding. They found seats at a table in a corner with other couples and families. Boze was aware of himself chewing and swallowing, he was aware of his fork scraping the glass plate; he was very aware of Elizabeth unzipping her jacket and her beige shirt and the slow way she chewed her food as if wringing the taste out of every bite.

Boze asked her, "What do you think of their chances?" He was deliberately non-referential, because it was a dangerous question to be posed in this barn on this night. But Elizabeth knew exactly what he meant.

She made a sour face. "I don't think so," she said. "Not too long. Five years tops. What do you think?"

Boze hadn't even considered it, but now that she threw his dumb question back at him he felt somewhat affronted. Didn't he have to defend them? Wasn't he, as best man, a conscript of the union?

"Eh...I think so, I think they'll make it. Look at them...." Boze gestured with his head, but since he had no idea where he was sitting or where William and Marla were, he ended up indicating the stone wall. "But," Boze continued. "Maybe not. I don't know. I suppose ultimately it all depends on whether William has grown up or not."

The remark surprised Boze and he was sorry he said it. Elizabeth arched an eyebrow. "Well," she said. "I guess we'll find out." She reached across Boze's plate and took his beer without asking. She took several long swallows and Boze found it difficult to not stare at her neck. When she was done, she put the bottle between them and said, "William and I were going to get married at 38 if neither of us got married to anyone else."

"One of those pacts," Boze said nodding. "I think everyone's got one with someone."

"You too?"

"No. I didn't mean me. Everyone else."

"Well, ours was just a joke. William and I were just kidding about our pact."

Boze shook his head. "One thing I know for sure, Elizabeth, is that there are no jokes. Only truth. The more hurtful the truth, the funnier it is, the bigger the laugh."

"You're some joke expert or something?"

"Funniest guy in my graduating class. 750 people and I was the funniest. So when I tell you something about funny, believe me, I'm accredited. I know funny. I'm not just some frat boy telling a lightbulb joke."

She twisted her lips dismissively and asked, "How many boring people does it take to screw in a lightbulb?"

"How many?"

"One."

"Knock knock," he said.

"Who's there?" she asked.

"Interrupting cow."

"Interrupting—"

"Moooo," he said, and reached for his water glass, which was a nervous tic he had whenever he made a joke—a retreat so as not to hover during the presumptive laugh.

"I've heard that one," Elizabeth said. "But you're right. Our pact was real. That spring break when William and I went back to where you all grew up, and the three of us looked at the Lloyd Wrights,

William and I even slept in the same bed to see if our bodies were compatible. For sleeping, I mean. Nothing happened between us."

"Nothing happened?" Boze leaned in on his joke. "Now I'm not sure you've ever met either one of us," and took another sip.

The tables were cleared away by a phalanx of aproned employees, and the buffet table pushed back to make room for dancing to the faux swing music from a CD player. Boze went to get another beer. It took him some time, and when he returned, shaking his arm to let the cold water from the tub wick off his fingers, he was glad to see her standing and waiting for him.

"Took you long enough." She took his beer from his hand and drank.

"I couldn't find it. They're hiding the tub from the prom kids."

Elizabeth had not heard about the prom, though she had seen some snazzily dressed teens walking around the premises. Boze told her that the prom was going on right under his room. "They've got the place all done up in streamers and linen on the table. There's a huge glass bowl of pretzels."

"Pretzels? And they're worried about those kids crashing *our* party?"

"You want to go see it?"

They stood in the foyer. Elizabeth rubbed her palms together as if she were cold, and Boze wiped the sweat off his forehead. The back wall of the dining room had been opened to a large tent. A few of the kids sat by themselves, either on the steps across from the dining hall or in at the empty tables. Their faces, stoic and empty, gave no clue as to why they were alone. Most of the other kids were under the tent where a band played synthesized dance music with a heavy beat. A cabinet of lights chaotically flashed a multitude of colored jellies. Boze felt the beginnings of an allergy attack and sneezed twice. He rubbed his nose surreptitiously on the sleeve of his sweater.

"You know I'm renting my room out to these kids for a hundred bucks a pop."

"Come on," Elizabeth said.

"That's how I'm paying for the weekend." Bottle, sip, swallow.

Elizabeth grinned and moved so that Boze had to put his arm

around her. He cleared his throat. "I've finally taken a girl to prom."

"Never been to prom?"

"Hard to believe, a real looker like me. Kidding. Actually, the girl I really wanted to ask went with William. No surprise there. And then the girl I *did* ask who was an ex of his—again no surprise—was too worried about seeing him there and couldn't work up the courage to go. Though let me tell you, she kept me dangling for quite some time while she made up her mind."

They watched the dancers and Elizabeth drank from his beer bottle. She took it out of his hands without asking and didn't wipe the mouth. It reminded Boze of the casual familiarity William enjoyed with girls in high school. He could reach into their lunches and take chips without asking and he never said thank you for rides or gifts. He floated through high school with a fully realized sense of entitlement which made him even more attractive to girls. When Boze tried a well-studied imitation, he found nonchalantness to be unnatural. It was like trying to use someone else's private jokes in the wrong crowd. Elizabeth had that same natural, off-handed confidence that he had admired so much in William.

"Do you dance?" she asked. "Most guys I know hate to dance, which is something that's always baffled me."

"I'm married. It's kind of beside the point to show up somewhere with your wife and then dance with her."

"You're kidding of course, but I can tell you know what I'm talking about."

"Soooo...." He stretched his arms behind him which he hoped would convey indifference. "Let's go out and show these kids how to dance." When she didn't answer he quickly added, "It's my first prom." It sounded desperate, even to his ears.

"I'll tell you, Boze. Thanks for asking but I've already been to prom. Ask me to dance tomorrow," she told him.

They were quiet walking back to the barn. Boze was already thinking about dancing with her when he was startled by the lack of familiar pull in his front pocket. He thought for a second that he had lost his keys, and it wasn't until he slapped at his thigh that he remembered he was only carrying around the room key and not his Palatine house and car keys. He had to resist the urge to take Elizabeth's hand and skip for joy across the estate.

Boze considered himself faithful to his marriage, although he did maintain a few titillating chat-room relationships. More than anything, he liked reassembling himself to a new chat partner, lowering his height a few inches to lumber less, taking 30 pounds off his weight, changing hair and eye color indiscriminately.

In his room that night he thought about buying condoms, though a girl like Elizabeth would surely be on birth control or carry a diaphragm. Besides, she would be smart enough to know that married men don't travel with condoms. The wedding would be going on just below them, but the bed—he bounced on it once—could take whatever might happen. It was a great piece of luck that William had gotten this room for him.

When Boze closed his eyes now he felt the twists and turns of the Pennsylvania Turnpike in his gut. He slept, but he woke just a few hours later sneezing and coughing, half in a dream state. The men in coveralls were in his room and directed him into the bathroom, where he leaned over the toilet and spat beads of green phlegm. Sweat poured off him and his eyes were fractured with red cracks and fissures. Snot ran from his nose faster than he could blow it. He took three Sudafeds and washed them down with water from the tap. When he felt as though he might have gotten a handle on the allergy attack, Boze crumpled two balls of toilet paper and inserted one into each nostril to stop the deluge of mucus.

At his bed he saw that the bottom sheet had come completely off the mattress and was tangled up with the top sheet and blanket. It had disengaged from his shifting and flipping. The arduous retucking process, hoofing around a bed that size, yanking here, jerking there, only revealed that the sheets were not the right size; not too small or too large exactly, but an off-shape, a goofy hexagon or pentagon. It wasn't a sheet at all but just a piece of fabric that someone had folded and tucked in opportune places to make it look like bed linen. He gave up on fixing it and reinserted two new wads of Kleenex into his nostrils.

As gingerly as a man of his bulk could, he lay back down on the bed. Unfamiliar rumblings and clanging beyond his walls kept him from sleeping, so he inserted the ear plugs he brought with him, producing the welcome buzz of his tinnitus. And while he was up, he unwrapped his sleep mask from the cloth sheath and placed that over his eyes, just in case the morning was bright. His only connection to the world now was through his mouth, and he breathed through it deeply. Having his senses blocked gave him a pleasant feeling of disembodiment, as though he were spilling over the walls of his flesh, uncontained. He floated now above Pennsylvanian mountains and watched the turnpike workers. They too wore safety goggles, face masks, ear protectors. He caught sight of his own car heading back from the wedding. He moved closer and could see that Elizabeth was in the passenger seat with her head against the window and her eyes closed. The vents in the dashboard were all pointed at her, and the breeze from the fans kept her skin fresh and cool. In the driver seat, Boze sipped at tepid coffee through a plastic lid and squinted against the glare of the road. He nodded to the turnpike workers, who paused in their gesturing and directing to consider the large man behind the wheel. Hadn't he been alone last time? Couldn't he follow directions? But they were all secretly pleased for him to be returning with such a prize.

THOUGH the magnolias were in bloom, a light but incessant drizzle spilled the pink and purple petals, and by mid-morning the grounds were covered in them. By noon the only topic of conversation was whether the plans for the outdoor ceremony should be scrapped or not. The decision was put off until the last possible minute in deference to Marla, who, it was often noted, had wished for an outdoor wedding ever since she was a little girl. By the time the 5:30pm deadline had been reached, the pessimists had carried the day, and the folding chairs were brought into the barn. The black and white plastic bunting which had previously festooned the gazebo was quickly stapled-gunned, damp and saggy, to the rafters in the barn.

Boze marched down the aisle, his tuxedoed arm linked to Marla's blue sun-dressed maid of honor, and then took his position behind

William. He stood stiffly, hands at his side. Only his index finger moved, tracing the outline of his room key in his pants pocket. When asked, Boze handed the rings to the efficient, forgoing any pocket patting or other canned comedic response. Clowning around during a wedding ceremony was like having a funny message on your answering machine: strictly for the amateurs.

The bridal party led the processional back out of the barn and onto the lawn, where the sun was making its first unabashed appearance of the day. Marla reproached the sky, asking who it was up there that hated her, which got much sympathetic laughter. When Elizabeth found Boze, he was already in the dining hall eating a stick of chicken satay, contorting his lips so he could pull off the meat near the bottom, and holding a napkin under his chin to catch the drippings. She stepped out of the crowd, and came towards him. She was wearing a silky green sleeveless dress that came down to her knees, with white hose and green pumps. Her stomach protruded slightly in a self-confident manner that made Boze even more nervous. And unlike last night she was wearing make-up: red lipstick and dark eyeliner. She opened her arms as if to say, *How do I look?* He was glad to have a mouthful of food so he didn't have to say anything right away.

When she reached him, Elizabeth said, "You look great," and she ran a hand from his shoulder down his lapel and kept her palm on his chest a few seconds longer than necessary. He felt a bit suffocated standing next to her. When she took the chicken satay, he dropped his free hand to his pocket and touched his room key. She finished eating and handed him the empty stick without a word.

"I saw in the program," she told him, "there aren't any assigned seats so we can sit together."

"Great," he said. This was a date. He was really on a date.

"If you give the toast before we get our seats, I'll wave so you can find me."

"The toast?"

"*Champagne toast Boze Cunningham.* That's you right? The best man always gives a toast."

"I don't have anything prepared."

"But you're the funniest of 750 suburban kids. You'll think of something."

Boze did have some ideas, some one-liners that he had been mulling over in his head, and felt confident that when the moment arrived he would ad-lib and be brilliant. It would be the adrenaline that would make the toast; the laughter would spur him on. That was how it always worked. Planning ahead only confused him; he always stumbled over prepared material. It was his ad-libbing that he could count on. Nevertheless, he feigned terror. He told Elizabeth that he was afraid of crowds and that he knew, just knew he was going to humiliate himself. She rubbed his back and cooed little platitudes, sotto voce.... *You can do it.... Just relax.... It'll be fine....* And her breath tickled his ears.

The plan was firm now: he would make a killer toast, the funniest ever heard in Bucks County, and then he would come back to her and say, *You were right, you believed in me and gave me the courage....* And she would be so honored that she would suggest right away that they go up to his room. Everything in the room could be part of the seduction. *Ever see walls this red?* She would laugh because it was true.The walls were overpoweringly red. *Ever see a bed this big? Crazy. And look at this sheet.* He could pull the covers off and show her the misshapen bottom sheet and explain how he had watched the chambermaid's tortured ministrations trying to get it to fit properly. *Once it's messed up it's messed up for good, ha ha ha. Try to straighten it out.* She wouldn't be able to. And he would make his move then, spin her around to face him and plant one right on the lips. She would take her shoes off and step out of her dress and when she reached up to remove the necklace, he would put his hands on her hands and say, *Leave the chain*; he would say it just to say it, and she would do it because she would do whatever he told her.

The back doors of the dining hall slid open and the crowd was herded into the tent toward the waiting tables to the sounds of slow, moody jazz. She asked, "Where do you want to sit?"

And he told her, "You pick. But let's not rush over. I don't want to get trampled like those kids at The Who concert."

They weren't holding hands like some of the couples, but they were walking together, he was sure of it. It's better than prom, he thought. The wait was worth it.

She picked a table at the edge of the dance floor, right next to the small table with two seats which had been set aside for the bride and groom. The band—seven or eight guys, guitars, keyboards, drums and a few horns—radiated heat. The air wasn't moving very much under the canvas and plastic, and Boze felt a sneeze forming at the very back of his mouth. After settling herself down, Elizabeth looked over at him and told him to take off his tuxedo jacket. She stood and pulled it off for him, and arranged it neatly on the back of his chair. He thought of a joke about the chair looking like him now, big bulky thing with arms at its side, but William appeared. He scratched disinterestedly at one of his sideburns and told Boze it was time for him to make the toast. William looked bored. He had the air of a professional *maitre d'* reduced to seating people at a chain restaurant. Elizabeth stood and helped Boze put his coat back on. William said, "You two are getting chummy." Boze left Elizabeth to respond to the charge. He walked forward to the stage.

"You the best man?" the bandleader asked him.

"Well, I'm good," Boze told him, winking.

Boze looked out at the tent. The tables were arrayed like water lilies in a pond, and there was William, taking his seat at the small table with Marla. The chatter turned to shushing and then a low murmur and finally near silence. The band had no singer and there didn't seem to be a mic stand. One of the horn players handed him a microphone, and Boze brought it to his mouth and heard his breath mingle with the hum of the public address system.

"I feel like a lounge singer holding this thing," he said. Someone behind him laughed. It was good to get the band on his side in case he wanted rim shots or something. He took the mic even closer and sang, "Doobidee doobie doo," and heard more laughter. "So time for the toast...oops."

Off mic now but only slightly so he can still be heard, Boze announced, "I need some champagne or something, a glass of something so I can toast." He put the mic on the stage and hopped off. William and Marla were both laughing as Boze strutted past shrugging his shoulders. Because the bride and groom were laughing, so did many others, and Boze walked to his seat and took the glass Elizabeth handed him.

"Here you go, honey," she said.

"Thank you, sweetie," he answered.

On the way back he looked to a table of complete strangers and pointed to his glass. "Forgot my champagne," he said and the table broke up laughing, pleased to be in on the joke.

Back up front, microphone in one hand, champagne in the other: "Okay, got the champagne now, champagne toast, and you all have yours?" People raised their glasses and some yelled, *Come on....Get on with it....Let's go already....You're holding up dinner.*

"Great. Hey thanks for coming out. I'm not a professional entertainer but still it's hard not to say that stuff: thanks for coming out and let's hear it for the band. Hey! Let's hear it for the band." Only a few people clapped. "Come on now, I'm serious. Aren't they great?" Everyone started clapping. When the applause started to die down he said, "These kids are going places. And how about a round of applause for the staff here at the estate. It's a hell of a place for a wedding and as anyone who ate here this morning can corroborate, they serve the finest cinnamon rolls on the Delaware. So good that people eat them all day. And the scuttlebutt is that they're coming out with dessert tonight, so save some room." Nonplused, most people clapped politely, though some, thinking they were in on a joke, over enthusiastically cheered, *Cinnamon rolls!*

"I drove here from Chicago—the suburbs, Palatine—where William and I grew up. My plan was to write the toast while I drove but what happened was that someone—" (The someone was his wife, but he glanced down at Elizabeth—she had moved and was now crouched with her camera by the bridal table to be closer to the stage—and he didn't want to remind her that he was married.) "...someone gave me this book on tape to listen to, *Horse Town*, and I figured since I wasn't ever going to read it.... That's my rule: only listen to a book on tape if it's one I'm never going to read. I know I'm never going to read this one because I tried when it first came out and couldn't get into it. It got good reviews and all that, but it's a western—you know, pastiche—

and when I was reading it and I got turned off by the frontier dialect. Even the narrator says y'all and yep and darn tootin'. Came off just a tad cornball to me." He was getting some laughs, just a few chuckles, but they were definitely listening.

"Brad Pitt does the narration on the tape. He's a big star, a professional entertainer unlike me, so I gave it a listen and it wasn't bad. It's a love story, a tragic love story—star-crossed, the whole bit—but anyway, half the dialogue is this woman. And she's beautiful of course, sultry, part Mexican I think, and so Brad has to talk like her. And he gets all low and whispery when he does her voice and he sighs a lot too. Like this, 'Ohhh big boy....'" Big laughs now. Boze paused a moment, before continuing. "It's hard to do a woman's voice, and Brad seemed like he was a little embarrassed. So that was funny. You know, real good-looking guy like that, always getting the ladies and stuff, and here he was humiliating himself on tape."

Elizabeth had her camera up to her face so Boze paused, grinned and froze like an 8X10 of himself. It looked strange, but when Elizabeth flashed the camera and everyone realized he had been posing for her, a big laugh broke out. He nodded towards Elizabeth to thank her for helping, but she was looking at William and he was looking back at her crouching on the floor by his feet and they were laughing with each other. "All this is to say that I have not written my speech and so sort of just winging it here."

From his seat William yelled, "It's a toast, not a speech!"

"I'm getting to it. Okay. So I've known both William and Marla for a short time, and just William for a lot longer. And let me tell you, I like William and Marla a heck of a lot more than I like just William." The tent leaned in with anticipation: he was about to break bad on the groom; it was going to be one of those toasts. "Being William's friend has definitely benefitted me, don't get me wrong. I never would have met any girls in high school if it wasn't for William. He attracted women like, well I don't have to tell you all. Even though William had a way with ladies, he had me—fat and sweaty Boze—as his secret weapon. I made him look even better. Women would check us out and say: Look at that fabulously good looking rakish fellow with the eyeliner and spiked hair. What a hunk, especially compared to that mongoloid he's with." Big laughs. "But anyway, the girls all tried to get to him through me. I'd get calls from the most popular girls in high school. They'd be like, oh Boze, how are you, what are you doing tonight? And I'd say well I'm, dot dot dot, whatever, and they'd say gosh that's interesting. Can I come over later? I'd be like, abso-loot-lee, and then they'd be like, 'Can we call William and invite him too?' and I'd say sure, whatever you want. You know, I'd be in la-la-land. And William would come over and soon he and the girl would disappear into my bedroom. I'd just stay downstairs and eat snacks or whatever and look up at the ceiling and try and imagine all the things going on up there. My bedroom saw more action than any other teen's on my block, but unfortunately for me, I wasn't involved in any of it." Laughter. Marla put her hands on her hips and leaned away from William with her mouth hanging open. William shrugged his shoulders playfully, then Marla laughed and leaned in and gave him a big kiss and everybody went *Awwww*.... "And that was before puberty," Boze said, which made everyone laugh again.

"Actually, I remember one girl, Daisy was her name, and she looked like a Daisy—"

"Get off the stage," William shouted. Boze laughed and Marla yelled, "Let him speak. Let's hear about Daisy."

A couple others echoed Marla, *"Let's hear about Daisy....Let the man speak...."* Boze took a noisy slurp from his champagne glass.

"Okay, Daisy. We, William and I, were on a marathon walk to raise money for Jerry's Kids. It wasn't just us, but lots of 7th and 8th graders from the northwest suburbs. And Daisy met up with us. And by 'met up with us,' I really mean she took one look at William with his Mork suspenders hooked to his parachute pants, and long feathered hair, and she started talking to him. I fell and twisted my ankle around the second or third mile. I can't remember where exactly because they measured in kilometers since this was the early eighties and there was a lot of talk about us, the whole country, going that way, metrics; and also we got money by our sponsors paying us by how much we walked and by using kilometers instead of miles—it's like two, two and a half kilometers to the mile, so we got more money. A little deceptive but for a good cause and no one minded. But I was about to tell William, you know, my ankle's twisted, you have to go on without me, it's for the good of the cause, but he was already gone. He and Daisy never even noticed I fell."

Marla had taken a bread stick and was whacking William on the head with it. "But don't be mad, no, wait everybody, hang on a sec. Because when he was finished with her, Daisy ended up calling me all the time. William's exes all called me, whether it was to make him jealous by paying attention to me, or just to show him that they hadn't committed suicide...which wasn't the case with all of them, but no need to mention that particular ugliness on this occasion. And I told him, Daisy's been calling me, and he was like, I don't care, do what you want, and blah blah blah. I was getting all primed up, had the whole evening planned out in my head. Daisy comes over, we drink a few beers, only I ended up ralphing all over my basement. I didn't know what happened to Daisy but my parents saw the puke and freaked out. Somehow I played it off, you know, said I've got the flu or something, Mom. And then I get up to my room, and hello! There she is, and what do you know? There's William. All of the sudden he was interested in her again. I didn't even know she had called him." The crowd was reacting, but it was disorganized, cacophonic. There was laughter but he also heard tisking and voices engaged in regular conversation as if he wasn't up there at all.

"And Marla, I don't know as well. But I can tell you this much, she's nice as hell. Sweet. Beautiful. I'm sorry he didn't dump her so I could get to know her better. Kidding. So at these affairs you always spend a lot of time calculating the odds and this one's no different." The tables hushed. Elizabeth sat motionless on the floor. William and Marla were expressionless. This was for Elizabeth. He looked right at her and felt dangerous. "And the consensus is unanimous: success. These two are going to make it. And so at your fiftieth wedding anniversary, which I know for certain you will have unless one of you is dead or both since you're already in your thirties, I'll get up and make a toast. And I promise to be more prepared. See you in fifty blissful happy married years."

Cheers! Skoal! L'Chiam!....

He handed the microphone to someone, he didn't know who,

and people were talking and animated; he felt good. As he walked by William and Marla's table he shrugged his shoulders and said coyly, "That was the best I could do."

William said, "That was exactly what we expected from you, Boze."

"Hey, that could be interpreted as an insult," Boze called back, but he was moving to his table now, and as soon as he got in the orbit, Elizabeth was up and patted his back. She pressed close.

"Hey, you really *are* funny," she said beaming.

"I told you. You didn't believe?"

"You've been amusing, but you really pulled out the big guns."

"I'm a subsistence joker; I use what I have, I have what I need, I get by. I store some of the good lines for the winter...." Boze was aware of his whole table watching him and maybe even a few faces from adjacent tables. A man from a few seats clockwise reached across some plates to put his hand out.

"Good job."

"That's very nice of you...." He wanted to relive the whole toast with Elizabeth right away, have her say her favorite parts back to him, but he also didn't want to be rude to this man who was obviously an admirer too.

"The Brad Pitt stuff was really funny," the man continued.

"Brad Pitt?" The opportunity. He turned towards Elizabeth. "Did I talk about Brad Pitt?"

"You did," Elizabeth said, pulling at his jacket so he could remove it. "You talked about him and you said you were listening to a book on tape in your car and that's why you hadn't written a real toast."

"Well," Boze said, now feeling like just Elizabeth's attention wasn't enough and giddily addressing the whole table. "I have no memory of saying any of that. I can scarcely believe I did, except that clearly something happened in the room, I can sense—"

Boze realized with a shock that he was shouting and the rest of the tent was silent. On the stage now was William's stepfather, the Colonel, standing erect in full military dress uniform. His legs were like twin oil rigs, his arm extended out to the crowd and in his hand was a glass of champagne. He might have been posing for a statue—

The Toast of Iwo Jima—and he had a mic stand! Where did he get a mic stand? Had he brought his own? The colonel cleared his throat and made a noise like a pristine Indian Motorcycle turning over.

He said, "I wasn't there when William was born, (pause) or even for that matter when he was conceived, but..." He let his voice trail off as a huge laugh erupted in the tent. Boze was stunned by the noise and the vibration; nothing he had said had gotten such a strong reaction. The Colonel was waiting sternly, not really acknowledging the laughter, and only a slight flicker of pleasure on his lips told the crowd that he was having fun too. He waited for the laugh to diminish but not die out altogether, before raising his stentorian voice. "But William does feel like a son to me." A few in the tent went: *Awwww*.... "And Marla," the Colonel paused; he wasn't sobbing, but for one syllable his voice had caught, and his lips tightened and then hardened earnestly as if he were trying to overcome great emotion. "I consider you my daughter too.... *Prrrr-osit!*" He had cocked his drinking arm while trilling his Rs, and now threw back his head and poured the glass into his mouth. Everyone followed suit, and when they finished drinking, they began applauding like mad.

Boze raised his glass but it was empty. The Colonel marched past on the way to his table and Boze tried to catch his eye, *We did it, we done good*, but the Colonel didn't notice. Jenny and Debby got up. They both had pink and purple dresses with matching scarves and shoes. They hugged their father, and then one pulled his chair out for him and the other made a big show of shaking out his cloth napkin and placing it on his lap. This made the Colonel and everyone at his table laugh.

Elizabeth said, "That was a beautiful toast; funny and touching."

"It was a good toast," agreed Boze quickly. "But you know, he's the stepfather, so he's got that edge. He can say, you're *like* a son to me. Like a son. It's even better than *You are my son*, you know?"

Elizabeth tsked at him. "Boze," she said.

"No wait, I'm just saying. It was a good toast, but William's real father, if he were here, couldn't have said, 'You're *like* a son to me.' That would be rude. And 'You *are* a son to me,' somehow that doesn't sound as complimentary, that's just biology. So this guy, he's really got a good toasting edge to exploit."

"You could have said, 'He's like a brother to me,'" the man from across the table said.

"I did say that," Boze told him. "Didn't I?"

Elizabeth shook her head.

"It was implicit. I implied that William was like a brother.... But you're missing the point; *like* a brother, any schmoe can be *like* a brother. Two guys in the same prison cell might be like brothers. Like a son, now that's special. Touching. I had the hard job; I had to be the clown and crack them up. Anyone can make them go awww...."

Another man at the table chimed in, "Heading up a blended family can be quite challenging."

"I'm sure it is," Boze said. "And not to take anything away from that achievement. And even though the Colonel came on the scene at the end of high school and William never really lived with him, I'm sure the influence is there and he really does feels like a father to him and God love him for it. I'm just saying he could have dug a little deeper."

AFTER dinner, Boze and Elizabeth danced. It was awkward for him at first. He had put one arm around her back and extended the other forward so that when she placed her hand in his, they advanced on the floor with their arms extended forward in a wedge, like birds flying south. He bobbed and weaved a few times before Elizabeth pulled her hand free and placed both arms on his shoulders. Boze's newly freed hand caused him a moment of panic. He kept it aloft as though waving to someone, then placed it on her hip, then shoulder, and finally curled his whole arm around her back. This had the desired effect of bringing her even closer, and with their bodies rubbing together, stomachs tangent, legs brushing legs; the resulting pleasant frottage produced for Boze a slight fluffing—nothing offensive, he was sure—just enough to let her know he was paying attention.

Debby and Jenny rushed the floor. Each one held a hand of the Colonel's, who was being dragged between them. He made a face of feigned weariness, but when they reached the center, he stood sharply at mock attention. He thrust his arms forward and Debby and Jenny squealed in delight and clapped their hands. He reached up over Debby's head and she took his hands and spun herself underneath him, purple scarf twirling in the air. In the meantime, Jenny held his torso, clinging to the right side of his body, and they swayed back and forth, keeping perfect time. Like intricately crafted gears in an old time piece, the Colonel brought Debby in while spinning Jenny out for a dramatic turn of her own. Boze had never seen anything like it. They were all so devoted.... Boze wanted to look away but found himself riveted, and soon Elizabeth was watching too. The Colonel took a step away from his daughters and threw his arms out and tossed his head back, and the girls rushed towards him and reached out and he spun them at the same time. It all looked effortless.

Boze felt a sudden rush of gratitude for the woman in his arms. He wanted to spin her the same way, but instead his arms squeezed her padded torso even more tightly. He breathed deeply, letting her scent envelop him. She smelled like lilacs, possibly, or some other light flower. Elizabeth was going to change everything for him. He might have kissed her right there—he saw the turnpike workers waving, *this way buddy, slowly, lean down, pucker up*—but the music stopped and he reluctantly let her go so they could clap.

"I'm going to get some water. Want anything from the bar?" Elizabeth asked.

"No thank you. I'm going to check out the sweet table. Should I get you some cake?"

She coyly shrugged her shoulders. "See what's there," she said. "Maybe a cinnamon roll if they're as good as you say...." She winked at him, which normally Boze thought a little corny, but when she did it, he reeled like a drunk.

A series of long tables had been erected, sheathed in white cloth and then covered in multicolored petit fours, grisly puff pastries heaped with powdered sugar, chocolate half moons oozing almond paste, raspberry buns, blueberry torts, peach cobbler, vats of vanilla pudding, lumps of dough perfused with corn syrup and glistening even under the soft lighting of the tent. Boze made a slow pass, inspecting the troops, and found it all satisfactory. Near the end was the plate of cinnamon rolls piled into a pyramid of caramel brown spirals and white frosting. By the time Boze had cantered back and gotten a plate from the other end of the table, the rolls were nearly gone, but he managed to snag three of them, leaving only garish white frosting smears, as if they had slid off the platter like snails.

The infusion of sugar into the proceedings had a noticeable effect. The assembled were up and animated, the dinner groupings had disbanded, sorted and regrouped into new teams. Boze went to his table but recognized no one—or perhaps he was mistaken and it wasn't his table—without Elizabeth he couldn't be sure. He continued threading his way around the tables looking for a spot. All the empty seats had sweaters or purses hanging off the backs. One chair looked promising at a far table against the wall, and it was even between people he already knew.

"Hey Debby. Jenny. Anybody sitting here?" He didn't look either one in the face because he wasn't sure which one was which.

"Go right ahead," one of them said. "Daddy can find a new seat."

Boze, who had pulled the chair out and was about to lower himself, stopped short. "No, no. I don't want to take anyone's..."

But the girls were pushing their glasses and nudging their plates away from the empty space to make room for him. The other sister sweetly said, "First come first served." They were both smiling, and so Boze put himself on the seat and pushed up to the table.

He nodded to the group, which was composed of women and children, all with Debby and Jenny's frail waifish bodies, the same lips, eyes, and black hair, with only slight variations owing to age.

"What an honor," one of the middle-aged women said. "Joined by the best man himself."

"I'm good," Boze said addressing the table. "I don't know about the best...."

"We thought your toast was really funny."

"You did?" He gave a confused look: the joker's version of 'This old thing?' Boze never enjoyed a conversation more than when people were reminding him of funny things he had said. Laughter was all right, but tended to fade in memory. One could never get that moment back. But a verbal acknowledgment...an admiring description of just how funny he was...that was something you could hang on to, something to remember. But before he could mine the depths of the woman's admiration, William approached the table and trumped him.

"What an honor," the same woman said. "Joined by the groom himself."

William laughed. His sideburns flared out of his head and as he stood behind one of his stepsisters he looked like a puppet that someone was working from below. William waited a respectful amount of time and then said loudly to Boze: "So Boze, Elizabeth tells me that you made a little money yesterday...."

"That's right. Because of prom..." Boze jumped into the joke even before he knew quite what was happening. "...renting my room to the kids."

The laugh that shook the table was like a thunderclap. Because of the toast, he had established himself as a wit and raconteur, and now people were just happy to be in his company. He no longer had to compete with every wise-ass in the joint.

When they were kids, William had always set Boze up for laughs; he had been a good and conscientious straight man. William even had that look again, a certain sort of impish, dopey expression. Boze was ebullient and suddenly felt for William the dormant loyalty he had when they were growing up. For years he had been holding something against William, nurturing an unnamed, low grade hostility. He wasn't sure why. But he thought now that it was time to let it go. Boze wished now that he had taken the toast more seriously, that he had made it clear that being William's friend had meant something to him.

"You could still rent your room out," one of the stepsisters said. "Now you could rent your room to us for the bathroom so no one has to stand in line."

Boze leaned in to layer the joke, to quote a price according to bodily function so that the last laugh would be his. A group joke was like a land grab, only unlike real estate, it was the last man on the scene who got the deed. But before Boze could execute, William was calling his name.

Boze shot him a look. *Can't you see I'm working here?*

"Let me borrow your key."

"Sure. Sure. Just put the lid down when you're done." Boze reached into his pocket and handed the key over Debby's head.

Boze returned his attention back to his admirers but found all heads turned away from him. Two small children, a boy and a girl were arguing, and the mother of one—or possibly both—was trying to settle them down. The boy ran off laughing, while the girl pouted, but was persuaded to sit in her mother's lap. The girl looked at Boze and she pointed to him and whined, "But *heeee's* got cinnamon rolls."

The mother told the girl that she had to be quiet, but the girl pointed to Boze's plate and said, "He's got *three....*"

An older woman, a grandmother version of the Debby/Jenny prototype, tried to get the table past the awkward moment. She smiled at Boze and asked genteelly, "Where did your wife go?"

"My wife isn't here," Boze said.

"He didn't come with his wife," the stepsister on his left said, and she gave the piece of melon on her plate a significant look. The remark made everyone even more uncomfortable, and they began eating their desserts in earnest. The only one still looking at him was the little girl, her eyes narrow and lips parted revealing two clean rows of tightly gritted teeth.

He was too big for the table, twice the size of anyone else—his mass was awful, stupefying—and the tuxedo added more thick layers. He was so sweaty now that even his wrist and fingers were damp. His nose tickled, and when he brought his hands up to press against his sinuses, he smacked the sisters on either side of him with his elbows.

"I'm sorry—"

"What's Daddy up to now?" one of the sisters asked.

Heads craned. The Colonel stood at the sweet table addressing a waiter. "No cinnamon rolls for the colonel?" he shouted.

Oh no.... People from nearby tables were joining in.... *Don't want to upset the Colonel.... Better get some in a hurry....*

The waiter shrugged and made some remark which did not carry over the noise.

"Back to KP!" the Colonel barked gesturing with his index finger towards the kitchen. "I'll have you peeling potatoes until your fingers bleed!" Though he had seemed genuinely frightening, he winked lightly to the waiter who gave a fake salute before rushing away. The Colonel turned and advanced towards the table. Boze tried to casually wipe his mouth on a napkin, and realized with horror that he hadn't brought a napkin and the cloth on his lips had probably been the Colonel's.

His time with Elizabeth had confused him. He had mistakenly thought the confidence and bravado he felt in her presence were portable commodities; that he could walk away from her and be the same Boze. When this night was over, he decided now, no matter what happened he was going to stay close to her. They could meet in chat-rooms...or maybe he could even see her in person. Where did she say she lived? Chicago? Hadn't he asked? Boze stood up and nodded to his table, though no one noticed. He would be able to come up with excuses and get away every few weekends. He would drive wherever she lived. He was not going to give this up. He walked away from the Colonel's table and didn't look back.

She wasn't on the dance floor or at the sweet table. He nervously patted his empty pocket, as if the constant checking might bring the room key back. When he looked in the dining room he found Marla instead. She was on an old heat register painted the same off-white as the walls. Her dress had been altered, and the long train was gone. A bevy of swooning children sat cross-legged at her feet. Marla clinked the ice in her small glass and took a sip through a coffee stirrer and screwed her face as though drinking moonshine. As Boze approached she puffed her cheeks out and exhaled dramatically.

"This is Boze, William's best man," she told the girls, who twittered and squawked.

Boze lowered himself and tried to cross his legs like the girls but eventually settled for knees bent and sitting on his feet. The little girls were breathlessly reeling out scenarios for weddings, each one telling Marla in detail about what she was going to have: huge cakes, movie star grooms, decorated mansions....

"I'm going to have pizza and ice cream at my wedding," one girl was saying.

"Ohhhh...." Marla leaned down and spoke in an exaggerated tone. "Well you know what? You'll be too busy talking to people to eat your pizza and ice cream."

The girl looked flummoxed.

"Isn't that right Boze? What did you have at your wedding?"

"I don't remember," he said.

"I do," Marla told him. "Chicken patties."

Boze rolled his eyes and Marla smirked.

"Why didn't you marry him if he's the best man?" one of the little girl asked.

Marla laughed broadly. "Aren't they precious?"

Boze got up on one knee. "Because the groom is better than the best man," he told the girl who stood close and looked into his face.

"Will you be my groom?" she asked him.

Marla gasped and roared so loudly that the little girl who asked jumped up and ran off. *Attention.... Attention please....* Boze glowered. He wanted to know what exactly Marla found so funny about the question. Was it funny because it came from a little girl, or was it funny that someone would want to marry him? *If I could just have your attention for one moment....* Surely Marla had noticed Elizabeth's more than passing interest in him. *Can we get the bride on the dance floor please?* Marla squealed and handed her drink to one of the girls and flitted quickly back into the tent. Boze followed behind her.

William was standing alone on the dance floor. He looked proud, still in his complete tuxedo, flushed with pleasure, and he put his arm out as Marla rushed forward. The band worked into a slow atmospheric ballad.

William's ardor seemed to have a new intensity. His affection, which had been playful before—a showy you-may-now-kiss-the-bride kiss during the ceremony, mock passionate kissing during the mealtime glass clinking—had now lost its stench of irony. William was really holding Marla tightly. He gave her a buss on the neck when she rested her head on his shoulder. The little girls followed Marla on to the floor and stared moony-eyed as they danced. It was just as they had always pictured it.

"Look at that," Elizabeth said to Boze. He was startled by her voice and the hand that clasped his arm. He hadn't heard her approach and had no idea how long she had been there. "All those little girls would give anything to be her tonight. They see a princess getting her picture taken, all the attention. And the cake. The biggest damn cake any of them have ever seen. They're all dying to get married. If only they knew."

"You're pretty jaded for someone who isn't even married yet," Boze said.

"It's not jaded to call this whole thing a sham. Honor and cherish."

"It's a necessary sham," Boze said, shrugging his shoulders. "Propagation of the species and all that."

"Really. And how long until they show up to other people's weddings and not dance with each other? Or better yet, one of them doesn't even go."

The bride and groom kissed while they danced. The floor was ringed with cameras flashing.

"I'm leaving," Elizabeth announced and let go of his arm.

He turned sharply and faced her. "I...did you want to dance? I was going to ask you to dance again."

"Thanks anyway," Elizabeth said.

"I wanted to show you the room." He felt himself pleading. "There's this enormous bed.... It's wacky. And you shouldn't be on these dark roads now when you're so tired. Stay here for the night." His throat caught on the last few words but he pressed on. "I've got a king-size bed, huge like in a museum. It's funny and it'll be funny. You'll really laugh."

"That's very sweet, but I'm going to go now."

"Just like you and William over spring break," he told her. "The same nothing will happen, just like that."

She made a face that he had not seen before. Her lips thinned and eyelids lowered; it lasted just for a second before she turned and walked for the door. He was going to have to live with it now; he had no more tapes to listen to in the car. He was going to have to live with *this*. He walked through the ring of onlookers to the dance floor. The flashes stopped and the children watched in horror as Boze put a hand on William's shoulder and stopped the dance and asked for his key.

WHEN he pulled at the bedspread he saw his bottom sheet was untucked. He gave it a little yank before noticing that all the linens were tangled and even the blanket was balled up. He smelled sweat and a familiar floral fragrance. In one swoop the comforter and sheets and pillows were off the bed and piled at his feet. Grunting once, Boze got down like a quarterback and shoved the mattress. It hit the far wall and stopped half off the box spring. It bent under its own weight and stayed in that position, half on the frame and half on the ground, like a playground slide. Boze went into the bathroom and took a dry washrag from the towel rack and stuck one end into his mouth. He bit down as hard as he could, until his jaws ached and the rag had absorbed the moisture from his mouth and his tongue was dry and he could no longer tell where terrycloth ended and tongue began. He kept his mouth clamped tightly and lay down on the mattress. He lay still with his arms at his side and his palms down and fingers splayed against the slope of the mattress. He was quiet. The music from the band gently rumbled and vibrated in his room like deep, sonorous laughter. His senses were sharp now. He could smell powdered sugar from the wedding and the sweat of dancers and even whiffs of cigar smoke from somewhere on the grounds. He could hear every word of every conversation below ...*Does anyone know where they're going to honeymoon....The food here got a wonderful write-up....I wonder what they're serving for breakfast....* The lights from the tent flickered and played tricks in the shadows. Something would move—a head, a gesturing arm—and he'd turn to look but see only pulsating red paint. He wasn't sure how he'd feel in the morning.... He'd feel foolish, he knew that.... But then again, it might just all seem funny in the morning....a good story for work. He'd have to wait and see. In the meantime he could stay like this, mouth shut, lips locked around the rag to mute any inadvertent sounds.... He could drive like this on the turnpike...through the dark tunnels...over the mountains...towards Palatine.... He would keep his mouth shut all the way to the front door if he had to. He'd just have to wait and see how it felt in the morning.

Ultralight

S<small>AL</small> tried to turn his head but the branch was faster and it drew little gashes of blood across his face with its shark-toothed prickers. The stalk was on its way down anyway but Sal was so pissed he stomped on it with the heel of his work boot for good measure. It felt good to at least get the last blow. The sun was going down and the air was slightly breezy which would have felt great if he hadn't worn so many layers—overalls, long sleeve shirt, hat—not that any of it was keeping him from getting nicked up. The chore du jour was the multiflora rose, an Old Testament-sized bush of fiery blossoms and vicious thorns. Sal Montgomery had cleaned chicken coops as a kid and dug ditches in Kuwait as a reservist and he had even recently spent an entire afternoon with his arm in a cow's uterus turning a calf, and all those jobs sucked in their own ways, but nothing sucked quite like removing the multiflora rose, and his procrastination was half of why the bushes were as overgrown and gnarly as they were.

The canister strapped to his back had gotten tangled in some of the shrubs, but Sal pulled the spray nozzle over his head like a samurai warrior and squeezed the trigger, dousing the hacks he had just made. Multiflora rose grew back twice as big if left untreated. The cut stalks could reroot as well, which was why he was going to drag the whole tangle into the pasture and let it bake in the sun for a week or so and then burn it.

The stems themselves gave satisfying little gasps when he ripped through them with his loppers, like slicing watermelon. He wasn't a philosophical man like his father had been, always jotting down notes for his journal or sketching the sky with chalks and brush paint, but Sal did appreciate the tranquility. Even with this pain in the ass job, hearing only the mourning doves cooing their resignation and the occasional rip of screeching hawk, it was decidedly, gloriously, endlessly quiet. He took the gun and sprayed another generous swath of herbicide.

A different noise suddenly intruded: a distant, low drone. A wet raspberry puttering across the sky. Another goddamned ultralight. Every fricking night, some yuppie buzzed across his sky with one of these giant toys. With the sun setting behind him Sal could just make out the machine, a motorcycle hanging from a parachute and a giant fan roaring behind it. If a hundred mosquitoes descended on you at once, the drone might come close to the irritating sound of an ultralight. It was a good quarter mile off still, just crossing over the lowlands where Sal's cows were no doubt taking last pulls from the round bales and drinking at the creek.

Sal ignored the violation at first and pushed his dirt-caked glove through the weeds, cut another stem, squirted Roundup. But finally, as it always did, the noise, the offense, the *unfairness* got to be too much and Sal raised himself toward the sky. He gaped the way his cows did when they peeked their heads up from the grass at a car going by, blankly monitoring its progress. Cars were a rare sight this far into the country, but these ultralights were more and more common. The yuppies drove out here from the suburbs and flew over his land because Sal had kept it pristine instead of developing.

The noisy machine farted along, making a sharp turn toward the edge of the timber where Sal was working. So far his strategy for combating the ultralights was to wait for them to leave, to stand stock still with as much dignity as he could muster, in the hopes that it might shame the pilots. *Here is a man at work*, they might think. *I am a man of leisure and money, and here is a man working, and I am disturbing him.* So far the plan hadn't been too effective.

Sal figured it was just fifty yards off now. The pilot—if that's what you called them—was wearing dark leather, head to toe, like a motorcyclist. He had a helmet which probably did a good deal of the work to cut down on the noise, even as those below were stuck listening to it. The pilot raised his arm off the joystick controller, and waved vigorously. This happened occasionally, a pilot showing off, usually when Sal's son Mikey had his friends over and the kids were encouraging the pilots. Sal understood the impulse to show off. Sometimes a subdivision kid would wave to him when he was driving his tractor and he would blow his air horn in response.

Sal gripped his lopper low, keeping his arms at his side to ensure nothing he did could be interpreted, even at this distance, as a friendly gesture. The guy was lucky it wasn't a rifle Sal was clutching. The noise whorbled and shifted as the ultralight chugged overhead. Sal looked up at the wheels and the skeleton from below and saw the parachute billowing under the enormous force of the fan. He turned back to the bush now. Not remembering where he had left off, he was forced to respray the gashes. It was expensive stuff but he couldn't risk leaving even one untreated stalk. He was losing the sun now to boot. He'd like to sue the yuppie for the cost of the Roundup, but how would he ever find him?

The buzz had been fading but suddenly changed again. Sal gritted his teeth. He could hear the ultralight turning rapidly over the timber. He was going to come over *again*. The gun lurched in his hands and Sal splattered his leg with the herbicide. He wiped at the residue with his glove but he reeked of the stuff now.

Then a yawning silence cut through the motor. It was quiet suddenly and it struck Sal like a thunderclap. He wriggled himself free of the long tendrils around him and looked into the sky. The ultralight was pointed down but still sailing, the parachute open but the fan still. Sal had to step backwards, away from the timber to be able to see it clearly over the tree line. The ultralight cruised now, gently descending.

The machine was only twenty feet over the canopy when the motor suddenly roared to life again. Sal danced around to see through the trees. The ultralight pointed down and picked up speed, but the chute crumpled like a ball of paper. Sal felt his heart pound. Something was wrong. The machine dropped like an ice cube and disappeared from view, leaving only the terrifying sound of splintering wood followed by an even more terrifying silence.

Sal unclasped the buckles of the canister on his back and tossed off the tank. He ran as fast as he could in work boots. It barely seemed possible that he had just seen what he thought he had seen. It had happened without warning or notice; the thing had simply dropped. Sal got down and rolled under the barbed wire fence protecting the timber. If he had strung the fence it would have taken more time, but this section of the woods had been turned over to a government preservation program and they hadn't done such a good job. A sickening crunch under his foot startled him. A red reflector. A few feet over, like a snake, a dark timing belt, and next to it a metal plate, a manifold cover or something like that. The smell of gas kept Sal from approaching too quickly.

Though he had played near here as a child—his first tree house was around somewhere—Sal had not been this far back in the timber for years. It was silly, but if you declared some of your acreage a preserve, the government tended to leave you alone, even look the other way if you burnt leaves in the fall which you used to be able to do whenever you wanted before all the subdivisions came in and brought the precious asthmatics with it. A man couldn't even fish his own crick without a license anymore. And when Sal moved his farm machines—his combine or his tractor—from plot to plot, the subdivision people honked and cursed as they pulled past. Then at the end of the day they got in their noisy machines and admired his unspoiled land from the sky.

Sal moved cautiously over the damp gulch. Even the crickets and cicadas were conspicuously quiet. A blue heron's nest had been built somewhere in the center of one of the dead trees, but they weren't squawking either.

By the time Sal came upon the chassis, its nose buried in the mossy ground but the back end sticking up with the twisted fan still slowly spinning, he was having trouble breathing. The pilot was gone, as was the parachute. He must have escaped; he must have made it free at the last second. Sal was grateful to be spared the sight for moment, but as he stepped back something brushed against his face: yellow cord hanging from the trees. The woods were thickest here, tall oaks and some newly planted baby pine. He took a step back.

Daniel S. Libman

The chute had ripped to shreds and small scraps dangled everywhere from the canopy overhead. Colorful bungee cords hung like vines in a Sharper Image forest. The pilot was hanging from one of them, about five feet off the ground, wet and pulpy. It was too dim to make out the details, but Sal was pretty sure the overpowering metallic smell was blood. One foot was pointed in the wrong direction and a large branch had pierced his arm. He seemed to be mostly hanging from a tree by something poking through one of his thighs. A branch. There was something permanent about him, not like he had just dropped into that position, but deliberately placed, like an offering for some ancient God.

"Hey?" Sal said quietly.

That was foolish. Dead bodies didn't answer back and if this one wasn't dead it was going to be soon. But Sal did think he could hear something, a little gurgle from inside the body. The phrase "death rattle," came to him. Or maybe the pilot was still alive. But he wouldn't survive the night. He looked out at the tall dead trees beyond the clearing where Sal and Tilly, from another hill on the property, could observe the blue herons. It looked like the ultralight had plowed right through the nests. If the birds hadn't been killed they probably were so frightened that they might never come again after this. Did birds have memory like that? He wasn't sure.

It was nearly dark by the time Sal retrieved the canister and made it back past the shed to remove his work clothes. The house was bathed in grey, energy saving light. Tilly and Mikey were in the den. Mikey's TV shows were on now but they were still working on math figures. Sal could hear Tilly explaining something, could sense by the way the boy was breathing that he was not happy to be getting another lesson. But he wasn't protesting; he was a good boy. Neither of them said anything to Sal when he walked past the door. They hadn't seen it go down obviously, hadn't heard it. Something like this could traumatize a boy. Sal himself felt queasy in his stomach from the blood, the battered body.

Sal ran his finger up and down the phone. He didn't have a lot of medical knowledge but he had seen enough injured cattle, enough sick animals to know that even if he picked up the phone, dialed 911 and got everyone out here, the pilot was still going to die.

If Sal waited...people would search for him, take some time to find him, a day at least. The pilot's body would decay. It would make the papers about the condition of the corpse. But if he called now the other pilots would thank him for acting so quickly. They would think this was a safe place to fly, that the stupid farmer was watching out for you and would call an ambulance if you got into trouble. The farmer must not mind emergency vehicles tearing up his land. The pilot would be dead whether Sal made the call tonight or not. With the blunt pencil by the phone Sal struck a line through *multiflora rose* on Tilly's TO DO list.

After showering and picking out his nightclothes, Sal changed the television to the news channel. Mikey was in bed now and Tilly was folding laundry in the mudroom. He could wait a little while, let the guy dangle, and still call tonight. He wondered if he was doing the right thing, but a moment later knew it was a silly question. Surely not; but was it so bad that he could never be forgiven? He pulled the afghan to his chin and turned slightly so that the lamp wasn't directly in his eyes.

When he woke up it was dark in the living room. The news channel was still on but the volume was off which meant Tilly had gone to bed. It was 3:30 a.m. according to the VCR. He remembered the pilot and nearly jumped out of his skin. That was a terrible, terrible thing he had done not making the call. But if he phoned now it would raise questions. He was stuck; a bad decision to wait, but really he was stuck. He got into bed and spooned Tilly, who shifted a little but stayed asleep. He hadn't really *decided* not to call. He had been trying to make a decision about whether or not to call but fell asleep. Well, that was a hazard of flying over a farmer's land. Sometimes the landowner was going to be too tired to make a phone call to help you out. Sal grinned despite his nerves. He wasn't going to fall asleep, he could tell. He put his hand in Tilly's nightgown and reached around for her. He rubbed her for a time until she finally turned over. They were quiet and didn't turn on the light even when it was over and she got up to wash.

HE drifted in and out of sleep and got up when Tilly did, putting on fresh overalls in the dark. The smell of the fabric softener was pleasant but embarrassed him vaguely. In the kitchen he ate toast and the hard-boiled egg that Tilly had made for him. She smoked a cigarette.

"What're you doing in the morning?" she asked.

Sal chewed slowly. "Check the coon traps. Got to *release* anything I find," he said pointedly. Tilly had insisted he buy Have-A-Heart traps that held raccoons alive so that bleeding hearted farmers could return the predators back into the wild. Of course they would just come back and eat the crops and kill more chickens, which is why Sal had been indulging Tilly with the traps but then plugging the raccoons with the rifle when she wasn't around.

"Oh," he made sure she was paying attention now. "I've got to check the fence around the timber. I think the cows might have stomped through some of it." He imagined himself "discovering" bits of the ultralight and following the trail of debris into the woods and making his terrible discovery.

Tilly stubbed her cigarette. "I ask because I need the truck. It's a market day and me 'n' Mikey are volunteered with the PTA."

"Go ahead take it," Sal told her, pulling the straps on his overalls.

EVAN Rose breathed deeply. He held the air in his lungs and let it out slowly, waiting for the inner tranquility to arrive per dictum of his yoga teacher Dale Barkin. This was supposed to create harmony, inner peace, and since Evan was caught in his own wires, dangling off a tree, hanging over the ground, bone poking out of his skin *everywhere*, a little inner tranquility was due. Amazingly, it was the memory of the mistake that was most painful: he should have accelerated after the whip-stall, but he hadn't been able to make himself do it. It was basic: accelerate during free fall and get lift in the chute. He had trained and trained, but when the moment finally came he had let himself drop. And it wasn't just his pilot training that had failed him. His level of panic was also an indictment against the yoga classes. If he ever got back home, there was going to be an awful lot of litigation before this would be settled.

Evan was further surprised, but only momentarily, to see several frontier women of the early 1840's sitting in the box elder tree before him, arrayed like bird's nests. Pepper Parker was there and Caddie McGraw in her dark overcoat, and Polly the Beast with her pinched and severe expression under a wide-brimmed hat.

He attempted a wave and even though his arm moved, it didn't exactly wave. His fingers mostly wiggled and shot searing rivulets of pain up his arm.

"Ladies," he said instead, by way of greeting.

The frontier women hooted and cackled as was their way. Being dead for a hundred and fifty years hadn't dampened their mordant senses of humor any.

"Look-ee the mess Evan got hisself into now," Caddie McGraw hooted. Although you wouldn't call any of them exactly sensitive to the suffering of others—the trials of being frontier women pretty much beat that out of them—Caddie McGraw took particular delight looking at pain, famously replacing healing elixir with hair tonic just to watch the cowboys writhe in agony when being worked on by medicine men.

Ole' Grandma Bearsly lifted off a back branch and floated to Evan to get a closer look. She hovered inches from his face and scowled darkly.

"Foo-ool," she spat. "Now what you gonna do?"

Evan tensed; Bearsly did not suffer foolish behavior very long. She had stopped speaking to one of her own children because he had gone to New York City to study finances. Evan knew this, as well as facts from the lives of all the frontier women of the early 1840s from a book he had discovered on his mother's bookshelf when he was twelve years old. The photograph on the front was of Adelie Olson, reputed to be one of the fiercest frontier women of the era. In the grainy black and white picture, her eyes were like pits of tar and her hand clutched the barrel of a rifle, her fingers curled around the butt. A single bony finger was cocked and raised as if she was warning the photographer not to make any sudden moves.

In those days, he had casually played with himself while reading, ejaculating for the first time while staring into the empty eyes of Adelie Olson. He had been astonished, and even somewhat alarmed by the mess, but took solace in the bravery of the frontier women. In fact one of the women, Mariposa Sanchez, had actually whored her way through the wild west, killing some of the men and amassing a small fortune.

During adolescence the book had remained under his mattress where Evan took it out at night to read the exploits of the women and masturbate. As he grew older and became more experimental, using for his onanistic activities magazines containing women who were not only contemporary, but also not adorned in several layers of impenetrable fabric, he still kept his copy of Frontier Women of the Early 1840s and looked at it occasionally, the way a baby bird will return to the nest where it was born for security. Even now the book was still on his shelf at home where the occasional sight of its cracked binding could spring upon him a youthfully solid erection. So while in a way it was a surprise to see the women hovering in the trees, it was also true to form that they would show up now, with Evan moments away from what he was sure was his mortal coil shuffling. Since their bearing and firm countenances had brought him from childhood to manhood—many times—it was only fitting that the frontier women should be the ones to escort him into the next life as well.

"We've had a good run, ladies," Evan muttered.

Adelie Olson spat a wad of tobacco juice in his face, a move that had actually landed her in a jailhouse for two months when she did it to the mayor of Scubbs, Oklahoma.

"What gives, Adelie?" Evan asked, wishing he could move his arm enough to wipe the brown slime from his face.

She hovered close, baring her brown teeth. "If I'd a known you was such a snot, such a giver-upper, I wouldn't a never let you spunk on me." She turned her back to him.

"It's a bad spot I'm in, Adelie," he called to the retreating figure.

Maureen the Mick moved swiftly from her perch and touched a finger to Evan's face. The book had a photograph of her gesturing like this to a child in a classroom. She had been a teacher in Ireland and it was the only existing photograph of her. She later went on to live with the Navajos in the southwest where she became the first white woman to run school on a reservation. Her hatred for the American white man was fierce. If a wagon train rolled on Navajo land she encouraged the Navajos to beat their drums and ride around whooping until the settlers were too scared to continue. In one of his more intense fantasies, Maureen the Mick found Evan cowering in the corner of a wagon after having killed the driver, and took pity on him and gave him a hand job.

"Use my knife," Maureen the Mick now told him. She tossed her Swiss knife into the air where it landed cleanly in the carrying case on Evan's belt.

He began to protest. "Sorry Ms. Maureen. I appreciate the effort but I can't even move my—"

But his arm was moving. It felt cool now and he could see the faint outline of Bertie Hack clutching his arm and gently directing it to his belt. Evan could barely believe his luck. Unlike the other frontier women, Bertie Hack was a sickly, pale woman who became famous for enduring an entire wagon ride to California, only to be eaten by her own party during a snowstorm in the mountains near Big Bear. Her chapter was among the shortest in the book and had no photograph.

Bertie coughed. "Can you take the knife now?"

Evan moved his fingers and was surprised to be able to fumble with the snap.

"I think I've got it," he grunted. He looked away from Bertie's pallid face. He was ashamed of the way he thought of Bertie, mostly imagining her already dead and using the uneaten part of her hand to grip his cock. He didn't use that fantasy often, and if she was angered by it now, she didn't let it show. She manipulated his fingers now so that he clutched the knife.

"I've got a good grip on it," Evan grunted.

Two more hands enclosed his arm and raised it over his head. Evan screamed. He thought he might pass out from the pain.

Blackie Jennings was suddenly in front of him. She did a somersault in the air and then gripped his head in just the way rumor had it she was clutching her baby in her grave. Dying while pregnant, the legend was that after she and the baby were buried, she had reached into her own belly and delivered the child herself.

"Shhhh," she said. Blackie Jennings cradled Evan's head to her breast, the way same way he used to imagine her doing to him, their two bodies pressed together copulating in her coffin.

"It hurts," Evan muttered into her heavy bosom.

"Shhhh," Blackie whispered maternally. "Let us do our work. It's the only egress."

His arm was sawing through the bungee cord that kept him bound to the oak. He slipped a few feet down and Blackie Jennings muffled his scream before he could take a breath.

"A bit more," she cooed.

"I won't make it," Evan gasped. His heart was pounding and he could see the rocks and gnarled tree roots on the ground below.

"Be brave," Pepper Parker cautioned, buzzing inches from his feet. "We gonna catch you. Now!"

Evan cried out as he dropped, his arms and legs like sacks of sand. Suddenly they had him—the frontier women of the early 1840s had caught him just above the ground. Evan spun helplessly in their hoary grasp, and slowly they lowered him, face down, gently, to the earth. They placed him next to the back wheel of the ultralight.

When Evan raised his head the women were gone. A heron's cry startled him. Evan looked to see the prehistoric bird with its needle nosed beak take flight from a nest he had not been able to see in the dark. The sun was just coming up and he could see that he was in a glade, and his chute was in tatters, fluttering in the trees above him. He was disoriented but not uncomfortable. He thought for a second that this might be a nice place for a nap, until a ghostly boot appeared before him. Squinting into the sun he could just make out Adelie Olson, lip curled, looking as angry as she did on the cover of the book the very first time he had ejaculated on to it. Adelie leaned down as low as her stout frame allowed.

"Now git!" she screamed.

Evan bent his knee. His body was useless; worse, it was keeping him from moving. But he had one good arm and he clutched at the earth and moved himself a half foot. His stomach lurched and he followed, one jump, another, and another. He moved like a snake, and he could taste the grass and the dirt and it was about the most wonderful thing he had ever tasted in his life. He remembered to breathe, to use his yoga training whenever the pain became too intense. During one session Evan had managed to support himself on one hand. Sure, Dale Barkin had been next to him, steadying him when he teetered, but Evan had done it, and he would get out of this as well. He was thirsty. He needed water. And there it was, up ahead. A river. A sparkling, babbling river. He crawled another inch toward it.

No one would see him of course, but Sal practiced his response anyway. *My God*, he said out loud, imagining coming upon the wreck sight. *I'm going to get help!* He would turn and run back to the house. *Tilly, Tilly, call the police! Call an ambulance!*

Sal rolled under the barbed wire again and walked almost gaily toward the center of the timber. *No, I didn't hear nothing last night or the night before, but from the looks of it he musta been hanging for sometime. Is he going to make it?* He would be sure to use his countrified farmer tone, the way he talked at the feed store. Use *ain't* and drop Gs. It would make him disarmingly folksy.

It took him a few seconds to reckon what he was seeing at the crash site. The ultralight was still in place, the cords dangled from the maple trees. Where was the fucking pilot? Sal looked around like a silent movie thug. He *had* to be here! The grass was flattened at his feet. The guy might have fallen but he couldn't have crawled away, could he?

Sal followed the trampled grass. He approached on the tips of his feet, quietly, pushing the scrub weed out of his way as he went. Up ahead, nearly at the clearing, he saw a backpack, rising and falling, humping through the tall prairie grass like a nylon animal. He picked up a thick oak branch the size of a walking stick and approached gingerly. The pilot turned suddenly and looked right at him. Sal felt his jaw clench, and a shiver of disgust ran up his back, the same shiver he felt when the raccoons shrieked from the haymow: *We're here now, you can't stop us.* Sal forced himself to take a breath and tightened his grip on the wood in his hands.

One Indiscretion

ONE night, dark bedroom, a few months after the wedding, Colleen held Hen's penis while complaining vacantly about work. "No one accountable in Asia..." She was on her back with an arm stretched to his lap, lightly stroking with the side of her thumb every couple of sentences. Hen knew she was using her hand as a way of keeping his attention while she talked, but just the possibility that it might lead to something—even a distracted something performed as a courtesy— kept his attention riveted. He tried to be as quiet as possible.

After a few moments without speaking, Colleen said, "I used to have a crush on this girl Wendy. I don't know why I'm thinking of this now. I knew her in New York. She lived in my dorm. Once, she told me she liked women, and I got...aroused when she said that." Colleen moved her hand quickly for him and when it was over Hen told her, "That was great. I've never felt one like that before. All the way down—I know this is a cliché—but down to my toes! Something about the surprise of what you told me. And when."

"Glad you liked it," Colleen said.

"Is there more? Stuff you haven't told me about?"

"I'll save it for later."

Hen didn't want to seem too eager, but he thought about it the next day at work selling water filters and the whole time while they ate cold lasagna across from each other at the kitchen table. They watched a TV movie and Hen made popcorn with the air popper and warmed butter in a saucepan and mixed Parmesan cheese flakes into it and brought it out to her in their large wooden salad bowl. When they got into bed Hen kissed her on the neck and cleared his throat and casually said, "So...."

"I knew it," Colleen said. "Being so nice all night. You want to hear more about that woman."

"Just a few more details," Hen told her. "I've been horny all day. I hate that word, *horny*—doesn't seem right somehow, doesn't fit. How else do you say it? Turned on? That's not much better, but at least gets to it somehow—you can picture a switch that literally gets, quote, turned on.... But horny...where's that even come from? Let's leave it that your story was a real turn-on."

"It turns me on too," Colleen said. "Telling you about it. And we can keep talking about it as long as you don't tell anyone. Not that I'm ashamed, but it's private. I don't want your bar- buddies talking about me, and certainly no one in my family can know, especially not my sister because you know how she is with the religion."

"I promise, of course. I don't even have bar-buddies, as you know, so I think you meant it just as an expression. But whatever we discuss is just between you and me. Talking is the best part of a relationship."

"Yes," she said quickly. "I think so too."

"My parents were always shooshing me," Hen continued. In fact, *quiet* was their definition of a good boy. They'd say, 'You were a good boy today: real quiet.' And then give me a piece of cake or something. Positively reinforcing my quietness. Is that the right phrase, *positively reinforcing*? I've heard that before and always assumed I knew what it meant, but now that I use it in speech I'm not so sure it conveys—refers—to exactly the thing I'm thinking: that my parents liked for me to not talk."

"You've convinced me." She shifted and reached for him. "No pajamas tonight?"

"Too presumptuous?"

She took his penis and talked about the woman in college. Wendy, her name had been. She was tall with frizzed hair—brown and curled tight—and pretty green eyes. Colleen told Hen about how they were at a party in Brooklyn, she and Wendy, and there was some alcohol, and some pot.

"Could you speak this part more slowly? Huskier too, the way a smoker would."

She tried to slow it down a little. "The guy who was hosting the party got both of us, me and Wendy into his bed. Want me to describe him?"

"No. I'm just going to picture me."

"The guy didn't look anything like you, but I can see why you would want to do that."

Hen nodded quickly. "The story..."

Colleen continued. "All three of us were in the bed fooling around, but it was obvious that he was less interested in me than in Wendy, who was very good looking in a flashier sort of way. In fact, he finished himself off with her. At that point I took Wendy's hand and sucked some of her fingers, just to show him what he was missing. Wendy tried to pull back but I sort of yanked her to me then and put my mouth on hers. I even got my tongue in for a few seconds. When the kiss was over we just went to sleep and no one messed with anyone anymore."

"Any other...encounters with this woman?"

"Not really," Colleen said. "I guess we were a little too shy."

"Okay, then," Hen told her. "You keep doing what you're doing and I'm going to close my eyes and run that back."

When he was finished, Hen said, "That was something. Really something. I'm glad you told me about this. But I have a question, a clarification: do you feel bad about that guy because he was more interested in Wendy and not you?"

Colleen thought for a second. "A little maybe. I was hurt at the time, but I've gotten over it. I don't think about it much, apart from these last few nights." She shifted her weight back to her side of the bed. "Now do something for me. Tell me a story. Tell me about what you did with your other girlfriends."

He put his hand between her legs. "My first girlfriend was Fran. We met in high school and then took classes in junior college together and she went off to study in Michigan."

"Could you just go right to the sex?"

"We had to do it quietly in her house or mine and sometimes in the car. The first time we tried it was in the alley behind Ned

Duncan's parent's house. I don't know why we chose his house. I guess because of the alley."

"Hen. Please."

"It was winter and we had the heat on full blast and she took off her pants and her panties—now there's a dumb word, *panties*. It's too silly-sounding to be sexy, like every time you use it, even in a dirty context, you're winking at the person and saying, sorry but that's what they're called."

"So call them underwear."

"Okay. I took off her underwear myself."

"In a sexy way or just regular?"

"Just regular. And I got between her legs, which was very strange place to be, I remember. They were pressed on my bare skin because of the narrow space in the back seat. I couldn't get in because she wasn't at all aroused, not that we called it that."

"You don't like the word *aroused* either?" Colleen's voice was all edge.

"No, it's fine. I just mean it was too sophisticated for where we were in life. I think we said wet, if we even referred to it at all. It was a very difficult and discouraging evening."

"Then pick a different story, a different girlfriend. Go right to where you knew what you were doing."

Hen told her about Lisa and her thing about wearing garters and stockings and how she made him put baby powder in his ass because she didn't like the smell, and when Colleen reminded him that she just wanted details about the sex he said he couldn't remember too much. It had all been regular and average. Eventually he lapsed into a long silence, but kept his hand moving, and Colleen finished up anyway.

Hen asked, "You liked that? I want to ask because I'm curious, not to study it or analyze the life out of it. But when I was telling you those stories, were you picturing me with the women, Lisa and Fran, or were you picturing yourself doing those things to them, or was it just the women you were thinking about?"

"You and the women, just how you described. It was a turn-on to think about you doing those things. Don't ask me why. And you're right about it not being a good idea to think about it too much, or I might decide it's too weird."

Later in the week she told about a girl in camp when she was very young. They had ridden together on the bus for a trip somewhere, the zoo or maybe one of the many trips to the public pool. The girl and Colleen hadn't been friends because they were from different cabins and so different teams (Colleen's group was the Badgers and this girl's group she had no idea) but they ended up sitting together for some reason, Colleen on the aisle and the girl by the window, and of course they were both wearing shorts, and Colleen could remember the girl pressed her leg against Colleen's, and they rode like that the whole way, bare leg against bare leg. This was before they were at the age of shaving so their legs were smooth, skin-tight, and young, and the bus shook and shuttered, so their legs were rubbing, and Colleen said she could remember thinking that she should move over and give the girl more room, but she didn't want to break the contact so she didn't. Sometimes the bus would bump and make them separate for a second, and Colleen would slide closer until the other girl was squeezed between the window and Colleen. They never did talk. Colleen never even looked at her but she got the impression that the girl was uncomfortable and would have liked for Colleen to back off a little, but that just made Colleen press closer and even move her leg so there was more rubbing. Colleen wasn't even really sure who the girl was, so she couldn't sit next to her again, and even if she had known, it really wasn't good form to not sit with the other Badgers unless circumstance made it so you couldn't, like it had on that day.

Hen also liked hearing about how Colleen had sexual feelings for one of her co-workers, a tall woman named Ruby who was really competent with numbers and all the vendors admired. Colleen and Ruby had traveled to many places together, Europe and Asia. A few times because of various problems, Colleen and Ruby had to share a room, and once they shared a bed. Nothing at all had ever happened, but Colleen found herself surreptitiously watching this woman when she dressed or did her stretching exercises in the mornings.

"Did you have any...what's the word? Urges toward her?" Hen asked.

Colleen thought a minute. "Not really, I guess. I mean, not at all. But, that doesn't titillate so much to say that."

"Let me just think about her," Hen said nobly. "Just keep going with what you're doing and let me think about her...."

In about a week, they had run through her near misses and female crushes, and everything she had stored up. Hen asked her to make something up.

"I see a girl and we're both wearing shorts and we're next to each other in a movie theater," she said. "The movie starts and our legs brush against each other."

"This is the girl-on-the-bus story again, only now you're older and in a movie theater."

"But this time I'm going to go in the bathroom stall and she'll follow me."

"Oh, okay. That's good. Tell me what she looks like, and say it slowly."

Colleen lowered her voice to a whisper. "She's got frizzy blonde hair, and green eyes."

"You're giving me the same description as Wendy."

"Wendy had brown hair, and the one in my story now is blonde."

"Yeah, but the word *frizzy* is too similar. I'll just picture who I want. A movie star, but I won't say her name because I know you don't think she's talented. Is that okay?"

"All right, I guess. If it does the trick. So she follows me into the bathroom stall and then we kiss. And then we do it."

"Describe it, give me details."

"I can't give you exact details. I don't know the logistics."

Colleen took her hand off him, and Hen looked over. Even though his eyes had adjusted to the dark, he still couldn't see the expression was on her face.

"You tell me a story now," she said. "Since you're not into what I'm saying. Maybe it'll give me some ideas for my stories."

"Okay. Well, Lisa was a fantastic kisser—"

"I don't want to hear that," Colleen said quickly. "It's too intimate.

Just tell me about sex with her. What did she do?"

"Just the regular stuff, mostly. I would come up from behind her and hold her breasts and kiss her neck. She liked that."

"You do that with me. Do you just have a set of standard moves that you always use?"

"Actually, yes," he said.

"Did anything unusual ever happen?" Colleen asked. "Ever pay for it?"

"With a prostitute?"

"I guess that's the only way you can pay for it," Colleen said.

"No," Hen answered. "But I always really wanted to, and I almost did once."

"What stopped you?"

"Don't get mad, but it was the night before we got married."

"What stopped you?"

"I had the *Free Weekly* and they had all these ads for escorts. I almost called, but then I thought maybe the police put in a fake ad or two to catch people. I didn't want to get into any trouble. Are you sure this doesn't bother you, especially since it was the night before our wedding?"

"Prostitution doesn't bother me anymore, since I started traveling for work. I've seen all sorts of women doing all sorts of things for money. Some hotels—some of the nicest ones—have hookers in the lobbies." Colleen exhaled loudly. "Sometimes when I'm alone in the evening I think about those women down in the lobby and I get pretty hot and bothered. I've thought about it: going up to one and paying her to come back to my room."

Hen repeated, " 'Hot and bothered.' Isn't it something how dumb this all sounds when you put into words? But getting back to what you said about being hot and bothered. You understand the impulse, then. Because to be honest, I drove to the bridge on North Avenue that same night. And I was all set to do it, talked myself into it, and the girls were there, walking back and forth. But the first problem was that I didn't know how it all worked. How do you get a hooker standing on the bridge into your car? Do you stop traffic? Do you honk, wave, wink? I didn't know. Also, I thought, what if someday someone asks me if I've ever been with a prostitute? Just like you just did. If I had gone through with it, I couldn't say no. Or I could deny it, but then I would have to lie, and I'm terrible at lying. I always pause, or shift my eyes, or something like that. And if I ever told the truth about it, like if I was drinking with someone and the subject came up, or maybe a psychiatrist if I ever had to go to one, then I'd have to convince that person that I'm really a good man, who just happened to have visited a prostitute once. And then whoever I told might tell someone else, but not explain how I was really a good man but had succumbed to a curiosity just that once. You wouldn't want your whole life represented by one indiscretion."

Colleen shifted and grabbed his penis. She held it tightly the way she would a hammer.

"Do it now," she said sharply. "I want you to go get a prostitute and tell me what happens."

"Okay," he said.

"I don't want you to make a habit of this, and you can never ever have an affair or sleep with someone I know. But you can go and find a clean woman, use a condom, and pay her to have sex with you."

"What would she look like?" Hen asked.

"I don't know," Colleen said in her normal voice. "Whatever you like. Not too young."

"Wait a second," Hen reached down and stroked her hand slightly hoping she might let go or soften her grip. "This is just bedtime talk, right? You aren't serious?"

"I'm one hundred percent for real."

"You talk big now," Hen said. "But after I do it you'll get jealous or mad."

"I don't think I will. We've been married less than a year and I know you had sex with plenty of people before. One more isn't going to hurt, and especially if she's a hooker and you pay for it."

"It's too weird. I haven't had sex with plenty of people, and I'm sorry if that disappoints you. If I inventoried right now...I have problems coming up with an exact figure because that word *sex* is too vague these days, does it only cover coitus or does it include anything? Anytime I was with someone and came? Because sometimes, early now, high school and college, especially the summer before college right after high school, I was doing a lot of groping with a neighbor girl who was older than me and sometimes I ended up—half the time she didn't know it—but we'd be making out I would just start—"

"Hen."

"I'm sorry and I appreciate the opportunity, and I know a lot of guys would give their left arm to have a wife so understanding, but I just couldn't. What if she did those corn-ball movie things like calling me baby, or saying I was real big? It would ruin it all for me. Or what if my hands started to sweat? You know how clammy they get when I'm nervous. And God, what if she's a cop! If it gets into the papers I've sold my last water filter, that's for sure."

Colleen left the bed and seconds later Hen heard the shower going. He smoothed the comforter on his chest. She was mad and not saying it. When she got back she spent a few seconds arranging her pillows, pulling some of the comforter her way, fiddling in the dark with objects on her night stand. Hen concentrated on not making any noise, being as still as possible, trying not to upset her.

Married But Looking

What do you expect, one is what one is, partly at least. —Beckett

It starts with a house on fire. Love is often called a house on fire, and it's true: love can start small and burn for a lifetime, or it can be stamped out but smolder unseen, raging back to life on the whisper of a breeze. But this is the other kind of house on fire: the kind that includes a frantic call to 911, pumper trucks screaming down the streets, and neighborhood kids dancing rapturously in flashing lights.

"This is from your basement wall." The biggest of the firemen holds up a gnarled chunk of wood, leans in close to be heard. "See what I mean?"

Silvers doesn't. "Yes I do," he says.

"What I'm talking here, the singeing going through the grain. Slow, smoldering cancer."

Silvers is nauseated, can keep from throwing up only by talking. "Sorry to get so many of you out here for something this small."

Yellow reflector tape gleams in stripes around the fire suit, makes him look like a shimmering demi-god. "It's only small because we removed what was spreading in your floorboard. Know what a back draft is? Don't catch this thing early you lose everything."

"I'm sorry," Silvers repeats. He apologizes the next day to his insurance agent's secretary and then again after the beep when she puts him through to voice mail. He apologizes to the contractor, actually an older neighbor who's handy and owns tools and seems to be enjoying himself.

"Not a problem," Bill indicates with his head for Silvers to hold the end of the measuring tape. "I can get new drywall up in a half day. Lick a paint, lick a paint, spackle. If you help, Guy, why we get the whole thing done in a weekend."

When the adjuster phones, Silvers begins apologizing all over again. "Oh gosh," he says when he hears the settlement figure. "It's too much."

"Mr. Silvers, the Work Order lists you as needing a new door and a new frame. Those sidelights on the right have to be replaced, new basement ceiling tile, plus a contractor's labor...."

"My neighbor Bill's going to do the work. For free—well, beer. He already fixed the door, which only needed propping, and he cut a threshold from wood lying around his garage. Some paint on the frame, a lick, and I have half a can leftover from last summer. As for the basement, the sheetrock already had holes in it, so I wonder if maybe the claims inspector looked in the wrong place."

A sigh. "That's the amount County in-sure is issuing Mr. Silvers, whether you elect to get the repairs or not. Check's already dispatched so the case folder is officially closed, unless you decide to contest the settlement in which case you have a year to file an additional claim. As for the money itself, if you decide not get the work done, go ahead and do whatever you want with it."

I⊤ is Valerie who suggests Paris, who arranges for her parents to baby-sit the children for the week, and who invests in a Rick Steves. It's not nearly enough for a four-star hotel or first-class airfare, but Silvers does manage to book well enough in advance that they can be alone in a row that has only two seats and extra leg room. Silvers works diligently on a Sudoku while Valerie reviews from a phrase book. *Un ver de l'eau*, she mutters. *L'addition, s'il vous plait. On attend tres longtemps pour notres plats, monsieur.* He looks over at her from time to time, finally noticing red lines fracturing the whites of her eyes.

"Have you been crying?" Silvers asks.

"No," she reaches into her carry-on for a bottle of Visine. "The bad air on the plane is drying me out."

She trades the bottle for a large pair of dark sunglasses, despite the fact that the shades are drawn and the cabin is depressingly dim.

Silvers suggests Rock-Paper-Scissors, which Valerie goes along with despite a mild embarrassment that Silvers can read even through the opaque lenses. They trade a few victories back and forth, and then after a long string of ties (scissors, rock, rock, scissors, rock), Valerie announces, "I'm going to throw paper next. Paper."

She pumps once but pauses when Silvers doesn't make any motion.

"You don't trust me?"

Silvers crunches the possibilities. If she is telling the truth then he should match her paper with scissors to win, but if she's lying—too strong, if she's *being tricky*–then she'll know he's about to throw scissors to cut her paper, so she'll throw rock to blunt scissors and he'll lose. In order to win, he's got to be the one to throw paper to wrap her mendacious rock.

Silvers pumps. "Rock, paper, scissors...."

His hand comes out flat and so does Valerie's. Both are showing paper.

"You should have trusted me," she teases without much interest. "You would have won."

Three hours later they are in Paris.

HER fluency in French is something Silvers always *knew*, the way a manager knows what college an employee attended from reading a résumé. But it isn't until he sees her in action, checking them in at the hotel, giving locations to cab drivers, arguing about stamps in the post office, that Silver really gets it. It's impressive to him, like going to a casino with someone you've known all your life and finding out they can count cards. Silvers finds himself enjoying the unusual feeling of total reliance.

"Ask the waitress for water when she comes back," he tells Valerie. "No gas."

As with all the cafés on the street, a row of tables has been positioned tightly under an awning, edging over the lively sidewalk. Silvers and Valerie sit on one side, shoulder to shoulder so they can watch the street as they pick over lunch.

"I've never been to a place more geared for human interaction,"

Silvers says between bites of a crusty ham sandwich. "When you hear a horn honking, half the time the driver is just waving to someone he knows on the sidewalk. Even the cigarette smoking, which I normally object to, is just part of this whole conviviality."

Valerie sips at her espresso, her dark glasses silently facing the intersection.

"It's a good trade, cigarette smoke for conversation," he continues. "I'd be willing to put up with more of it if it meant we could sit for hours talking."

Valerie dips a sugar cube into her cup and then sucks at it. This afternoon she is wearing her dark blazer with the sharp white piping, because, as she told Silvers before they left, one should "dress it up a little" in Paris. It wasn't like walking around their neighborhood in Chicago where one could look like a vagrant and still be welcomed in a nice restaurant. Silvers had left all his shorts and gym shoes at home in favor of tan khakis and earth-toned walking shoes.

"Also, I'm not the first to say this—" he wipes his mouth with the back of his hand— "but have you noticed how beautiful everyone is here? Women and men. But the women here are particularly incredible. Have you noticed? Where do these women go during the day?"

She turns her dark lenses toward him.

"That one walking her dog, for example. She's gorgeous. You telling me that somewhere in some office she sits down and answers phones or puts price tags on ashtrays in some store? Ashtrays are probably a big seller here. And there's another one across the street, and look, that one on the bike! Where are they housing all these women?"

When the waitress comes, Valerie crisply tells her to clear the plates, bring another glass of water, and tabulate the bill. Surprised, Silvers moves quickly to finish his sandwich.

"Want to hear my theory?" He leans in while chewing. "Because it's Paris, the most beautiful, sophisticated women in the world are drawn here for fashion work and such. Then they breed, and this has been going on for centuries. It's the only way to account for the quantity of stunning people. Men too, Val. Hey, I'm mostly trying to be funny here. No?"

"I'm getting tired."

In fact, since they bought the Paris Museum Pass, Silvers had been dragging them around trying to maximize the fee. They saw the Louvre on the first day as well as the L'Orangerie and then the next day he made her go immediately to the D'Orsay, the Hotel of the Invalides, and the Musée Rodin.

"I'm going to spend the afternoon in the hotel room," she tells him crisply. "I'm going to take a nap. You don't mind do you?"

Actually he is glad for it. Having read a bit about *flânerie*, Silvers harbors a fantasy of being—for one afternoon—a man of leisure, walking around the city aimlessly, letting himself be swept along by what interests him. Crossing the street, they hold hands as far as the lobby of the hotel. Silvers watches her in the window chatting with the desk girl before taking her key. Even though the hotel employees speak English, Valerie speaks in French and Silvers again marvels at her ability, this confidence that he's been so unaware of. All he can do is make dumb observations about cigarettes and beauty from his outsider perspective.

It's a struggle to keep himself paced to a brisk walk. He feels like the kid running through Paris at the end of *The 400 Blows*. Or was that at the beginning? The kid runs at the end of the movie, he recalls, but not in Paris. In the beginning is when you see the city streets, but that kid isn't running on them, right? In any event, even with the laminated Smart-Map, Silvers soon finds himself lost among the narrow walkways and intersections tucked in all the grand, wedding-cake buildings. Rue Montmartre becomes Boulevard Haussmann without actually turning, Rue de la Chaussée morphs into Rue Blanche and before Silvers locates it in on the Smart-Map, he's walking Rue Jean-Baptiste. He spends more time in the map then he does on the streets, folding then unfolding, orienting himself, forgetting the names of the intersections in the time it takes him to read a street sign and then get the map unfolded. Earlier Silvers had joked to Valerie that they should just officially rename the city, "Rick Steve's Paris," but now Silvers seems to be the only tourist on this curvy little Avenue Frochot, lost and unsure of himself. Up ahead is

Pigalle, a district that rings a bell from his reading, and Silvers finds himself *flânering* a bit faster toward the lights.

Facebook. Inbox. (3) Messages for Valerie Silvers. Reply.

My Dear Scudder, I didn't mean to get you to change your official home profile picture, though I must admit the new one is much better and if I have to write only to a photo I'd rather it be this. You look younger—maybe ten years away from college, though of course you were already older—a grad student!~in our venerable ol' acting department.

Yes, mon cher, I am still in Paris, and no I did NOT not write you because I've forgotten you (hardly!) but because Guy has kept me so busy during the day that it's been difficult to steal a few minutes to be alone. :>(This day he allowed me an afternoon, and here I sit in chamber 39 of the Hotel Vivienne, the finest two-star hotel we could afford on Guy's insurance settlement. Actually it's not too bad, I have a balcony with a view of the Bourse and much of *l'arrondissement deuxième* where my husband wanders at this very minute, probably getting whiplash in an effort to take in the beauty of "gay par-ee." Ever notice how beautiful French women are? Guy maunders endlessly about the women we pass on the street, staring after each backside in the most undignified manner. Perhaps he even thinks he's being amusing as he regales me with his ideas on how the French became such luscious hotties. (It has to do with "breeding.")

So as you can imagine I was very happy to see you (and your new pic!) in my box. :>) (I know, there I go again with the saucy double-entendre. ;>)) And lest you ever think you were ever far from my mind while maintaining radio silence, I have something to tell you which will prove quite the contrary.

I don't know if you ever heard of Walter Benjamin, but I had to read about him in one of those auditorium classes one takes to round out the Gen Eds. He's a philosopher who wrote about small things being more important than the large ones, a thing taking on an inverse significance to its size. (He's on my mind since discovering this hotel abuts one his beloved Arcades.)

So, I was in the Maille Mustard shop across from the monstrous Church of the Madeleine on Boulevard des Capucines. Guy was ecstatic about all the varieties, because, as he reminded me several times, he's really a "big fan" of mustard. He was asking me to translate one label after another, and though my French has reappeared in a rather muscular fashion, I couldn't help the feeling of being miserably yoked to such an undignified display of hick-xuberance, as though this were the first time he'd been allowed off the farm. Before we went I asked him several times to try to learn a little bit of useful French, a phrase or two here and there, what to say in restaurants, that sort of thing. And while it might not have helped in the Maille where even *I* strained to decode some of the more complex labels, he might have at least made that one slight gesture to me, one small indication that we were going on a vacation together, instead of putting me in his employ as his personal valet and translatrix.

While I was dwelling on all this, there I happened to spy a small clay mustard pot which reminded me of you for many reasons, not the least of which is its vague resemblance to a heart, and the warmth I felt while holding it, imagining myself placing it into your hands someday filled me with a sudden— oh, not to be over dramatic about it—but a sudden *broader sense of purpose* as Walter Benjamin might have put it. (But I don't think did.)

It's a burgundy mustard filling your clay pot—you recall sharing a bottle of cheap Burgundy with me under the bleachers near the running track in college. Has it really been so long since we were at school?! I thought I would have a trophy case full of Academy Awards and you were going to be a famously prickly but talented visionary, directing me in films and Broadway. Now I'm in France on insurance money and you're waiting tables. (I know, you're manager at a swanky joint. Still...) But listen, though we haven't seen each other in over a decade, and won't again in god knows how long, you should know Scuds, when our paths do cross, in five years or ten or even twenty, I will place that mustard pot into your hands. I'll be saving it for you until then, hiding it from the world, keeping it safe, for that time when we should meet again in some more corporeal milieu than this damned website.

Don't make me wait too long to hear from you. ~V

THEY spend the next morning in Pére LaChaise, stepping on the cobblestone walkways, touching tombstones and monuments. At first they wander aimlessly, awed by the names on the stones in front of them, but then Silvers buys a guide and scans an alphabetical list of the dead.

"No Beckett," he tells her.

Valerie is tracing the flat surface of a grave with her palm. "No," she tells him. "Beckett's in Montparnasse. Why are you looking for him?"

"You have his books, I remember. You like him, right?"

Her face softens as she nods. She playfully takes his arm and Silvers, feeling suddenly confident and happy, leads her along to Rossini and then Proust and then Wilde.

"I have to admit I feel a little disappointment at each one," Valerie says, stepping carefully toward Chopin's elaborate monument.

Silvers has felt that too. "Because you want to see the actual people." He gazes into the eyes of a cement angel poised over a chiseled musical score. "But they're not here, of course. Not the body of work you admire. Not even the corpses anymore, really."

Valerie looks up from the inscription. "But for the composers at least, you can hear the music. That's a gift. I'm hearing a mazurka in my head. Number four, in A flat minor. Opus eight. You know that one? Bah dah deee..."

Silvers considers, nods. "I like that sentiment. Hey, you think all those dopes hovered around Jim Morrison have his crap in their heads?"

She makes a face, and then she is laughing. They have always had this together, a shared disdain for things everybody else likes. He reaches around for her and croons in a low voice, "*This is the end... my friend... doo-bid-ee doo... the end...*"

Valerie wriggles free. "Stop! I don't want drug music crowding out Chopin."

Silvers continues singing, "*The blue BUS is calling US...*"

Valerie gives him a small shove. Earlier in the morning they walked to the cemetery through a depressing neighborhood along Avenue de la Republique, and Valerie was whistled at, so Silvers took her hand to pull her along faster. Both of them had been rattled and nervous. After a few seconds Valerie had wriggled free of his grip because his hand was moist. Now she laces her fingers in his and they're both laughing, he deliberately mangling lyrics, "*Girl could we get the funeral PYRE any HIGHER,*" and she pretending to be in worse physical pain upon hearing each one.

Back near the gates they mutually agree it's best to not walk through the questionable neighborhoods, but disagree about whether they should take a cab (Valerie) or the bus (Silvers). They're near a stop on the #69, which is listed in the Rick Steves as being the best public transportation route for seeing the sights.

"And rubbing elbows with locals," Silvers points to the page in the open guidebook.

Only once they're actually on the bus Silvers notices that nearly every "local" is clutching a Rick Steves. They ride as far the Rue de Rivoli.

"My feet hurt," Valerie says irritably as they walk through Les Halles toward Hotel Vivienne. "I've had about enough for the day."

"It's those fancy shoes you brought. Anyway it's not walking, it's *flâneuring,*" he tells her. "We're strolling Paris, just like intellectuals have been doing for centuries. Not that we're intellectuals by any stretch."

Valerie's lips thin. "Fine," she snaps. "But when we get back to the room I'm going to rest. You go wander around—*flâneur*—by yourself."

In the hotel lift she tells him, "You know you don't need to shout. They speak French, they're not deaf."

"What do you mean?" The lift creaks and shudders its way to the sixth floor.

"*Trent-neuf! Trent-neuf!* You shout it like a child begging for ice cream."

Silvers shoves the lift doors open, deflated. Along with *bier* it was the only French he had picked up, and it was true, he did ask for the room key with a tad more exuberance than the interaction called for.

Valerie opens the small window so the breeze comes in but the heavy curtains still keep the room dim. Silvers stays by the door. He's looking forward to his afternoon walk and doesn't want to get caught in the bickering that seems to be brewing. Still he can't help taking a shot.

"Your dream vacation is walking back and forth from the tub to the bed in some hotel room, going out occasionally for protein and sugar."

"Hmmmm," she gives him a dreamy smile while taking off her shoes. "Why are you taking your backpack?"

"I want to sit and read in a cafe like they do. Not sure what though. Hemingway? Queneau? Might be fun to read *Zazie on the Metro* on the metro."

Valerie settles herself on the bed, arm draped over her face, shielding her eyes. "Leave your laptop," she tells him softly. "I might want to go online."

Silvers pauses.

She stirs awkwardly. "It's been a couple of days and I want to catch up a little."

He feels something go hot and then fingers of ice moving up and down his spine. More than anything he'd like to not say what he's about to say but he can't help it and it's done before he can stop it. "Are you...you're not E-mailing him here, are you?"

Valerie looks wounded. "Take your laptop."

"You didn't answer me. Here too? On our vacation!"

"No, Guy. I am not. Take it with you."

He makes a conciliatory face even though she's not looking. "I just want the books," he says, reaching for the top paperback from the pile on her bedside, unsure what it even is. "I'll leave you the laptop."

She says quickly, "Remember, I was going to check if they have standby seats at the *Comédie Francaise?*"

He kisses the arm lying over her eyes. "You can still rally and take a walk with me. It's our last day here."

"When you come back we'll walk around Saint Germain. I'll be rested."

"Ever," he says. It's coming out edgier than he'd like. "We're not ever *ever* ever going to come here again. So you shouldn't spend your last afternoon *ever* in Paris up in this shitty room by yourself. Could be your last chance to use your French."

"Maybe you'll flood the basement someday. Guy, let's not fight. Give me an hour or two to rest and I'll be sharp for tonight."

The sad little lift and threadbare carpeting in the hall reminds Silvers that he lost some ground with her, and anyway, walking across the lobby he sees the bank of computers provided for guests. He can't keep her from doing what she wants. The ice water in his arms and legs begins to ebb only out on Rue Vivienne as Silvers pulls the pack straps tight across his shoulders and chest. The streets are less crowded, rain a distinct possibility, and he walks in the same general direction as the day before. He lets his hand brush against the smooth stone of the buildings on Rue Lafayette, walking through the late afternoon espresso crowd.

In front of a brasserie Silvers takes a wide berth, avoiding two shaggy men who have stopped to exchange drawn out cheek-kissing. He's jealous of the free-flowing amiability the French reserve for each other but withhold from everyone else. All those Eric Rohmer movies he crammed had given Silvers a false sense that he was, if not French, at least someone who could be recognized by the French as a sympathetic spirit. If he can find someone who would speak to him in English he can explain that he isn't like his countrymen: Silvers understands the debt owed by every American for the statue of Liberty and soft cheese and the Enlightenment. Jealousy ripples each step he takes now, jealousy of the French and jealousy of Valerie. It's true that he is only pressing his nose against the window, peeking in on Valerie's vacation. She walks around with a royal letter of introduction and he is, at best, her valet.

But it's different in Pigalle, where Silvers now finds himself striding under porn marquees, ignoring the Irma la Douces calling to him from storefront windows.

Alloo sir! How are yooo Mister...

Silvers waves and keeps walking. Pigalle is the one place in Paris where people will talk to him, where he is wanted. Here Paris feels like those old Doisneau photographs, edgy but inviting. The sky has prematurely purpled, the rains are coming finally, and all the light has gone gauzy and tawdry; it seems to be coming from headlights and street lamps as in a faded postcard. Silvers soaks it in slowly, savoring the feeling of attention.

"Hey you."

A warm hand on his arm, fingers soft like dinner rolls. "Remember me? You are the American from yesterday. 'I don't speak French,' remember?"

Silvers is amazed. "Mona?"

Mona wears an even tighter top than the day before, brown and slinky, and her stomach pooching out in a sexy, inviting manner.

"That's right. You remember me," her eyes twinkle, not exactly with joy but with a sort of satisfaction. She digs deeper with her nails and when he tries to pull his arm back, twists so that he's looking directly into her cleavage. "Tell me your name."

"I don't want to, Mona."

"Ahh..." she rolls her eyes comically. Her accent is strong and she makes her lips into an overly fake pout. "Make zee name up," she tells him.

"Uhm. Yorick."

Throaty laugh, like a low gurgle. "Very good, Yorick. I like this name." She reaches up and cups his chin, long nails tickling his stubble. "I know you well, poor Yorick. Forty Euro I can know you much weller. Eh?"

"Forty Euro? It was 30 yesterday."

"For Yorick the fool I reduce price. Okay, 30. For 30 you come in and I show you around the club and the nice girls. Lots of girls and I will show you."

"If I wait until tomorrow it'll be 20."

"Twenty then," she leans and whispers, holding his arm now with both hands. "Don't tell my boss inside."

"I need to think about it," he struggles to break her grip. "I'll come back." Thumping bass comes from inside the Moulin Raunch, as does the smell of cigarettes and *bier*. The other girls on the street— seemingly as ubiquitous as café tables near his hotel—make catcalls, insulting him or maybe offering Mona encouragement

"I'm bringing you in now, Yorick," Mona tells him. Taking hold of the strap of his backpack, she pulls him slowly like a small poodle, and Silvers walks with her.

Facebook. Inbox. (1) Messages for Valerie Silvers. Reply.

My Dear Scudder: I'm glad too that you remember our "date" under the bleachers with the Burgundy. Those are good memories, and while they don't match 100% with mine, I acknowledge that's what a memory is, the infinite representation of a finite moment. (That's W. Benjamin again, this time talking about M. Proust.) And while in my most ugly moments I think that you have confused me with another girl, I do acknowledge at least I was living in DeKalb that summer, even if I can't quite remember that rainstorm, seeing that movie with you, or owning that kind of car. 'Course, m'dear old Scudder, it would be a lie for me to tell you that I ALWAYS think back to what happened between us with what you called, "warm fuzzies."

Fuck it, Scuds. I'm feeling guilty. Guy asked me about you again—not exactly, but let's just say "it came up," and that for a moment you were as present in this room as all the Parisian femmes who turn his head. And I lied to him. I told a bald-faced, plebeian, lie. You and I have not heard each other's voices, not touched, not set eyes upon each other apart from these awful stamp-sized avatars in over 10 years. So then why do I squirm when the subject of our communications comes up? It's to spare Guy, I used to think, because he would get upset if he knew, and he doesn't need to get upset because *nothing* is happening. I dissemble to protect.

Daniel S. Libman

But then I think of that badger.

You remember I chose to inhabit the body of a badger for Animal Pantomime Workshop? I borrowed your Apple IIe to copy out everything I knew about badgers: grist for the actor's mill, as I believe we said in those days. You were dubious about why I needed a computer just to "get down" some ideas about badger-performance. Rightfully—as it turns out—so. Mostly I desired an evening in your apartment, which I remember with some delight, ended about the way I wanted it to. ;>)

Funny now the badger returns. As I wrote that night, all I knew from badgers was that in Plum Creek, one of the Little House on the Prairie books, Laura writes about succumbing to a temptation to visit a deep swimming hole which surely would have swallowed her entirely, calico dress and all. She is saved by a hissing badger, which blocks her path and frightens her to running back home where "Pa" tells her that once one is no longer trusted, one must be watched.

So I say to you what I say to myself and what I should have said to Guy: I am doing nothing wrong; we are doing nothing wrong. If anyone is going to get hurt, it's me for starting back up with you, for unlocking so much of what has long been hidden, for bringing it out into the light of day and exposing it to you. For ignoring the atavistic hiss I can hear in my head.

You are in Ohio, not really holding my hand in the Tuileries, not really offering an encouraging push as I trot in heels to keep up with Guy so he can get to the Louvre while the backpack check-in line is short. Write me and reassure me that I'm right about this, that we're doing nothing wrong, And write me soon.
—V

It takes a moment or two for his eyes to adjust to the darkness. Mona has the Euros crumpled in her fist and passes it on to a dark man just inside the curtain. His face is blotchy and round as a dinner plate, and his lips quiver knowingly before shooting Silvers a final look and disappearing behind another curtain. In fact, Silvers sees now that the narrow space is full of curtains, like a poorly conceived haunted house. Mona winks on her return, flips her curly hair over her face like a hood, takes his hand and pushes them through another set of curtains, behind which is a tiny stage, a foot off the ground and about as wide as a phone booth. It's gloomy and hot behind all this fabric, and it takes Silvers a moment before he sees the three benches arranged like a triangle around the small riser. Mona lights two table candles on the stage, giving the room an odd, flickering red caste, and arranges Silvers on one of the narrow benches, setting his backpack next to him. She takes both his hands and kneels in front of him, arms draped casually on his khakis. After offering a brief sexy smirk, she pushes herself between his legs, but stays back near his knees.

"We start for 40 Euros," she says loudly to be heard over the thumping bass.

"I just paid you."

She strokes his hands with her thumbs. "That gets you in the door, Poor Yorick." She puts a hand on his thigh. "With the 40, you'll get what you want."

"You don't know what I want."

She laughs, running her finger down his arm before squeezing his hand. "Of course I do. And you can have *eeet* for 40."

"We're going...all the way?"

Mona scrunches her face. "All the way? What means this? I still study my English mornings so I don't know all the words. 40 Euro you will be happy."

He reaches into his pocket and brings forth only the top two bills. Mona hops up as soon as she has the money and pivots behind one of the curtains, leaving Silvers alone with the two empty benches and his backpack. He's nervous now, wondering if he could even figure out which curtain leads to the exit if he has to run, like if Mona suddenly pulls a gun or if there is a fire. He clutches the strap atop his backpack. Valerie is probably just now getting out of the tub. He can still leave, cut his losses, no one will ever know. Everything would still be exactly as he left it at the Hotel Vivienne. He doesn't have to go through with this. Silvers vigorously wipes the sweat from his face as Mona reappears from behind a curtain, holding out a small glass of yellow beer.

"One *dreenk* minimum. But I buy for you. For Yorick I know well. I buy it for 10 Euro."

He takes one sip—it's warm and flat—before putting it on the bench. He thinks suddenly of the warnings to women to never to drink from an open container given by a stranger. His passport is in the hotel and all he has is a pocketful of European money. He suddenly wonders how they'll know to contact Valerie if he's discovered face down in the Seine.

"Say Mona—"

"I will return."

She's gone another eternity, during which Silvers zips and unzips a couple of pockets on the backpack as though trying to find something. If he's being watched he doesn't want to appear as miserable or as nervous as he actually is. Silvers jumps when the music gets loud and Mona is in front of him suddenly wearing only a bra and panties and a little gold chain around her waist. He leans back on the bench, glad that at least it's a solid wall behind him. He's nervous, and she dances very slowly in front of him, mostly putting her weight on one foot then the other like a cat working over a pillow before settling down to sleep. It's so dim he can barely make her out, but he thinks she is pretty and it is sexy and he smiles politely.

"Oooh la la. Right Yorick?"

Silvers glowers. "I don't think like that! I know you French don't say *ooh la la* and I know you don't laugh through your noses. I'm not some schmoe tourist."

"*Eeet's* okay," she says soothingly, stepping forward to sit on his lap, nudging the backpack a few inches away to make room. Her bare legs rub against the khakis, and she brushes her kinky hair against his face.

"I'm not one of those Freedom Fryers," he says directly into her ear. "I know French fries are from Belgium. Give me *some* credit."

Mona steps back off his lap but keeps her gaze on him. "I give you a leeettle credit. Come on now Yorick. You're ready for some real fun. I need 80 Euros from you."

"That's it for the 40? You said I would get what I wanted."

"You only paid 30 because I had to buy the drink for 10. Geev me

80 Euro you get me in the back room. Very private, very fun."

"80 Euros? I mean, with the exchange rate...it's really quite a bit of money. And for the 80 do we actually, do you promise we'll do it?"

"I can't understand your meaning with my English," she says brashly. "You *will* be happy. That I know. Don't you like girls, Yorick?"

She puts a hand on his pants and Silvers realizes for the first time that he is soft. Nothing happening. Maybe it's the drugged drink.

"Are you worried about your wife?" Mona taps his wedding band. "But when in France, eh? You know this expression? You do as the French, and in France, a man has many mistresses. A man can be a man."

He wonders now if Valerie is online. He has the urge to tell Mona about it. She speaks English, the only one in France who deigns talk to him. Why isn't he getting hard? Mona rubs him through his pants more vigorously and Silvers tries to will an erection.

"A man can be a man in the France," Mona whispers.

Silvers nods, feeling nothing, talking to cover it up. "It's certainly different here with respect to affairs and matters of the heart. Even your president had a girlfriend. Left his wife for her, right? In my country the president just got a blowjob and the nation was paralyzed for over a year. You're much more civilized. Still, God, you have to sort of feel bad for his poor wife!"

Silvers puts his face into his hands.

"Oh!" Mona squeals. "Yorick, why? Why are you crying?"

"Oh god," he says, trying to wipe away the tears. But it's all happening too fast. "God, Hillary. Chelsea too. What did they do to deserve it? It's such a mean thing to do to Hillary. And your lady. Your first lady here in France. I don't know her name. Your president left her for his mistress. The... first lady... what happened to her...."

Mona throws herself next to him, patting his head. "Shhh, Yorick. Shhh...shhh..."

"It's so mean. So mean. The worst thing you can do to another person. It's being told you're a loser by the one person in whole world who actually knows whether it's true or not."

"They're going to make you leave, Yorick," she whispers. "You have to calm you down. The boss, he is looking at us and you are not behaving right. Shhh... He's not from a Western world and he doesn't know about men who cry. Shhh, Yorick. Stop crying. Pay me 20 Euro and we will go to that booth and I'll put my dress back on and you can lie down on top of me and you can cry and I will hold you and tell you everything will be okay."

Silvers never wanted anything more in his life. "I'm sorry Mona. Can I just give you 20 and you can let me go?"

They stand together and Silvers is covered in moisture, tears and snot on his face, her musky sweat on his arms and pants, and though it's hot in the lounge he's shivering. Mona seems an apparition in the darkness, hovering near like an otherworldly visitor. "Drink your beer, Yorick," she coos. "You'll feel better after that." The gold in her chain catches the candlelight, glinting mutely.

Instead, he's swinging his backpack over his shoulders, moving through a curtain where the man startles and takes a step back to let Silvers run past. On the street he's surprised by the rain, but it is a sweet relief, cooling him, a gift from a mean, grudging city, and Silvers all but jogs down Rue de Martyrs, big rain spattering the sidewalk, the tears only now stopping their run down his cheeks. Unable to keep his chest from heaving, Silvers wipes his face against his sodden sleeve in front of a bookseller: an honest to goodness, real-life warm, well-lighted place. To get dry he enters and walks around the stacks, twisting himself through the narrow aisles to keep his wet backpack from dripping on any of the merchandise.

And there are books from all over Europe, British writers and German writers, but there are also African writers, Australian writers and Middle-Eastern writers, Canadian writers and Mexican writers, all translated into French, and Silvers thinks glumly how much they really do hate Americans here. Good to fleece at the fake brothels but not good for anything else. They won't even read our literature. Everyone else's but not America's.

And he is about to leave when he sees an American flag and an arrow and so turns a corner, and there it is, a whole book case, practically a wall, a small wall but a whole wall of books displaying

American authors whose works have been translated into French. He doesn't recognize the French in the titles—printed upside down on the spine the way they do here—but the names! Auster, Bukowski, Carver, Dixon, Elkin, on and on, G, H, I, one American writer after another—translated into French!

Silvers touches the cover of each book, pulling one forward, trying to read the next, heart pounding and hands sweating. He thinks of the way Popes kiss the ground when landing back in Italy. He fears he might actually kiss the Roths or the Updikes or Capotes. The French did at least have some use for Americans; here was the proof. Taking a Norman Mailer off the shelf, Silvers gives into the urge to participate and goes to the cashier. When he takes his change and the clerk gives a heavily-accented "Thank you," Silvers feels that such an enormous kindness has been extended him that he runs from the bookshop afraid he might burst into tears again.

Trotting down toward arron-diss-ment doo-zee-em, Silvers is happy, really happy thinking about Valerie resting in trent-neuf, waiting for him to come back so they can dress up and walk toward the Seine, arm in arm, huddled together under an umbrella, *flanéuring* their way across Pont Neuf, walking in the Saint Germain. She'll find a crepe vendor and ask, in her perfect French, for one with Nuttella—her favorite—and he will feel proud to be the one in France with Valerie, and he will pay with the leftover Euros from his pocket and she will eat some and hold it for him to take a bite and taste the warm hazelnut paste and they will be together, one last night, their final night in Paris.

Facebook. Inbox. (0) Messages for Valerie Silvers. Reply.

Scudder: I haven't given you time to write me back and answer my question, it's been less than an hour since my last e-mail, but I think perhaps I have come up with some answers on my own. I do wish I were speaking to someone instead of typing in this frankly sophomoric networking website. Guy has pointed out how much *talking* the French do with one another. I've been speaking French with people and it's a wonderful feeling, but it's still not exactly communicating when all you're doing is arguing about which postage stamp goes on which postcard. Maybe it would have been different if he had at least made a cursory attempt at learning some French.

Did I write last time that Guy and I went to Pére Lachaise? There was a slight chill in the air and the old necropolis really felt prophetic. Your idol Morrison is there, of course. I remember listening to your Doors records and the enthusiasm you had while pointing out the "real" poetry in all those dopey, juvenile lyrics of his. It was one of the few times I felt that I wasn't admiring you, just sort of putting up with you. I wonder now what you think when you hear those old songs, if you still listen to them with the same reverence. If you were here you could tell me, but these conversations are slow and linger, we savor them because they take so much time, so much headspace when we're not in front of the screen. But is it real?

These e-mails are like Benjamin's small things that become large. Guilt is even more destructive than anger, Scuds, for forgiveness can be freely given, but guilt is an insidious little bastard, like Guy's cinder that burrowed its way through our floorboards. I remember Guy kept saying he was sorry to the fireman working so hard to save our house, and they *were* forgiving, but not enough to soothe Guy. I don't have an answer to the questions I'm posing. In fact, I don't even have questions for the confusion I'm feeling. You're not here. And I lied to Guy because what you and I do on-line isn't real. It doesn't matter because it is nothing. But the mustard pot is not nothing, it's in a bag in my chamber and it is very real. Ergo if it's real in part, it must a priori be real in sum. Finally then, what you and I do on-line is not quite at the level of being something, but it isn't true to declare it nothing either.

I'm tired and anxious and I find myself looking forward to my husband's return tonight. Does that surprise you as it surprises me? Maybe it's just easier, marriage. Not perfect but cleaner, liminal, with a set of parameters and an order of gestures decipherable only by the two partners. Marriage doesn't negate what comes before it, obviously, but it should alter boundaries for what comes after. Learning those boundaries might be the whole purpose of the thing, making "a marriage" to be the one thing so fragile that it exists only as the two people involved recognize it to exist—regardless of its legal status.

Which is why I might take a break from Facebook for awhile, maybe a long while. Or maybe tomorrow I'll feel different again and decide that no break is necessary and I'll carry on as though Paris never happened. Amazingly, I have no idea which way this will go right now, but I feel strangely eager to see what happens. And hopeful. I have a mazurka in my head. Talk later, perhaps. ~Valerie S.

HE waited until they were on the plane and nearly already home, before showing the book to Valerie. "Look at this," Silvers held the paperback like a trophy.

"What are you going to do with that?" she asked.

"Read it."

"It's in French, to state the obvious."

"Well," he shrugged. "I've decided I'm going to learn French. You said I should before we left and I didn't, but now I think I'll listen to those CDs, maybe even take one of those night classes. I mean really learn it too, not just pick up some travel phrases."

"That's a lot of work to read a book that was written in English in the first place. What's the point since we're not ever going back to Paris anyway?"

"I was just mad. You know that. We'll come back some day. And I won't set a fire to get us there next time. I'll learn the French and we shall return. It might take five years or ten or whatever, but I promise you when we come back you won't have to do all the heavy lifting."

When the flight attendant announced the meal he lowered both their trays. Valerie had her face pressed up against the window for a time and only turned when the sandwich, tightly wrapped in cellophane was placed in front of her.

"Wow," Silvers said, looking at her eyes, which were red and puffy. "Bad air on the plane drying you out?"

"No. I was crying." She took a bite of her sandwich. After chewing for a time she said, "We can make this better."

From her carry-on she pulled out a small box wrapped in her laundry, clawed open some gift wrapping and pulled out a Maille mustard pot. He watched her struggle to pull the cork out, not saying anything, not quite sure what was happening.

With the plastic knife she glopped enormous quantities of mustard on her sandwich and the same amount on his, scraping the sides and bottom of the pot finally so that there was none left, and she squished the tops of their sandwiches and jammed the first bite into her mouth and spoke to him between chews. "Eat your sandwich," she told him.

All he could taste was the coarse mustard, acidic, tangy, more mustard than he normally ate in a month, but he understood that it was important to choke down every bite, and even after signaling for a second bottle of water he couldn't get the taste from his tongue. And after they finished and wiped up the drippings, Valerie dumped their trays into the plastic bags offered by the attendant and Silvers didn't say anything when the ceramic mustard pot went with it, gone with the rest of the garbage. Later on when they played Paper Rock Scissors, she told him exactly what she was going to do before she did it. *I'm going to throw paper, now I'm going to throw rock*, and he believed every word she said, meeting her scissors with rock and her paper with scissors, and in this way Silvers found it possible, at least for a little while, to feel like a winner.

author photo: Rhoda Schulzinger

Daniel S. Libman is the winner of a Pushcart Prize for fiction as well as a *Paris Review* discovery Prize, now called the Plimpton Prize. His story "In the Belly of the Cat" has been anthologized many times and translated into several languages, most recently Russian for the journal *Inostrannaya Literatura*. He has published stories and essays in many journals and magazines including *Details, Other Voices, Columbia, The Paris Review, The Baffler, Santa Monica Review,* and *The Chicago Reader*. Winner of a writing grant from the Illinois Arts Council, Dan is currently holed up in rural Illinois with his wife, two kids, a dog and a cat, and chickens too numerous to count.